I0659630

Heartfelt Cases:
Book 1: The Collins Case
Book 2: The Kiverson Case

By Julie C. Gilbert

The Collins Case Copyright © 2012 Julie C. Gilbert.
The Kiverson Case Copyright © 2014 Julie C. Gilbert.

Large Print Heartfelt Cases Books 1-2 © 2019

All rights reserved.

Aletheia Pyralis Publishers
www.juliecgilbert.com/
sites.google.com/view/juliecgilbert-writer/

Love Science Fiction or Mystery?

Choose your adventure!

Visit: http://www.juliecgilbert.com/

For details on getting
Free books

Dedication:

The Collins Case:
This book is dedicated to all FBI agents.

Special thanks to the FBI personnel who fielded many questions, Supervisory Special Agent Joseph Lewis and Public Affairs Specialist Mrs. Linda Wilkins.

Special thanks Ken Dalenberg and Mike.

The Kiverson Case:
To Timothy Sparvero

Table of Contents:

Prologue:

Parker Residence
Piscataway, NJ

"Jon? Jon, are you in there?" Elizabeth Parker called out, growing more worried with each passing second.

Where is that boy?

Elizabeth knocked but received no answer. Cautiously, she opened the door and peered into her son's dark room. "Jon?" Everything except his computer desk was a mess. She quickly spotted the note lying on the keyboard. Frowning, she picked it up and read:

Mom, I won't be a burden to you. Don't worry, I'll be fine.
Your son,
Jon

Sobs jammed up in Elizabeth's throat, strangling her momentarily before bursting forth in a tortured cry. The divorce had been rough on all of them, but she had never dreamed it would turn out like this. If Jonathan didn't want to be found, nothing could be done. Heart heavy, she called the police.

Chapter 1:
Peaceful Night

Collins Residence
Fairview, Pennsylvania

Rachel Collins had a perfect life. She loved her job as a medical doctor at a small, private practice in Pennsylvania. Her husband—Dr. Christopher Collins—was easy on the eyes and wonderful in every way that mattered. Their two young children brought much joy—and good-natured chaos—into their lives. God had certainly blessed them as a family. At least, she thought so anyway. Though he never put down her religion, Chris never promised to believe a word of it either.

Thank you for being good to us, Father, Rachel thought, tilting her head to the side and watching her husband crawl around on the floor with the children. She only wished that nights like this weren't so rare. She kept fairly regular hours, but Chris worked at Millcreek Community Hospital, so his schedule had to be a little more flexible.

Sandy probably gets to see the kids more than we do, Rachel mused bleakly, thinking of the girl she hired to watch the kids while she worked. Tonight, Chris had persuaded a friend to switch shifts so he could spend time at home with the family.

What did you use to bribe him, Chris?

"No, Emily. Not yours," said Jason, green eyes ablaze to make his point.

Rachel smiled, amused by the strained patience in her five-year-old son's tone as he addressed his little sister.

"I have?" asked Emily, tears welling up in her warm brown eyes. The child's bottom lip stuck out, and she shoved a finger into her mouth. Her brother grunted irritably but let her keep the building block clutched in her chubby right hand.

It amused Rachel that Emily, at the ripe old age of three, could manipulate her brother so well.

You'll break hearts when you're older, Emily Adele Collins.

Rachel smiled down at her daughter, admiring the waves weaving through the child's blond hair. The pleasant golden color of both children's hair came from Chris, but the waves were definitely maternally inherited.

Chris's hair wouldn't know a wave if a curler attacked it, Rachel mused.

"Here, Jay, finish this tower," said Chris, drawing Jason's attention away from Emily and the borrowed block.

Seizing upon the opportunity, Emily snatched up another block. Rachel's smile twitched even wider at that, and she shifted her gaze to her husband. He kept his straight hair cropped short, revealing a broad, expressive forehead that usually announced his moods. His sea green eyes were set deep in his face, lending him a mysterious air that always fascinated Rachel. His nose might have been too large if his pleasant mouth and lips didn't immediately call attention away from it.

The night had gone well so far with meatloaf and mashed potatoes for dinner followed by three-quarters of a Disney movie and some time with the building blocks. Next, would be story time followed closely by bedtime. Rachel would savor this night for a while. Though it was getting late, she stood another minute observing her husband and children.

When it looked like a round of horsey

might break out, Rachel intervened. "I think it's time for two little people to be off to bed."

"No bed!" cried Emily. She dropped the blocks she'd been guarding so jealously and clapped her hands to either side of her face.

Jason went with a soft groan and a deep frown, but his disappointment was just as clear.

Rachel looked at their crestfallen faces. "What's with the long faces? You'd think I'd just sucked all the joy from the world. Come on, let's have a smile." She broke Jason's serious face by tickling his tummy.

Laughter replaced the mournful silence.

Chris swept Emily up off the floor. "You too, Princess, time for the Bedtime Express."

Motioning Jason toward the stairs, Rachel turned to lead the way.

"Oww!" Chris cried.

Rachel whirled and smiled at the sight of Emily giggling and squeezing Chris's nose.

Chris gently extricated his nose from the child's grip. "That's no way for a princess to act." Without further comment, he buzzed and beeped his way to the bathroom for teeth brushing and potty time.

Hand-in-hand with Jason, Rachel followed her husband into the bathroom for the nightly adventures. Despite half the bathroom population being mini-people, lack of space made the preparations interesting. Still, it was a happy struggle.

Twenty minutes and two stories later, the kids were safely tucked in and kissed goodnight, so Chris and Rachel went downstairs to enjoy the rare chance to simply spend some time together. Rachel settled onto the couch and Chris joined her, pausing only long enough to turn the television to a classical music channel. Rachel leaned her head against her husband's chest and rested contentedly. After a moment, she reached past him and grabbed her old high school yearbook from the end table. She chattered about the pictures while relishing the feel of his hands stroking her hair. The music mixed pleasantly with her voice until she fell asleep in Chris's arms.

When she awoke hours later, it took Rachel's sleep-slowed brain a few moments to realize she was nestled in her own bed.

Chris must have carried me.

Thinking she heard something, Rachel

listened intently for several moments. Hearing nothing, she let sleep overtake her again and slipped into a series of peaceful dreams.

Her dreams would have been very different if she had known what the next few weeks would hold for her.

Chapter 2:
Bold Move

Wegmans
Erie, Pennsylvania

After work on Thursday, Rachel Collins stopped at the grocery store for basics and something special for dinner. Having heard many horrible stories, she didn't dare leave the children alone in the car. Warnings about best behavior fell upon deaf ears. Somewhere, she found the patience to tolerate Jason and Emily's childish antics.

"Why you frown, Mommy?" Jason asked.

"I'm just tired, Jay," replied Rachel. Her mind took a trip back to the office where a thousand little things had gone wrong. The secretary's morning car accident had added considerable stress to Rachel's hectic life. Her trust in God's sovereignty didn't make lousy days any easier to live through.

For years she had believed Christ to be mere church rhetoric. Finally, during a particularly rough college year, she had accepted God's gift of salvation through Jesus Christ's sacrifice. It pained her that Chris avoided church. Come Sunday, Rachel forced a bright smile, sang in the choir, helped in the nursery, and coordinated other children's ministries. In fact, she kept herself so busy with work, kids, and church that her spiritual walk floundered. Stress and bills were her biggest problems, but she understood that they allowed her family light, food, warmth, and a fine home in the great state of Pennsylvania. She knew the "could-haves" and the "what-ifs" could drive her mad so she decided not to worry about the future.

"When we get home, you need a nap," Jason said.

Her son's solemn suggestion drew Rachel back to the present. She chuckled softly. Children were a blessing, even if they did jump all over her nerves sometimes.

"Cookies!" Emily shouted, pointing with a tiny finger.

Annoyed at herself for wandering down the wrong aisle, Rachel winced at the volume, grabbed Emily's wildly waving hand, and said, "Hush, sweets, I see them."

That's what you get for not paying

attention. Oh well, the damage is done. The pantry's nearly empty anyway.

She let them each pick a favorite and finished the hike to the back corner where the main selection of milk and eggs were located.

Ingenious to put milk in the back, Rachel admitted.

Next, they swung by the fish department where Jason made a face.

Emily covered her nose and announced, "Stinky!"

Rachel quickly picked up shrimp for dinner, before speeding over to the bread aisle which offered a safer zone for their delicate noses. Perhaps she saw the young man watching her, but if she did, she thought nothing of it. Her children often drew strangers' stares just by being charming or crazy, sometimes both. Eventually, Rachel made it to the checkout lines. Despite the two extra packages of cookies and a last-minute addition of crackers, Rachel counted the expedition a success and headed for home.

***

Collins Residence
Fairview, Pennsylvania
Pulling into the garage, Rachel shut off the

car, unpacked the kids, and ushered them into the playroom where they would be safely out from under foot. This would make grocery unpacking and dinner preparations much easier. So far, the afternoon routine was going well.

On her way back to the garage, Rachel thought she heard a noise. She froze mid-step and experienced the creepy feeling of being watched. Observation in public was one thing, but being watched at home was downright disconcerting. Goosebumps sprang to life up and down her arms. Seconds later the air conditioning turned on, masking other noises. With a shrug, Rachel continued toward the garage thinking, *Scaredy cat.*

Paper grocery bags filling her arms, Rachel busily planned the evening's activities when a man's broad chest materialized before her. Reflexively, she stepped back. Her head snapped up to look at him.

Before she could scream, a rough hand covered her mouth. Another arm curled around her slender waist and drew her back a step. Stale breath washed over her in a nauseating wave. She screamed, but it came out muffled and ineffective. Fear fixed her hands in place. Her heart pounded and her eyes locked on the assailant in front of her. He was of average height with neat hair, dark eyes, and a clean-shaven face that could have been cut from stone.

Go away! What do you want? Rachel didn't get far with her frantic thoughts.

"Relax, Dr. Collins, it'll be far easier if you cooperate," said the first man. He took the two grocery bags from her stiff arms and placed them on the kitchen table.

I bet it would. There's about a snowball's chance in hell of that! Belatedly, Rachel realized that the time to make a move was over. *Oh God, help!* She struggled against the hands holding her.

"Calm down, Doc! The boss just wants to meet you," said the man behind her. He sounded young and frantic.

Frustrated tears welled up as the man tightened his grip.

I'm in a nightmare.

Sweat from her labored breath built up under the man's hand making it slippery. Desperately, Rachel twisted her head to the side, hoping to at least gain enough room for a good scream.

The first man's hand shot out faster than Rachel thought possible and closed around her neck. He turned her head so she faced him squarely, brushing the other man's hand away. "There's little time for introductions, Dr. Collins. Stop struggling and I promise your children will be fine."

The man's firm tone and cryptic words made every muscle in Rachel coil with tension.

What happens to them if I do struggle?

Her mouth was dry, and she could barely think.

The first man slowly released her neck and gently traced her jaw with his forefinger. "Now, I want you to be real still while I give you a shot. It'll just knock you out for a short nap."

Despite the man's soothing tone, Rachel's panic level spiked even higher. Then, she noticed that he wore a paramedic's uniform and some of her panic morphed into bafflement.

What in the—

"My partner will need to shift his grip, but it'll be over in seconds, I promise."

The other man's hand fumbled at her waist. He tossed her cell phone to his partner who dumped it into a grocery bag.

Rachel's stomach lurched as the sense of desperation hit her anew. She barely felt the sharp needle enter her upper right arm. Unshed tears stung her eyes and blurred her vision.

"Mr. Parker will explain everything later," said the other man, easing her toward the ground.

"Shut up, fool."

The hard-faced man's words stopped making sense to Rachel as her mind shut down. The urge to sleep was strong, but she fought it to think, *Jason, Emily, are you safe?*

***

Night rapidly approached as the two men carried Rachel Collins to their van.

Jense returned and coaxed the children out. "Your mother's very sick and needs to go to a doctor. Me and my friend are here to help."

"You're a stranger," Jason pointed out, studying Jense carefully.

"Call Daddy," suggested Emily.

Jense smiled at the small child and picked her up. "We will later, but now, we've got to get your mommy to a safe place. Come on, she'll want to see you when she wakes up."

Emily reached out and touched the scar above his right eyebrow then started crying for her mother. Jense held his hand out to Jason. Reluctantly, the boy took the rough hand.

As soon as the two Collins children were in the white van, Thomas Randle drove off. The entire operation had taken less than ten minutes, but he was anxious to get back to South Dakota. He had never liked kidnapping jobs. They rarely ended well.

Chapter 3:
Stressful Present

Millcreek Community Hospital to Collins Residence
Erie County, Pennsylvania

Doctor Christopher Collins reluctantly resigned himself to the fact that he would get home late. He took advantage of a brief break to call home and anxiously awaited Rachel's voice. When a more cheerful version of his own voice spoke from their answering machine, he sighed in weary frustration. "Hey, Rach, just called to say I love you. I'm going to be late tonight. Dr. Hidle stepped off a curb wrong and twisted his ankle. So instead of treating people tonight, he's receiving treatment. I've got to get back to work now, but I love you like crazy … okay, bye."

He finished his duties even later than anticipated because of an emergency call. An elderly woman had had a stroke, and Dr. Collins was the only one with free hands. Once he finished with her, he quickly escaped the hospital to avoid "just one more thing."

Chris kept just above the speed limit the whole way home. Being friends with a cop, he felt fairly certain he could get out of a speeding ticket, but he had no desire to go through the hassle tonight. He simply wanted to go home.

The kids will already be in bed.

Thankfully, the ride home passed without incident. After parking in the garage, he entered the house. "Rachel—" Chris broke off upon seeing the grocery bags on the kitchen table.

He peeked in the closest bag and frowned. One by one, he pulled out warm milk, pungent shrimp, and a package of eggs.

Seafood, milk, and eggs, what idiot packed that?

His hand brushed a familiar silver object. Grimly, Chris held up Rachel's cell phone as his mind flew to many troubling scenarios. Perhaps Rachel had taken a bad spill and knocked herself out. *No, she's too careful for something like that; besides, she'd be sprawled out here.* Maybe she just went out. *No, her car's still here.* Maybe she went to a neighbor's house to borrow something. *She just bought milk and eggs.* Something could have come up at work. *Her cell phone is here!*

Growing increasingly agitated, Chris tentatively sniffed the milk and abruptly recoiled. With his mood perfectly matching the milk's current state, he walked to the sink and poured it out, rinsing it down with copious amounts of cold water. Next, he put the eggs in the refrigerator and the shrimp in the freezer. He left the non-perishable food in the bags.

Where is she?

"Rachel? Rachel? Jay? Emily?" He called out futilely, knowing they weren't home.

Out of sheer need to do something, Chris searched every room thoroughly. He even checked under the couches. "Yes, they're hiding right under the couch," he muttered sarcastically, realizing the ridiculousness of his search. Finally, he called the police.

"Fairview police department, this is Officer Ebert speaking," said a crisp male voice.

"Hello. Is Officer Long available?" asked Chris, attempting to mask his agitated state.

"I'm sorry, sir, but Officer Long is off tonight. Can I take a message?"

"No."

Chris abruptly hung up the phone then called the Long home and immediately had his stressed nerves grated upon by a bubbly female voice.

"Hi, you've reached the Long residence. Amanda speaking."

"Is Ryan there?" he asked gruffly.

"Chris? Oh, it's lovely to hear from you. How's Rachel? How're the—"

"Just get Ryan," Chris interrupted, despite his efforts to choke back his anger.

"Oh, of course," Amanda said in a hurt tone.

Chris was too worried about his family to be guilt-stricken over his rudeness.

Soon, Ryan Long picked up the phone. "What's up, Chris? Amanda said you sounded worried."

Sobs burned Chris's throat making his voice hoarse. "I need to speak to you," he said shortly. Then, he hung up.

I shouldn't involve him.

The phone rang as he was returning it to its belt-clip home. His fist tightened around the phone and he stared contemptuously at it through half the happy ringtone Rachel had insisted he install. He grimaced because thinking of her hurt. His expression hardened as he opened the phone, and said, "Chris Collins speaking. What do you want?"

"Dr. Collins, you are a very hard man to get in touch with," said a young, cheerful, and thoroughly annoying voice.

"Skip it. Where's my family?" Instinct told him that the young man would have the answer to that question.

"Safe. Your cooperation will ensure they stay that way."

"What does he want?" Chris managed to say through clenched teeth. He was forced to ease the locked-jaw expression a few seconds later due to pain, but his mood remained foul. He had a pretty good idea who had kidnapped Rachel and the kids, but the exact motive remained a mystery. Chris's head pounded with fury and a galling sense of helplessness.

I told you I wanted out for good, Chris thought at his former friend.

"He needs your brand of expertise, sir," said the enthusiastic voice.

"And …."

"And?" the voice sounded confused. "Oh! You mean the rest of the message, right?

Sorry! Where is it? I just had it. Here it is. There are a few things here. Burn house, clear accounts, and meet Evan on the Brooklyn Bridge Saturday at noon."

The line went dead.

Chris wasted no time. Furious, he spent about twenty minutes packing the essentials he would need and trying not to think of the major task ahead. Finally, he went to his bedroom closet, broke into the hidden compartment, and removed the briefcase he had never wanted to see again. He stared at the case for a few minutes, fingering the locks and frantically thinking of another way out of this situation. This was the third time packing up his life, and it was the third time too many.

I'm sorry, Rachel.

Chris's expression settled into cool resolve. "This wasn't supposed to happen," he muttered.

The doorbell announced Ryan's arrival. Chris mentally cursed.

Ryan, you have really bad timing.

"Chris? Are you here?" Ryan's voice floated through the house.

Chris ran into Emily's room, knocking

over a lamp in his haste.

It wasn't supposed to be like this, his mind cried, echoing his earlier statement. Knowing Ryan would systematically check each room, Chris waited patiently. It wasn't long before he heard his friend's cautious steps. Chris watched his friend from the darkest part of the room, and as soon as Ryan turned his back, Chris made his move. Three quick steps brought him within striking distance. While his left hand firmly clamped over Ryan's mouth, his right hand squeezed a pressure point in his friend's neck. Ryan struggled fiercely but briefly before slumping in Chris's arms.

Sorry, Ryan.

Chris stuffed Emily's soft nightshirt into his friend's mouth and used the cord of her special bunny lamp to bind his hands. Next, Chris used his computer to push funds around. With that out of the way, he finished packing his suitcase and connected the last wires to the explosives embedded throughout the walls of his house. When everything was ready, he dumped Ryan behind some bushes in the backyard. His muscles ached with tension and anger fueled his steps as he walked to his car.

Two blocks from his house, Chris pulled out his other cell phone and set off the charges. His car radio was off, allowing the muffled booms to reach him. As he watched smoke and flames reach for the sky, tears for his lost peaceful life flowed freely. He stuck a piece of gum in his mouth and nearly swallowed it down the wrong tube. The mistake left him gagging and coughing for several moments. When he recovered a bit, Chris fixed his eyes on the destruction.

Rachel and the kids being taken. The house being destroyed. This is all your fault.

Negative thoughts haunted Chris the whole way to the bank. It was closed. He parked, slipped on rubber gloves, and strode to the automated telling machine. Well-placed chewing gum neutralized the hidden camera. Several minutes later, Chris returned to his car with $7,000. Sticking another piece of gum in his mouth, he shoved the cash in his bag. Twelve atms later, Chris had indecent sums of cash on him. His anger finally ebbed a bit, but hate still burned in his eyes. He hated the man behind this. He hated being manipulated, and most of all, he hated his failure to bury the past.

Chapter 4:
Shocking News

J. Edgar Hoover Building, FBI Headquarters
Washington, D.C.

"Did you hear the news?"

Special Agent Julie Ann Davidson looked up from a case file she was reading and eyed her partner. She didn't like his tone. It suggested trouble, something they didn't need to seek out. "No." Knowing her partner would eventually elaborate, she waited patiently.

It could be a long time. Patrick Duncan usually did more listening than speaking. While this made him a good investigator, it often made him a frustrating partner. Idly, Ann picked up her lukewarm coffee and took a sip. She studied Patrick while she waited. His lean, fit frame occupied the usual spot against the right side of the threshold of her cluttered cubby hole of an office. Although quiet, Patrick could be very expressive, and at the moment a deep frown dominated his face. He cocked his jaw slightly to the right, forming the expression Ann thought of as "worried to the point of peeved."

Finally, Ann couldn't take the silence. "Are you going to tell me what's up or am I going to have to beg?" she asked, setting the coffee down, folding her arms, and leaning back.

"You grew up out in PA, right?" Patrick asked matter-of-factly, fixing her with a very neutral gaze.

Ah, the poker face and a question; this could get interesting.

Ann's hair bounced off her shoulders as she confirmed Patrick's statement with a nod. She raised an eyebrow at the sudden shift in conversation.

Then, it was his turn to be confused. "I thought you never missed the six o'clock news."

Sighing, Ann uncrossed her arms and fiddled with her coffee mug. "Not normally, but my dog is sick and was busy hacking all over my new rugs. I had to make a few phone calls and pull in a well-earned favor to get a neighbor to take him to the vet today." She paused, reflecting on her miserable morning.

"In other words, I was a little preoccupied." She smiled somewhat grimly, feeling mild amusement duel with remembered irritation.

"Uh-huh. You once mentioned having a close friend out there." A distant look came over Patrick's face. He raised a rolled newspaper and gently slapped it against his left palm.

Ann thought hard. "Martha?"

He frowned and let his gaze wander the tiny office.

"Jana?"

Still, the frown.

"Rachel?"

Patrick's eyes snapped up to meet hers, though the frown remained fixed.

"What is it?" Ann asked, her tone now dead serious as concern replaced all traces of amusement. A detailed mental picture of her high school friend immediately came to mind. It wasn't hard. People had always commented that Rachel and Ann could have been sisters. *Except my ears are bigger, my eyes are blue instead of brown, my hair's lighter and straighter, my complexion's worse, my nose is funny, and—*

Patrick threw the paper at her, and Ann

27

interrupted her self-scrutiny to move her coffee out of the flight path. "It's all over the television too."

The paper landed in front of her with a splat. The headline read:

Suburban Home Explodes

Ann skimmed the article becoming more confused by the second.

"What's this got to—oh." A smaller headline caught her attention when she unfolded the paper so she could see the entire front page.

Family Vanishes

The paper had nestled a charming family photo beneath that ominous headline. Ann sucked in sharply.

Rachel.

With the same cheerful, intelligent brown eyes, flawless skin, and pleasant smile, Rachel hardly looked a day older than their senior class portraits. The way Rachel's head was tipped toward the handsome blond man next to her indicated that he was something special to her. Ann recalled old email conversations about the "world's greatest man."

28

Ann didn't get to study him too closely before Patrick said, "It's their home too."

"What?"

Their home exploded? That can't be right!

Ann's gaze fixed on the toddler and infant in the photo. Feeling the blood draining from her face, she sent up a quick prayer for the safety of Rachel's family.

"You okay?"

"Fine," Ann mumbled distractedly, reading the rest of the article.

"You want in?"

"Absolutely," Ann confirmed, reaching for the spring jacket she had brought out of habit.

"Thought so. Leave your paperwork on my desk."

***

Long Residence
Albion, Pennsylvania

It was a very long drive from Washington, D.C. to Western Pennsylvania, but thankfully, the six-plus hours of driving passed quickly. Unfortunately, the long drive gave Ann plenty of time to worry about Rachel. Actual travel time was lengthened by the need to refuel both herself and the car.

"Home sweet home," she muttered, nearing her destination. Ann's family actually lived in Fairview where the Collins family also resided, but Albion was only about a twenty to twenty-five minute drive away. She considered stopping by to say hello but figured she should try to talk to Officer Long first. Then, she could check out Rachel's wrecked house and see if there was enough time for a visit home.

Her cell phone played "It's a Small World," courtesy of Agent
Baker being bored and somehow getting his grubby hands on her phone.

Darn, I really need to change that ringtone.

Ann fumbled for a moment, trying to dig the phone out of her purse and simultaneously stay on the road. At last, she wrestled the earpiece into position and turned her attention back to driving. "Special Agent Davidson."

"Oh, you sound so professional!"

"Hi, mom," Ann said wearily, rolling her eyes.

"Did you hear the news?" Carol Davidson's tone turned somber.

"About Rachel?"

"Yes."

"I'm on my way now."

That piece of information took her mother by surprise. "This is *your* case? Oh, Julie Ann, I don't think I like the idea of you working on it."

"It's not officially my case," Ann admitted. "The Pittsburgh Field Office probably has agents on it, but Rachel's my friend. I have to help her if I can."

"Honey, her house exploded. This could be a very, very dangerous—"

"Mom, I'm still on the road. Got to go. Love you. I'll call you later," Ann said in one breath. She hung up before they could get into the much overdone "dangers of your job" conversation.

Sorry, mom.

Ann immediately wanted to call her mother back and apologize, but she knew the conversation would probably end poorly again. Groaning a little, she wondered if all female law enforcement officers had overprotective mothers.

As she pulled up to a pretty two-story house late in the afternoon, a barking dog three yards over caught her attention.

Dog ... dog.

"Ooohhh, crud! Danny!" Absently, Ann strode up the front walk and wrestled her phone out of its holder. Jabbing her finger at the button to ring the doorbell and mentally apologizing to her dog, Ann speed dialed her partner.

"Hi, Patrick, it's me. No, no, I'm fine. Listen—oh you did? Really? Thanks, I owe you one."

How does he do that? she thought, ending the call.

"Can I help you?" asked a woman, peering through the screen door.

A large German shepherd bounded up to the door and growled at Ann.

The woman held the dog by the collar, but Ann understood she had better be on her best behavior or else. She retrieved her ID badge from the depths of her suit jacket and flipped it open so the woman could get a good look at it. Maybe Ann was imagining things, but as she moved to put her phone away, the dog's growl seemed to turn more menacing.

"Good afternoon, Mrs. Long, I'm Special Agent Davidson with the FBI. I was informed that Officer Long was at home today. May I speak with him for a moment?"

"Do you have a gun?" asked a little boy, appearing beside the woman.

"Michael! Mind your manners," said Mrs. Long, mortified.

"It's all right," Ann assured, smiling at the child. Leaning down so that she was closer to his eye level, Ann showed him her badge. "Yes, Michael, I carry a gun, but the badge is just as important."

"Guns are cooler," Michael argued.

Chuckling as she stood upright again, Ann tucked her badge away. "Agreed."

"That's enough, Michael. Go play," said Mrs. Long, shooing the boy away from the door. She stepped back and motioned Ann into the house. "Please come in. I'll go see if my husband is up for more. He's already been questioned by the FBI, you know."

Nodding acknowledgement, Ann looked around, a stubborn but useful habit. She smiled to see the dog sit down and watch her carefully. She held out her hands. "You're a bit of a guard dog, I see."

"You wanted to speak with me?" A handsome man stepped into the room.

Everything about him, from the impressive physique to rigid haircut, said "cop" to Ann. The only thing that surprised her was his employment by a small town in Pennsylvania rather than a big city. Red rings still marked his wrists and lower arms.

Realizing she hadn't answered his question, Ann held out her right hand, and said, "Yes, sir. I'm Agent Davidson. I wanted to talk to you about your experiences last night."

"Ryan Long," he responded, shaking hands. "I spoke with the other feds already. Didn't you read their report?" His tone conveyed equal parts confusion and doubt with more than a hint of guardedness mixed in.

Ann didn't want to get into a discussion about her involvement in the case, but she saw no easy way out of responding to his question. "I'm from Washington. This isn't officially my case. I'm just here as a consultant."

A very unofficial consultant, she added silently. Ann avoided eye contact, glad when he didn't press the point of jurisdiction.

Officer Long led Ann to a sitting room

and gestured for her to have a seat on the floral printed couch. "I'll tell you what I told the other feds, my friends, and wrote in my official report." He sat on a two-person settee angled to facilitate easy conversation around a coffee table.

Ann settled herself on the sofa's edge.

"Would you like anything to drink?" asked Mrs. Long.

"No, thank you, ma'am."

"A friend of mine, Chris Collins, called last night," Ryan began, slowly rubbing at his temple like he had a headache.

"What time was this?"

"Around 9:30 p.m., I think. All he said was that he needed to speak with me. When no one answered the doorbell, I used my spare key to enter the house," Long said frowning.

His wife sat next to him and gently squeezed his right arm encouragingly.

The silence stretched.

"Was Dr. Collins there?" Ann asked finally, wishing she had Patrick's level of patience.

"No … at least, not that I saw."

"You have doubts?"

"*Someone* was there," said Officer Long. "I heard a noise from the second story. I'd been off yesterday, but I always carry a spare gun so I went to investigate. The first several rooms were clear. I was just ending my sweep of the upstairs when someone grabbed me from behind and knocked me out."

Ann struggled to keep a straight face. *Who'd want to take on this guy? He's built like a professional wrestler.*

"How were you knocked out?"

The man shifted uncomfortably. "Pressure point in the neck. I woke up when the explosions went off. My hands were tied behind me with a lamp cord and a shirt was stuffed in my mouth. I even had my spare gun back in the ankle holster."

Ann furrowed her brows.

That's strange. Who would knock him out and then return his gun?

The scenario would have struck her funny if she wasn't chatting with a man who had clearly had a bad night. Something was strange about the whole thing. After a few more questions, Ann thanked the Longs for their time and took her leave. She needed to stop by the Fairview police station to see if they'd let her see the official reports. Then, if she had time and sufficient energy, she would stop home and try to set her mother at ease.

It's going to be a very long weekend.

Chapter 5:
Hard Truth

Corra Compound
Stanley County, South Dakota
Rachel Collins woke up frantic.

Where are my children? Where am I? What happened?

The odd angle of Rachel's head caused a sharp pain in her neck and gave her a headache. Her limbs felt limp. She tried to lift an arm, only to have it flop down again like a dead fish. She was hot. Sweat and grime glued her to a lumpy mattress.

I don't feel good, she thought, sitting upright and immediately regretting it.

"Jason! Em!—owww!" Rachel swayed, ready to faint.

Where are you Chris?

With much effort, Rachel swung her legs over the side of the small cot and leaned forward, resting her head in upturned palms as she propped her elbows on her knees. She blinked, waiting for things to quit spinning.

Gradually, her eyes adjusted to the dimness. It wasn't pitch-black, only mostly dark. A bright beam of sunlight forced its way through a crack between the door and the ground, illuminating the small, dusty chamber.

Think. Think.

"Where am I?" Rachel mumbled, voicing earlier thoughts just to see if her vocal cords worked. She rubbed some sleep from her eyes. Slowly, her brain began to function properly. She thought about her children again. The sweeping urge to do something drove her to her feet. Strange light residues swam through her vision when she shut her eyes against the shooting pain in her head. She gently twisted her neck to the left. Five satisfying cracks later, her neck felt better.

Rachel glanced at the bed again. The pattern on the bright blanket draped over the horrible mattress reminded her of the one she'd bought on a mission trip to Mexico in another lifetime. She made a mental note of it and walked to the door. She hesitated for a split-second before trying the flimsy looking handle. To her surprise, the latch turned easily. The door swung open and Rachel found herself blinking against cheerful sunbeams. Her legs trembled, threatening to buckle. She leaned heavily against the door frame. Someone to her left gasped, but she didn't have the strength to lift her head and see the person.

"You're awake! I—I'll go tell Mr. Parker."

Rachel couldn't decide whether the speaker was male or female, but she noted that he or she sounded young and happy.

Strange. The way I feel, everyone ought to feel terrible. As she finished the thought, Rachel fainted. She fought for consciousness but only managed to maintain a semi-conscious, listless state.

Someone picked her up and carried her into another building. On the way to a small, spare room, Rachel noticed that everything seemed very clean and white. The person who carried her in deposited her onto a hard chair that aggravated her back. She glanced around in a daze. The room was approximately ten feet by ten feet, but the bare, metal table on which she slumped made it seem even tinier.

A confident, male voice addressed her. "Are you feeling better, Dr. Collins?"

Of course not.

Rachel took another visual tour of the room. It took her drug-muddled brain a few moments to realize that the sound emanated from the table itself. A thin screen rose out of the table inches from her head, revealing a shadowy figure sitting in a large chair.

Somebody's been watching too many movies.

"Mr. Hart said you had awakened."

Rachel managed a non-committal grunt. She would have cried if she could spare the energy, but she barely mustered a decent glare at the screen.

"I'm terribly sorry. How rude of me not to introduce myself. My name is Jonathan Parker. It's good of you to come, though I know you had little choice in the matter." He chuckled softly. "No worries, Dr. Collins. If your husband plays his hand right, everything will be fine."

"Where are my children?" Rachel demanded, a new strength entering her. "I want to see them right now."

"Do watch your tone, Dr. Collins. I have no desire to waste precious energy on your bad moods."

The lecturing voice made her angry, which was sort of good. The angrier she got, the more awake she became. "You must know that I'll be much more willing to listen once I know my children are safe," she snapped, staring daggers at the shadowy man.

Tell me where my kids are, you jerk!

Another infuriating chuckle emanated from the screen. "I see why he fell in love. I told him not to do that, but since when did he ever take good advice?"

What the heck does that mean?

"Very well, Dr. Collins, have it your way."

A click caused Rachel's heart to skip several beats. She feared the man had cut the conversation off for good, but after a few painful seconds, there was another click.

"Mrs. Hart will be there shortly with Jason and Emily."

Rachel flinched, despite the good news. Hearing the man say her children's names gave her the creeps. "You mean they're here?" She partially stood—ready to hit the nearest thing—not knowing how to take the news. Her elation over Jason and Emily's nearness was offset by horror of them being in danger. Rachel's right palm slammed down onto the table, causing a nice stinging pain that gave her something besides the grim situation to concentrate on.

God, protect them!

Rachel could practically taste the helpless terror consuming her from the inside out.

"Of course, they're here. You don't think your dear husband would listen to me for your sake alone, do you?"

The merriment in the man's tone irritated her. The headache returned with a vengeance, and exhaustion tugged Rachel closer to despair. Just then, the door opened. She squinted into yet more light and saw her children clutching the hands of a strange woman.

Before Rachel could move, Jason shouted, "Mommy!"

He ran around the tiny table while Emily took the shortcut under the table, latched onto Rachel's left leg, and cried.

Though the ruckus made her head ring, it was by far the best sound Rachel had ever heard. "Jay, Em! Oh, I missed you!" She stood up so fast the chair fell over.

Emily continued wailing, but let go long enough for Rachel to forget all physical pain, kneel, and sweep both children into a tight embrace.

I'm here, my loves. Hold on, mommy's here.

A minute later the man spoke from the screen again. "Are you ready to listen now? I hate to interrupt the happy reunion, but I have better things to do. And I'm doing you a favor by taking the time to explain things."

The strange woman who had brought Jason and Emily to Rachel gently pried her fingers away from them and led them out. "Your mommy's gonna be just fine. Don't you worry; we'll come back for a visit later. The doctor will need to see her soon."

That's a bold-faced lie! Rachel wanted to shout for the woman to speak sense. *I am a doctor,* she thought petulantly.

Empty arms sinking to her side, Rachel hugged herself for lack of a better thing to do with her hands. Slowly, she forced herself to her feet and struggled over to the chair. After righting it, she wearily sat down. "Start explaining," she said dully, almost as if she didn't care.

"That's better. This will go a lot easier with your cooperation, Dr. Collins. Some of this may seem incredible to you, but it's the God's honest truth."

Rachel's eyes pierced the screen at the mention of God.

Don't bring God into this, you big snake!

"I see I hit a nerve," the man commented. "Calm down, it's only an expression."

"Exactly," Rachel spat, strength entering from somewhere. She straightened in the uncomfortable chair. "To you, it's *only* an expression!"

"I don't have time for this," muttered the man.

"That's your problem."

A gentle laugh answered the obvious frustration in her tone. "You are a sharp one, my dear Dr. Collins." The man lapsed into silence for several long seconds as if deep in thought. Then, he shook himself like a man waking up. "Where was I? Oh, right, I was about to tell you about your husband."

"Chris?"

"You have more than one?" the man asked, amused.

"What about Chris?" Rachel's expression

added, *shut up or make a point quickly.*

The man's voice took on a serious quality that unnerved her. "He's not the man you think he is. Christopher Collins isn't even his real name. I bet you didn't know that. For now, we'll just continue to use his alias for convenience's sake. I don't owe you anything, Dr. Collins. Remember that. I think if we understand each other well, the coming months will be easier."

Months? If Rachel had been speaking the thought, her voice would have squeaked.

"What do you want from him?" Rachel asked, hardly daring to breathe for fear it would scare away an answer.

"I need him to perform a service for me."

"You're not going to tell me?"

"No, I'm not. All you need to know is that you're going to be my guest of sorts for a while. When I have my money—"

"Ransom?" asked Rachel doubtfully. She and Chris made decent money, but neither they nor her parents had enough money to warrant kidnapping.

Who are Chris's parents anyway? Are they rich? Is this scheme meant to get to them? No, if that were the case, wouldn't they

46

just threaten Chris?

Come to think of it, Chris tended to avoid conversations about his past.

"Something far grander, my dear," the man said cryptically.

"When will I see my children again?"

A click was all the answer she got.

Chapter 6:
Neighborly Chatter

Collins Residence
Fairview, Pennsylvania

On her way from the Fairview police station—where she initially got stonewalled—to Rachel's house, Ann stopped for some fast food. She would have to hurry if she wanted to get to work on time the next day, despite the fact that it was a Saturday.

Nobody ever promised working for the FBI would be a nine-to-five job.

Ann still had to contend with a six-ish hour drive home. When she reached the house, she said a quick prayer over her meal and took four minutes to eat. Wiping her hands on a fourth napkin, she grimaced at her grease-covered fingers.

What's that doing to the inside of me?

Checking to make sure her gun was in place, Ann climbed out of the car. "I'll need to run extra far tomorrow," she murmured.

The neighborhood was quiet, almost too

quiet. Yellow police tape surrounded the entire yard. Since this wasn't officially her case, she had no reason to duck the tape. Besides, she lacked a pressing desire to approach the burned-out wreck of a house.

Officer Long said someone left him out back.

Confidently, Ann crossed the street. She followed the taped path back to some disheveled bushes. Crushed branches marked the place where Officer Long had taken his forced nap. She bent over to take a closer look at the scene.

"What are you doing?" barked a harsh, elderly female voice.

Ann took a sharp breath and just barely refrained from pulling her gun out of the holster next to her right ribs. She spun around and put on a disarming smile. "Good evening, ma'am. I'm Agent Davidson. I came to look at the crime scene."

"You're a police officer?" the short, plump woman asked skeptically.

As she moved closer, Ann felt the woman's measuring gaze and gave the lady her own once-over. Alert eyes, jolly, somewhat abrupt manner, and even the way she clutched a damp towel said "perfect snitch" to Ann.

This woman seems to know what goes on around here.

Ann's smile broadened. "No, ma'am, I'm only an investigator."

Before she could continue the woman became more animated.

"Oohhh, like a private detective?" It was equal parts question and exclamation.

Ann shook her head. "No, ma'am, I work for the Federal Bureau of Investigation."

Who's running this interview anyway?

Ann stepped toward the woman, who was leaning over the deck attached to a small, quaint house with baby blue siding. "I'd like to ask you some questions about your neighbors."

The statement seemed to further excite the lady.

"Of course, my dear. Do you want some lemonade? I just made up a fresh batch. Do come up and have a glass. Come! Come." As she babbled, the woman's arms flailed in the general direction of her house.

I hope she doesn't have a heart attack on me.

Ann hesitated and her natural suspicions flared at the thought of consuming a stranger's beverage.

Yes, the elderly woman keeps a tiny bottle of cyanide around to poison random people!

Figuring she might learn something, Ann said, "Thank you very much, lemonade sounds wonderful." She followed the woman inside and sat down on a burgundy couch in the sitting room.

While the woman left to get the drinks, Ann gathered her thoughts and checked her surroundings. In addition to the couch, the room boasted a matched set of floral-printed armchairs and a brown leather recliner. A dark coffee table containing several bird books and a vase of fresh flowers dominated the center of the room. The wall opposite the couch Ann occupied had large bookshelves flanking a neat fireplace. Precious Moments figurines took up most of the shelf space, but cooking and gardening books were also well-represented.

"I've never met a government agent before—not someone who works for the FBI—I mean," the woman said almost shyly as she entered the room carrying a tray with two oversized glasses and a huge plate of chocolate chip cookies.

What ninety people is she serving tonight?

The lady balanced the tray on the corner of the coffee table while Ann cleared away enough room to slide the tray to a more stable position. Once the tray was settled, the woman held a large glass of lemonade out to Ann.

Grinning politely, Ann nodded her thanks and accepted the drink with both hands. At the woman's insistence, she picked up a cookie. "May I ask your name?" she asked her hostess.

The woman gasped. "Goodness gracious! Where have my manners skedaddled to?" In her excitement, she knocked her eyeglasses askew. She righted them primly. "Karla Banning. Mrs. Karla Banning, but you can just call me 'Mrs. Banning' or 'Karla' if you like."

"Very well, Mrs. Banning—"

"My husband, Jeffrey, died several years ago; he had lung cancer from smoking. Poor Jeffrey, he sure loved those smelly old sticks of his." The woman patted her snowy white hair and stared off into space for a moment as she sat down on one of the armchairs.

Ann figured she would have to control the conversation soon or risk hearing this woman's entire family history. She hid a smile behind her lemonade glass and took a sip. "What can you tell me about the Collins?"

"Oh, such a lovely family! They're both doctors you know. That young Mrs. Collins and I used to swap recipes. She makes a wonderful peach cobbler, but her spinach casserole could use a little help. Oh, but she is getting better—she just needs to practice more. Practice makes perfect, as my mother always said. And that husband of hers; he's as handsome as a man can be! If I were forty years younger, I'd be a mite jealous of the missus. Their two young ones are such sweet, darling babies. They remind me of my grandchildren. So fiery, especially the little girl. My but that youngin' can pitch a proper fit!"

At this rate, I may learn something in a year ... or three.

Before the woman could whip out an iPhone loaded with grandchildren pictures, Ann spoke up, "Mrs. Banning, did you hear or see anything unusual yesterday afternoon?"

The woman clutched her lemonade glass tightly as she concentrated, causing Ann to subconsciously brace for shattering glass.

"Hmmm, let's see," said Mrs. Banning slowly. "Unusual, you say. Did I see anything unusual? There must have been something out of place. This used to be such a safe neighborhood." Mrs. Banning paused for a long, fortifying drink from her lemonade glass. "Well, now that you mention it, I saw a white van in front of their house."

Ann's ears perked up. "What time?"

"Oh, around dusk, I suppose."

"Did you see the license plate?"

Mrs. Banning looked crestfallen.

Pushing down her own disappointment, Ann hastened to set the woman at ease again. "Don't worry about it. Can you tell me anything else about the van? Did you see the driver? Were there other people with the driver?" Ann considered biting into the cookie to cut off the flow of questions but settled for another drink of lemonade.

"I don't know what they were doing, but a fellow in a blue uniform was just shutting the front door. 'Now that's odd,' I said to myself. Then, that fellow was hand-in-hand with those precious little ones. My eyes aren't so good anymore. I might have gone out there and confronted that fellow myself but the children didn't seem upset, so I didn't think anymore on it. And then later that evening, those awful explosions made me forget all but my own name." A thought seemed to strike the woman, and she gasped again. "Is it important? Could something have happened to those little ones?"

They were good questions, but Ann decided to ignore them for the moment. The news reports had not mentioned bodies being found. While the police and fire officials might have suppressed that information, Ann doubted they would have been able to do that effectively if any bodies had been moved from the wreckage. "No one was in the house," she said soothingly. "Did you talk to the police yesterday?"

"Yes, yes. I told them all about the explosions. They were just awful. There were four separate ones you know."

Ann hadn't known because she still needed to see the official fire and police reports, but she filed the information in the back of her mind.

Mrs. Banning suddenly looked worried. "I forgot to tell them about the van! What if they need to know about it? Oooohh, I should call them right away!"

Ann made a placating gesture. "I'm sure they'll be glad for the information, Mrs. Banning," she assured. "Just give them a call when you have a chance. Now, was there anything else you heard or saw?"

After a moment's thought the woman said, "Well, one of those young police fellows was found tied up in the back. I heard him talking with another officer. Poor dear, even in the dim light and with my weak eyes, I saw the marks on his arms. They were from a lamp cord you know. Oh, it was about the saddest thing I've ever seen!" Mrs. Banning paused to set the lemonade glass down on the coffee table before continuing her report. Now that her hands were free, the narrative was punctuated properly with appropriate hand gestures. "Another young fellow picked up a lamp cord still attached to a fluffy bunny tail. I remember because those lamps are fire hazards. Have you ever seen one? Cute things, with pink and purple ears and a cotton tail and all, but they're fire hazards I tell you.

Anyway, a thing like that has no business at a crime scene!" Mrs. Banning declared.

Nodding agreement, Ann checked her watch; it was getting late. "Thank you for your time, Mrs. Banning. The lemonade was wonderful, but I must take my leave now."

"Oh, but you haven't even eaten any cookies!"

"I'm sure they're wonderful as well," Ann said, holding up the melting cookie.

"Take some with you!" the woman insisted.

Ann didn't protest as Mrs. Banning wrapped several cookies in a napkin and handed it to her. With another hasty thank you, Ann tucked the melting cookie into the napkin with the rest and stuffed the whole bundle into her suit pocket, making a mental note to move them to her purse as soon as she reached her car. They would not do well in her pocket during the long drive back to the D.C. area.

As she dashed to her car, the case details tumbled through Ann's head, making her worry.

Oh, Rachel, what have you gotten yourself into this time?

Chapter 7:
Bridge Rendezvous

Brooklyn Bridge to Parker's Base of Operations
New York City, New York

At precisely noon on that gloomy June Saturday, the week Chris Collins's life was once again upended, he waited on the Brooklyn Bridge. Rain started falling steadily, adding to his misery. Briefly, he pondered just jumping off and taking his chances with the long drop and swift waters. It would certainly solve his problems, but thoughts of Rachel and the kids kept him from embracing the irrational solution. He couldn't do that to them. He couldn't take the coward's way out and let them suffer at the hands of his former friend.

"Dr. Collins, I presume," said a youthful male voice.

"That's not funny," Chris said, turning to face the hooded figure that appeared beside him. "You must be Evan. I suppose you'll show me where to go."

Maybe I can redeem myself and get back at him.

"It's good to finally meet you, sir," Evan said.

Chris was surprised at the deep admiration he heard.

What's he been telling you about me?

It started raining harder.

"Mr. Parker says you have a lot to teach us." The young man shouted to be heard above the driving rain.

Very funny, Chris thought when he heard the name.

"He also says your family is fine and will remain so if you follow instructions. If all goes well, you'll be given a few million dollars and a ticket to anywhere in the world."

"What about my family?"

"Mr. Parker says—"

"I'm not doing anything until I know they're all right and I get his word that my entire family leaves with me!" The rain lost momentum suddenly, making Chris feel stupid for shouting.

"The details will be worked out later, but you can have your confirmation now," said the kid, handing Chris a cell phone. "It's only set to make this one call, and its mate is only set to receive this one call. You have five minutes."

Chris eagerly hit the "send" button. At Evan's suggestion, he pressed another button to set the phone to speaker status. He couldn't even tell which area code he was dialing since the phone's display remained disturbingly blank. His hand trembled and he felt about a hundred years old. "Hello? Rachel, are you there?"

At first nothing happened, but then suddenly his wife's lovely face appeared on the tiny screen. A burst of emotions rendered speech impossible. Chris spent the moments studying his wife, trying to absorb her wonderful features. Her beautiful eyes gazed back at him, and her expression said words were avoiding her as well. Tear tracks followed the curvature of her face all the way to the tip of her chin. Fresh tears suddenly gushed down those well-worn tracks. She looked physically and emotionally drained. Her lips were drawn into a thin line. Her hair was mussed, like she had just awakened from a series of violent dreams.

"How are you, darling?" Chris asked

softly.

Stupid, stupid question, he silently berated himself. Seconds continued to slip by. *You're wasting time!* Chris whipped his mind into sharp focus.

"Listen, I'm going to get this straightened out. I promise. Look, I know I don't deserve it, but I'm begging you to trust me. Please, Rachel, I've done some wrong things, but I swear I'll make everything right."

She was speaking but he couldn't hear her.

"Say that again."

"The audio connection's only one way," Evan informed with irritating good cheer.

Rachel spoke again. Chris wanted to read "I love you" on her lips but her message was more urgent. He missed it the first time but caught it the second and third times.

Clever lady; we'll get out of this yet.

"Believe me. I never wanted this to come back. I'm so sorry for getting you involved. I'll explain everything one day, I promise." A sob lodged like a ball of fire in his throat, burning him from the inside out.

"Times up in thirty seconds," Evan warned.

That wasn't five minutes!

Chris could see his wife weeping. Despite the minuscule screen, he read the emotions playing across her face: fear, love, joy, loss, and a whole host of others. Swallowing a painful lump in his throat, Chris said, "I love you. I'll do everything I can to get us out of this. Be brave for Jay and Emily." He saw her nod and wipe at more tears. "That's my girl. I love you, never doubt that." They spent the last few precious seconds in silence. Suddenly, Chris found himself staring at a tiny room. Pale dirt, lots of dust, and bits of hay and grass stuck out in his mind.

Thanks, Rach. I'll find you, I swear.

The screen went black.

Chris looked at Evan for further instructions. Without the rain, he could see that Evan was physically about eighteen, but the kid's cold eyes spoke of too many years of hard living. Slowly and painfully, Chris pushed thoughts of his family aside to concentrate on earning their freedom. "Lead on."

"Toss the phone," Evan instructed.

Chris did so promptly. He could have tucked the phone away and still made Evan think he was following the instruction, but he decided full cooperation would serve his family better for the time being. Besides, he'd gotten all there was to get from the phone. He wouldn't soon forget Rachel, her tiny prison, or her hidden message.

During the long trip to their Manhattan destination, Chris listened as Evan described Mr. Parker's wishes. Chris had conjured the original plan during a wilder time in his life, but then he'd met Rachel and decided to follow a different path. Obviously, his friend still thought it was a good idea.

Chris wore an odd combination of old jeans, worn T-shirt, and expensive suit jacket. As they walked through dangerous areas, he felt menacing eyes watching him. He almost wished somebody would try something, just so he could release some anger. He didn't look physically impressive, but he knew how to handle himself in hand-to-hand combat.

Finally, Evan entered an old, abandoned-looking building.

Just like him to choose such a cheery place, Chris thought as he followed the kid down a labyrinth of hallways.

At last, they came to a door sporting a fancy electronic lock. Evan calmly disengaged the lock with a long code, pushed the door open, and motioned Chris inside. There wasn't an abandoned thing about this room. It was completely modernized, right down to the clean white walls.

He was always obsessed with white.

The number of people strolling about surprised Chris. Men and women hurried around like they had pressing business.

Evan called the room to attention, and gradually, the din subsided. "Mr. Parker has finally come through on his promise. Ladies and gentlemen, may I present our tutor: Dr. Collins."

Chris ran a critical eye over his class. They were a youthful and colorful bunch.

He still likes his crew well-rounded, I guess.

To a man—or woman—they looked eager to learn and had a greedy glint in their eyes.

"I'm assuming you've been vetted for this. It's going to take some careful coordination. Rule number one, follow my instructions implicitly. One mistake can ruin everything." Chris sighed. "Okay, people, clear the room. Come back in half an hour. I'll give you each your assignments, we'll practice for three hours, break for dinner, and practice some more. When we get it right, we'll do the real deal."

Cheers and whistles rose from all around the room. Being back in command felt surprisingly good, but Chris couldn't shake the gloomy feeling of being manipulated.

Is this really the best way to save Rachel, Jay, and Em?

Chapter 8:
Strange Place

Corra Compound
Stanley County, South Dakota

Saturday morning, Rachel Collins woke up to find a woman holding a breakfast tray hovering near her bed. "What time is it?"

"Nine thirty-five," the woman answered automatically. Color drained from her face and she pursed her lips as if that could prevent more harmful words from slipping out. Casting one more frightened glance at Rachel, the woman dumped the breakfast tray onto the rickety little end table near the head of the bed and fled.

Shrugging at the woman's weird behavior, Rachel set the second time on her watch accordingly. Her hunger overrode picky taste buds. She ate the rubbery eggs and burnt toast and recalled her second wretched night in this place. As usual, questions held the key to her misery. *Why did they take me? Are my children okay? Did I do something wrong? God, are you there?* Self-pitying tears flowed freely.

About a half-hour later, three men with guns barged in. One tossed some clean clothes onto the bed. A second shoved a phone at her. The third simply stood in the doorway with folded arms, wearing a bored expression.

"What's this for?" Rachel asked, looking from one man to the others and back again.

They ignored her.

The phone rang, and Rachel suddenly found herself juggling the phone. Once she had it under control, she unfolded it and looked at the blank screen. A red light began blinking then stayed on once she'd accepted the call. Chris's voice floated out of the phone. He sounded far away and distressed, but the blessed familiarity of his voice brought happy tears to her eyes.

As he babbled about right, wrong, and love, she wondered if he could see her. On the off chance that he could, she lowered her head so that her hair flowed in front of her face. Then, behind that temporary veil, she mouthed the time. He asked her to repeat the message and she did so several times. Next, she let herself cry more freely and dropped her hand out of seeming despair. Surreptitiously, she twisted the phone so that the camera would catch as much of the tiny room as possible. She didn't know why she bothered, but it was the only thing she could think to do.

Three minutes later, Rachel Collins clutched the phone tightly and stared off into space. She didn't care that the three men still crowded her tiny room. Light from the open doorway flooded the room, and tiny dust particles danced about happily.

Now what do I do, God?

As if in answer to her question, one of the men spoke. "Dr. Collins, you're to come with us on a tour of Corra."

So they can speak. What the heck's Corra?

Rachel would have loved to give them a hard time, but she was all funned out from the emotional ringer. Instead, she meekly struggled to her feet.

"Lead on," she said, taking one step toward the door.

One man made a stopping motion. "Change first," he said, gesturing to the forgotten clothes.

Rachel gave him a pointed look.

With an acknowledging grunt, he nodded to the others, and the men exited the room.

Rachel longed for a hot shower. Nevertheless, the fresh clothes felt magnificent. Prying her tattered stockings off took a full three minutes. The new clothes were plain but comfortable. Beige slacks, a casual blouse, and flat shoes that fit her perfectly. She frowned at the thought of her captors knowing her clothes and shoe sizes.

Cautiously stepping into the bright sunlight, Rachel slowly stretched her arms above her head.

Hey, I can even stand up without falling over. What a wonderful improvement.

Looking around, Rachel saw eight identical, one-story housing units standing in two neat rows off to her right side. Straight ahead, she saw a large, plain building. Four more buildings rose up on her left. Her tiny prison aligned with two of them. She noticed the compound made a giant rectangle. All of the buildings were white, marred with dust and dirt, and had grass and hay scattered across their black roofs. The long stalks caused the buildings to blend in nicely with the wide expanses of arid grassland surrounding them in all directions. Shielding her eyes and looking diagonally across a large open space, Rachel noticed a well-kept house with what appeared to be former army barracks sitting next to it.

"Ready for the tour?" asked a man. He was actually sort of handsome, but the perpetual scowl didn't help him in that regard. His short, dark hair, coal-black eyes, and small scar above one eyebrow gave him the look of a pirate. He grinned nastily.

"Don't go gettin' no stupid ideas, Jense," warned a younger man cheerfully.

Rachel remembered the name. She did a double take and her hands formed fists. *Participate in my kidnapping, will ya?* She clenched her teeth to keep her tongue from getting her in trouble. *Leave revenge to God.*

Can't I have just one swing, God? With much effort, Rachel forced her thoughts away from the man with the scar and concentrated on the man who had spoken.

"The boss'll kill you if ya so much as look at the lady wrong," the happy guy continued. He was shorter than his companions, probably only about five feet, seven inches tall, and he was the only one wearing a smile. Soft brown hair poked out from under a wide-rimmed cowboy hat. His eyes matched his hair, and he spoke with a soft Southern twang.

He's a bit young to be mixed up with this nasty crowd.

Though Rachel only had a vague idea of her location, the wide open spaces and abundance of short grasses ruled out most Southern states, except maybe Texas. Despite the cowboy hat, Rachel doubted he was a Texas boy.

The third man, the one who had handed her the phone, had a much-abused nose that currently sported a butterfly bandage across the bridge. His blond hair was pulled back into a greasy ponytail. Rachel wondered if it had been washed in the last six months. He wore a gold earring and four chains around his scrawny neck. "We pass your examination, Doc?" he asked with a sneer. He made a hocking noise and spat, narrowly missing Rachel's left foot as she jumped back.

"That's right, Dace. Impress the lady with those fine spittin' skills. If she slaps you, I ain't saying nothin'."

The happy boy removed his cowboy hat and addressed her.

"Good morning, ma'am, I'm Logan Dales." He suddenly looked shy. "Sorry about all this, but Mr. Parker's got some business matters he needs yer husband's cooperation with."

Rachel didn't know quite how to answer that. "Um, thanks, Logan. This is a bit stressful."

I'm surrounded by ugly, gun-wielding maniacs and my children are out of sight!

Before she could object, they whisked her off on a hasty tour. Walking left, they passed more "guest" rooms, the bathroom, and the showering facilities. She let them explain but didn't pay close attention. Each building blended in with the surrounding area.

What are they afraid of?

Next, they walked by a storage barn. Then, they came to the computer lab. Rachel mentally noted its position. Here, they turned right and walked along the wall of the long building.

"This is home sweet home to me an' the rest of the boys," Logan said, dutifully playing tour guide. "That's where the boss lives with his mistress." They cut across diagonally to the largest building. "You'll be spendin' most of your time here," said Logan as they entered a long hallway.

"Time for work," Dace said, shoving Rachel through a doorway midway down the hall.

She stumbled over the threshold into a four-bed clinic.

Logan just shook his head sadly, and let it go.

"When will I see my children?"

"You just saw them yesterday," Jense pointed out. "If you're real good—"

"Shut yer trap, Jense," the young man said indignantly. "I don't rightly know much about the visitin' schedule, ma'am, but I'll ask the boss about it."

Mumbling thanks, Rachel tried to sort more thoughts about this nightmare. She had recognized the pristine white hallways as the ones she had been carried through before her conversation with Mr. Parker. Again, the building's cleanliness caught her attention.

Odd for a place stuck in the middle of dusty nowhere.

It didn't take a genius to comprehend

what her job would be. A nurse listlessly attended a Hispanic man with a bullet wound in his chest. Being a medical doctor in a private practice in Western PA, Rachel had little experience with gunshot wounds. The nurse brightened considerably upon seeing Rachel. Hastily, she finished wrapping the chest bandage.

After introductions, Nurse Megan Jenson briefed Rachel on the clinic.

The days slipped by fairly pleasantly for Rachel, considering the circumstances. The clinic work kept her hands busy as her mind formulated escape plans. Megan's twin two-year-olds caught colds, and the cranky boys kept both women jumping. Each afternoon, Rachel got to spend time with Jason and Emily.

Midday on the Tuesday before the Thursday that would mark the one week anniversary of the kidnapping, Megan suddenly stopped folding towels and sobbed. Not knowing what else to do, Rachel comforted her as she would Jason or Emily. She gently guided Megan to the nearest cot. The man with the gunshot wound had left the day before so they had the clinic to themselves.

"What's the matter, Megan?"

"Everything!" the woman wailed, shaking her blond head violently.

You can say that again.

"Sshhhh. Look, I think we're okay to talk here, but we've got to be careful." Rachel held her breath and waited to see if the woman would open up. Despite the fact that they had spent the last few days working together, they were still very much strangers.

"I—I want to tell you my story. I don't really know how it happened, but I know we stay because it's the only way to be together as a family."

Megan's initial babblings only made marginal sense to Rachel, but she listened patiently.

"We used to live in Oregon. My husband, Kyle, was beginning to distinguish himself in the computer world. He designs programs and tinkers with computers. I don't know how Mr. Parker even learned of him, and I wish he hadn't." Her dark brown eyes became distant as she said, "The boys were only infants when Parker's men came for us. I thought we'd die during those first few days, but then, Kyle showed up, angry and scared."

"That must have been awful," Rachel murmured. She found herself fighting mixed feelings of wishing her husband to her side and simultaneously hoping he stayed as far away from Mr. Parker as possible.

Heedless of Rachel's inner turmoil, Megan continued telling her tale. "It's been over a year and a half now, and we only get to see each other twice a week. Kyle hates working for Mr. Parker; I can see it in his eyes. He does it for us." She stopped as if embarrassed. "I—I just thought you'd want to know that you're not alone." Before Rachel could respond, Megan rose from the cot and began reorganizing a rack of medical supplies.

The woman's concern touched Rachel, but her story was disturbing.

Over a year and a half! I don't want my children to grow up here!

Chapter 9:
New Case

J. Edgar Hoover Building, FBI Headquarters
Washington, D.C.

Monday morning, the first thing that melted through the fog of Julie Ann Davidson's brain was the sudden stream of profanities that came from a side office she passed. Her eyes widened and she blushed, scooting by the door as quickly as possible. Two steps from her tiny office an excited voice grabbed her attention.

"Davidson, Duncan, East conference room. Big case coming up!"

Her partner appeared at her side, and they exchanged glances but didn't speak. Ann wasn't even sure who had originally spoken to her, let alone how to respond to them.

"Did you sleep at all this weekend?" her partner asked in her ear.

Ann couldn't decide whether to be flattered by or annoyed at the concern in his voice. She jerked her head in a quick nod, but didn't have time to elaborate. Inwardly, she cringed a bit.

So much for makeup's magic.

Ann had just decided to accept the concern graciously when she realized her partner was already halfway to the conference room where the meeting would take place. Rolling her eyes, Ann dashed to catch up.

The tiny conference room quickly filled with an odd assortment of agents. A confused frown crossed Ann's face as she carefully scanned the others. Klipper and Harding usually worked organized crime cases. Baker and Vice worked a lot with CART, the Computer Analysis and Response Team. Daniels and Porter were "crime in the suites" agents, who spent their time tracking white collar crime. Ann was amused to note that she and Agent Duncan seemed to be the oddballs, seeing as they caught all sorts of cases. Someone had once told her they were observation and methods personified.

Ann got so lost analyzing the other agents that it took her a moment to realize everyone had gone quiet. When she saw Assistant Director in Charge Lance Morgan standing there in their midst, she had to clamp her lips firmly so her jaw wouldn't drop. The tall African American man cast a powerful presence, and the fact that he was here to brief them in person was more than slightly unusual.

"Have you all checked your bank accounts recently?" AD Morgan asked.

The question blindsided Ann. It sounded strange enough to be a question her partner would ask. She silently shook her head with the rest of the room.

"Sir?" asked Hank Klipper, the oldest agent in the room.

"Saturday night, the largest bank robbery in U.S. history took place," Morgan announced grimly. "If you bank online with any major branch, you're probably out a few dollars. Hackers sliced into bank accounts and siphoned off anywhere from three cents to four dollars and thirty-three cents."

"Do they know how many accounts were hit?" asked George Baker.

A general buzz arose and Morgan shook his head.

Baker took a sip of coffee.

The marvelous scent wafted through the

room, playing tricks on Ann's nose. Noticing the coffee maker in the corner, she slipped over to it and fixed two cups.

"Damage?"

Ann smiled at the simple, pointed question that was so characteristic of her quiet partner.

Morgan's voice was grumpy as he admitted, "That's unknown at this time. Complaints are pouring in from all over the country. I've even got Alaskan banks barking in my ears."

Ann returned to Patrick's side and handed him a hot cup of coffee. He nodded his thanks.

After savoring a sip of warm, liquid comfort, Ann asked, "Do we have an origin point?"

Agent Vice shot her a mixed look of admiration and irritation that told her she had stolen the question from between his pudgy lips.

"The CART teams are working on it," her boss said wearily. "I expect a report from them sometime this afternoon. Because this is such a massive case, I want you four teams tackling it from whatever angle you see fit. I'm making Patrick the case agent, but you're still free to pursue leads as you find them."

The other teams nodded solemnly, but Ann exchanged an alarmed glance with Patrick.

Knowing he would just let it go, Ann said, "Um, sir, how exactly do we fit?"

"Report analysis." The assistant director gave her a teeth-filled smile and pointed to the others. "They'll get you the pieces. You just have to put them together." That said, he strode from the room looking like a burden had just rolled off his shoulders.

Great, now the burden's on our shoulders.

Slowly, Ann and Patrick walked to her office. She sat behind her desk, and he leaned against the doorframe as usual.

"You can sit down, if you want," Ann offered, knowing it would be futile.

Patrick declined with a shake of his head and downed the rest of the coffee. A thoughtful expression stole over his face. He walked the three paces to her waste basket, deposited the Styrofoam cup, returned to his spot in her doorway, and leaned there with arms crossed in a position Ann had dubbed his "thinking pose." She impatiently fiddled with a pencil, giving Patrick time to think.

When several very long minutes had passed and her coffee wasn't there to distract her, Ann gave up on waiting, and asked, "Where do we start?"

He gave her a *have-patience* look.

Slumping in her chair, Ann resigned herself to the irksome task of waiting for Patrick to say something. Bored with the pencil, she tossed it onto her desk and studied her partner. She despised waiting, but she had learned that soon after Patrick got that look in his deep blue eyes, which were several shades darker than her own, cases were broken wide open. His dark brown hair was a mite longer than was entirely neat but it fit nicely with his crisp, black suit. Ann admired his patience, not that she would ever tell him that. It infuriated as much as impressed her. He was only three years older than her thirty years, but at times, it seemed like he had about twenty years more experience.

"Want a cookie?" Ann offered, taking them out of her purse.

Patrick shook his head.

"They're kinda stale." Ann munched one of Mrs. Banning's cookies as she pondered the case.

Now I need milk.

The money motive was simple, but many questions remained. *How many people are involved? How was it coordinated? How did they pull it off?* Suddenly, Ann realized that she was assuming more than one person was involved. She contemplated that for a moment and then agreed with herself. *There must be more than one hacker, right? Nobody's that good.*

"We'll wait it out," Patrick said finally.

Ann nodded, mildly disappointed that he didn't spit out the criminals' names, birthdays, and favorite foods.

What else can we do?

"Did you find out anything about your friend?"

Shaking her head in frustration, Ann remembered the countless weekend hours spent thinking about the Collins case. Despite going to work on Saturday, her efforts had been consumed by the unofficial case. Taking a deep breath, she summarized her weekend. "When I got back home Friday evening, I did an internet search and read as many newspaper accounts of the case as I could. I spent Saturday bothering the Fairview police and fire departments. At first they were a bit wary about sharing details. I think they thought I was a reporter."

She made a face, and Patrick chuckled.

"Finally, Officer Long vouched for me with the police, and I assured both departments that my involvement with the case was purely unofficial. That seemed to soothe their rabid territorial instincts, and they were more cooperative."

"Who's Officer Long?"

"Oh, that's right. You weren't in Saturday. I forgot I haven't talked to you about the case at all. My trip out to PA was basically a waste of time, but I managed to talk to Officer Long, a Fairview cop who is also a friend of the Collins family. He had gone there that night because Christopher Collins wanted to talk. When he got there, he heard noises upstairs, and naturally, he went to investigate."

Ann shook her head sadly, as if to say *that was dumb*.

"Trouble?" inquired Patrick.

Nodding confirmation, Ann chucked the half-eaten cookie into the garbage.

Okay, really stale. I need more coffee.

"Somebody knocked him out, tied him up, and dumped him out back sometime before the house exploded. Judging from the timeline in the reports, I'd say it was only a few minutes between the attack on Officer Long and the house incident. No one knows who set the charges, but Chris Collins is the prime suspect."

"Did they run him through criminal databases?"

Ann winced, and Patrick nodded in understanding. The man in question was married to her friend. She desperately wanted to believe Rachel had better character judgment than marriage to a former convict would suggest. She frowned thoughtfully. "I don't think so, but I'll get one of the computer guys here to handle that."

Ann quickly put in the request before saying, "No bodies were found in the house."

"No bodies are good bodies," Patrick joked deadpan.

Smiling patronizingly, Ann continued, "I talked to a neighbor lady; nice, elderly, and very chatty. The important things I got from the rather drawn-out conversation were that Officer Long had been tied with a fluffy bunny lamp cord and a man in a blue uniform from a white van was seen that same day with the children, Jason and Emily, in front of their house."

Patrick nodded, still leaning on her doorway.

Doesn't his shoulder ever get sore?

Ann's phone rang, startling her. The caller ID told her it was Brad Matthews.

"Davidson," she answered, before listening to the quick explanation. "I see. Okay, thanks Brad. No, no—wait do me a favor. I want you to run the check again. This time do a face search for a picture I'm sending you." She pulled a photo of Christopher Collins from her purse. "Be right back," she said to Patrick.

Exiting the room, Ann dashed over to the scanner and sent the photo to her buddies down in the dungeons the Bureau liked to call computer labs. Mission accomplished, she returned to her office and slipped sideways past Patrick who hadn't moved an inch. "I asked around and found out several of the Collins family's bank accounts were emptied the same day the house exploded and the family disappeared. Also, the people at

Millcreek Community Hospital say Dr. Collins was there late."

"Mister?"

"Yes, they're both doctors, but only Christopher works at the hospital. He was there covering a staff shortage that night. Officer Long said he talked to Chris around 9:30. I checked with the bank. Their system shows that someone used the internet to access the accounts belonging to the Collins family and moved some funds to offshore accounts around ten. That's about as far as I got. Later, six automated telling machines had their hidden cameras covered and most of the remaining money in the accounts was removed."

"Strange."

"Very much so. No one knows who got their money. If it was Chris, then he had every right to access the accounts. But why cover the cameras? And why the rest of the cloak and dagger bit? On a hunch, I asked Officer Long to have the ATM machines dusted for prints. It was too late for four of the machines; they already had fingerprints all over the place." The inflection in her voice suggested there was more.

"Bet the other two had the opposite problem," said Patrick.

His ability to process things quickly was one more reason Ann liked him.

"Precisely. The one on Archer Street is rarely used because it's so out of the way. There were five partial prints, but the other buttons and all around the base had been wiped clean. The other machine had the same thing. Half of it was still clean of all prints, which tells us that either there are obsessive-compulsive bank employees out there or someone didn't want their prints taken."

"Brad came up negative on the criminal records?" Patrick inquired.

Ann nodded.

"Juvenile records too?"

"I didn't ask," she admitted.

He looked at her kindly. "Shall I?"

She smiled thanks.

"Please, but only if you can do it without making waves."

Giving her a good-natured salute, Patrick went to complete his assignment.

Suddenly alone, Ann sat at her desk idly tapping a pencil against her chin and thinking.

This could be even more complicated

than I'd thought.

More than four days had passed. Statistically, the odds of recovering kidnapping victims alive after the first twenty-four hours weren't stellar, and each extra day just made the likelihood of a happy ending more and more remote. With the new case they'd caught today, Ann wasn't sure how much time she could devote to finding Rachel.

Please, please don't become a statistic, Rach. I need you to be okay.

Chapter 10:
Satellite Snooping

Parker's Base of Operations
New York City, New York

Christopher Collins let his head slump into his palms, supported by elbows firmly planted on the desk. Since his arrival at the Manhattan hideout, he had taught hackers just enough so they could complete "Mr. Parker's" job. The first hit had been highly successful, netting about $237 million. Lacking the element of surprise, the second wave of bank account raids had required a great deal more care. The extra precautions forced them all to work longer and harder than they had the previous time. Chris fought down a flutter of worry that someone would catch his safeguards. He didn't have time for worry. The others had dispersed to celebrate their successful take of $289 million.

Chris could probably have used a good stiff drink to forget his troubles, but he needed a clear head to find his family. He spent the free time hacking into government files and satellite feeds. Rachel's mouthed message all those days ago had been a time: 10:06. That placed her in Mountain Standard Time.

Over the last four nights, Chris had stolen a few minutes here and there alone with the computers, but this was the first time he'd managed to devote a few hours to his search. He knew his former friend well enough to know that Rachel and the kids would be held in a remote compound hidden in plain sight.

Frustrated, Chris studied hundreds of satellite photos, systematically searching from south to north. After several false alarms, he found it, a tiny, square compound that blended in perfectly with the South Dakota landscape.

Thank you, suspicious, nosy government bureaucrats, he thought as he pulled up, cleaned up, and printed out the photo.

I've got to tell someone.

Chris hated to admit needing help, but he knew rescuing Rachel and the kids would require far more than a one-man crusade. His knees cracked when he stood up to stretch. Grabbing the printout, he stumbled to his room to rack his brain for ideas. He hid the photo and collapsed onto the bed. Soon, he drifted off to a dreamless sleep.

The next day the team rigorously prepared for the third and final wave. Or so they thought. Mostly, Chris had them working in circles.

That night, Chris continued his quest. He had spent much of the day thinking about whom he should contact. For some reason, his thoughts kept drifting to that last night with Rachel. He could almost smell her pleasant perfume.

What were we doing? After a few moments, Chris answered his own question. *Looking at pictures from her old yearbook. She was talking about something ... someone. Who was she talking about?* He closed his eyes and massaged his temple. *I should remember this!*

At last, things clicked together. With a few sure key strokes, he connected to a private search engine. Since his bank raids messed with people's money, they had generated a lot of media coverage. After scanning a few newspapers, Chris discovered a short interview with one of his neighbors who had belatedly reported seeing a white van outside of the house, pre-explosion of course.

Chris smiled genuinely for the first time in a long time. Next, he hacked into the government's personnel database.

Perfect.

A simple plan formed within minutes. He would get his help to come to him.

Chris set his plan in motion and found himself awkwardly praying. *Uh, God? I've never been much of a praying man, but please, watch over my family.*

Chapter 11:
Song Strength

Ann Davidson's Apartment
Alexandria, Virginia

As the one-week anniversary of the kidnapping of Rachel, Jason, and Emily Collins neared, Ann's anxiety level spiked. To make matters worse, the case of the internet bank thieves was going nowhere either. She felt like she'd leapt onto a case treadmill. This wasn't the first time a case stumped her, but by far, Rachel's disappearance was the most personal case to do so. It wasn't officially her case, but she and Rachel had been good friends once upon a time. Ann knew all too well the time sensitivity of kidnapping cases.

A conference speaker had once said, *"The more time that slips by, the more likely it is the victim will die."*

Ann couldn't shake the words from her mind. She had seen firsthand the devastation that a prolonged investigation could have on a family. As usual with kidnapping cases, Ann's thoughts turned to Gabriel Dawson, a boy about Jason Collins's age, who'd been missing more than ten months before surfacing as a broken body in a field half a state away from his Virginia home. Finding the Collins family murdered like that would be infinitely worse than a long wait, but the agony of not knowing what happened also cut deeply. The search for justice continued in the Dawson case, but it had long since gone cold.

I haven't forgotten you, Gabriel, Ann silently promised. She considered calling the child's mother, but couldn't bear the added emotional stress at the moment.

New stories like the spectacular internet robberies and the murder of a senator's wife made the media forget about the Collins family, but Ann couldn't forget the case. *Not enough people died to make it interesting,* she thought bitterly. The thought sickened her. *Lord, have we sunk so low, forgetting the pain of others if the story doesn't hold our interest?*

Currently, she sat on the sitting room floor of her Virginia apartment surrounded by a sea of papers. Danny, her hyper golden retriever, barked and whined from his kitchen prison. Although pretty much over the illness that had recently plagued his system, Danny occasionally experienced a gross leakage from one end or the other. This made Ann extra cautious, especially where her plush living room carpet was concerned. Annoyed at being ignored, Danny yipped and yowled impatiently.

Ann sighed, struggled to her feet, and walked to the kitchen gate to chat with her pal. "I know you're lonely, boy, but I've got work to do tonight." She leaned over the gate and patted his head while he looked at her with sad eyes. "Oh, don't look at me like that," Ann said half-heartedly. Finally giving in, she hauled herself over the gate and sat on the floor. Danny immediately climbed onto her lap. She laughed. "Okay, you can stay as long as you don't deposit your lunch on me and ruin my nice pants." She cupped his face and endured a sloppy kiss. "Whew! You have really, really bad breath."

Note to self, invest in doggy breath mints.

Danny stepped over Ann, turned around, tilted his head, whined, draped his paws over her left leg, and lowered his head in between his paws.

"Comfortable?" Ann asked. Receiving no answer from the dog, save for the deep, regular hushed noises of his slumber, Ann absently stroked his soft fur and let her mind wander back to her two main cases.

A half-hour later, her leg started to cramp. She looked at the microwave clock. "Dinner time," she muttered.

Do I have to get up? She grunted and dragged her stiff self to an upright position.

At her movement the dog stirred, repositioned his head, and went back to sleep.

Wish I could sleep like that, Ann thought, frowning as she recalled how little she had slept in the last week. She fixed herself a leftover meatloaf sandwich and sniffed at a takeout tossed salad that still looked edible. Since she couldn't remember when she had gotten the salad, she settled on an apple to accompany dinner. She prayed, but her heart wasn't in it.

After dinner, she took a shower, refilled Danny's water bowl, and returned to her piles of papers spread all over her living room. The bank case still had a position in the newspapers, but five minutes later, Ann's mind wandered as it often did when something

Julie C. Gilbert

deeply troubled her. She thought of an old song called "God Will Have the Last Word." She let the words tumble around her mind for a while before humming the gentle tune. Before she knew it, she found herself singing:

"As the world falls apart around me,
I think of this truth and peace comes:
God will have the last word!
He has in ages past, He still does today,
And the future's certain when it comes to this:
God will have the last word!
Our Mighty King came to earth
As a baby to live and love and die,
But that wasn't the end by far.
Jesus had the last word, when He rose again!"

As she finished the song, Ann's knees automatically shifted under her so that she was kneeling. As she spoke her heart, she forgot the papers around her. "Oh God, I can't do this! You do have the last word, but I can't see it. Forgive me for doubting Your sovereignty. Please be with Rachel tonight. I know she's alive. Help us find her, Lord, and please guide me and the others as we work on this bank case. I just don't know what to do.

98

Help us piece together these mysteries. Thank you for who You are. Thank you for—just … thank you."

Ann prayed some more with her heart and a poem called "Speak Soft Words" came to mind. She spoke the words as a part of her prayer:

"So, here I am again,
Baffled and confused,
Come before You, Lord God,
Saying please give me wisdom.
Please give me wisdom,
For my head is pounding with
The problems of the world around me.
Won't You please give me wisdom?
Won't You lead my heart today, Lord?

So, here I am again,
Worn and weary,
Come before you, Lord God,
Saying speak soft words to me, Lord.
Speak soft words to me,
For my ears are ringing with
The loud shouts of the world around me.
Won't You speak soft words to me, Lord?
Won't You speak soft words today?

Totally at peace
Is exactly where I'll be,
When the Lord God is near."

In her mind's eye, Ann saw Rachel smiling and laughing. "Thank you for always being near, Father," Ann murmured, recalling the long phone conversations and sporadic e-mails exchanged over the years since high school. "Place Your protective arms around the Collins family, I pray. Let Your will be done in their lives, and in mine. Amen."

Nothing radical happened. No lightning bolts containing the answers to the mysterious cases fell from the sky, but Ann had a keen sense of peace after laying the heavy burdens in her heavenly Father's capable hands.

Her eyes widened when she looked at her wristwatch and realized how much time had passed. Knowing she could do little more of use, Ann prepared for bed and slipped between the clean sheets. She fell asleep in record time.

Chapter 12:
Cloak of Peace

Corra Compound
Stanley County, South Dakota

Thursday morning, Rachel Collins woke up with a wave of peace washing over her. She lay wide awake in her bed and began praying softly. "Father, forgive me for all of my doubts. I trust you. I just hate feeling helpless. Please protect my babies. I know You're in control, but I'm still fighting You for that control. Help me to trust You more."

Throughout the week, she had been worried sick for her husband and children. It had gotten to the point that prayer had not even entered Rachel's mind. Every moment apart from her family hurt in a way she could only describe as a deep ache. Now, she felt starved for the Word of God. Doubting there was a Bible in the whole of Corra, she thought hard to remember some Psalms.

After a few minutes, Rachel remembered Psalm 18: 1-2. She whispered the words as a prayer. "'I love you, O Lord, my strength. The Lord is my rock, my fortress and my deliverer; my God is my rock, in whom I take refuge. He is my shield and the horn of my salvation, my stronghold.'"

Fortified by her short prayer, Rachel spent another half-hour in solid prayer. They were supposed to receive another "guest" today so she prayed for that too. "God, protect and keep this person. Give them the peace that you've given to me."

Soon after that, Logan Dales came to take Rachel to visit her children. After an enthusiastic greeting, Jason wandered off to play again, but Emily latched onto Rachel like a leech. Minutes passed while Rachel relished the reassuring weight of Emily in her arms. Just as sure as she felt Emily's thin arm gripping her neck, she knew the child would be sucking a thumb. Rachel had tried countless times to break the three-year-old of the bad habit, but she was in no mood to cause her baby any more distress today. Mrs. Hart had said Emily threw several fits, and Rachel believed it. Her sleeping angel could be a firebrand at times.

"I love you," Rachel whispered into

Emily's soft hair. She closed her eyes and imagined what havoc Emily would wreak upon entering those dark, scary teenage years. Would she grow up to be a rebellious young woman? Would she sneak out of the house and lie to her parents like Rachel had once upon a time?

Will you give me gray hair, Emily?

If they stayed in Corra, Emily would hardly have a chance to learn her letters and numbers. The more Rachel learned of this place, the more adamant she became about the necessity of escaping. Whatever they were up to here, it had no business being conducted around children.

Despite the long-term worries and missing her husband terribly, Rachel was finally at peace.

Find me, Chris. Better yet, find God. He knows where I am.

With eyes still shut against the world, Rachel held her daughter for a few more moments. Her arms started hurting, but she wanted to cherish the quiet, restful embrace for as long as it would last. A crash prompted her to open her eyes. Rachel whipped her head toward the disturbance then smiled at her son's frantic efforts to keep the Jenson boys away from the toys he had claimed. Jason was quite out of his element with the twins.

Poor thing, he's only had one sibling to contend with so far.

The rest of the morning playtime went smoothly. Jason and Emily didn't understand the situation, and Rachel kept up the illusion that daddy was simply "away." Their peace of mind outweighed the need for them to know the truth. To be honest, she didn't fully understand the truth anyway.

"Doc?" said a shaky voice from the doorway. "The men said you would be in here ... I—I don't feel good."

The newcomer didn't look so good either. Giving the girl a reassuring smile, Rachel said, "Go get settled on one of the beds in the clinic. It's two doors down on the left. You passed it getting here. I'll be over in a moment."

Poor child, how did she end up in this mess?

Reluctantly, Rachel left her children in Sylvia Hart's hands. The woman and her husband both worked willingly for Mr. Parker, which surprised Rachel. She had assumed all of the workers were either illegal aliens or people in situations similar to her own.

Stepping into the clinic, Rachel found the girl lying on a cot staring blankly at the ceiling. She took in the girl's curly dark hair and striking skin, which was the color of creamy coffee. When Rachel finished her observations, she said, "I'm Dr. Collins, but you can just continue calling me 'Doc' if you prefer. What's your name?" She picked up the girl's clammy hand and squeezed.

The youth looked at her blankly but said nothing.

Rachel gazed deeply into the girl's forlorn black eyes. *You have such beautiful eyes.* With one more reassuring squeeze, Rachel let go so she could retrieve a damp cloth.

After cleaning the girl's face and hands, Rachel said, "You don't have to tell me your name, but it sure would make this easier. I bet you have quite a story to tell." She forced a smile for the patient's sake.

A few moments slipped by in silence before the girl spoke. "Jenny—Jenny Hapler."

"Hapler," repeated Rachel thoughtfully. "Any relation to the Illinois senator?"

Jenny's weak smile confirmed Rachel's guess. "My father," murmured the girl.

Why would they kidnap a senator's daughter? Rachel recalled several recent newspaper articles talking about Senator Orion Hapler. *He was pushing hard for something. What was it?*

She absently checked Jenny's vital signs, still trying to remember the details.

It was something about strengthening borders ... Border hardening! Hapler's been bent on getting the Boarded Border Act passed. Or was it the Satellite Expansion Program? Either way, why does Mr. Parker care?

Rachel's mind hummed through things she had seen and heard in the last week.

Smuggling!

The answer seemed obvious once she thought of it. The new act—whatever its name—involved taking numerous satellite pictures of the U.S. borders and possible smuggling routes at random times.

Okay, so they're smugglers and photos would threaten their ring. What does that have to do with Jenny or us? How do Chris and I factor in?

"My—my mother is dead!" Sobs Jenny had obviously kept pent up for quite some time burst forth, shaking her body with painful force.

The statement slapped Rachel in the face. "How?" She breathed out the question, though she expected no answer. Tears stung her eyes as she watched the girl break down. Jenny couldn't be more than sixteen. Seeing her in so much pain broke Rachel's heart. Afraid the girl might choke on her tears, Rachel helped her sit up and held her while she cried.

When the stormy sobs finally subsided into a gentle stream, Jenny whispered, "She tried to stop them from taking me. It's my fault. It's all my fault!"

"No," Rachel countered. She pulled away enough so she could look the teenager in the eyes. Although her eyes glittered with conviction, Rachel softened her voice when she spoke. "Jenny, none of this is your fault. Never believe it. Your mother did only what a mother ought to do in that situation. God knew this. Despite what it seems, God has a plan for your life. That may sound trite, but His plan is perfect."

"He planned for my mother to be murdered?"

Rachel stopped to think before she got herself into trouble.

Father, speak through me.

"Jenny, there is evil in this world and suffering comes with such evil. But along with the pain of loss there is hope because God's love is perfect. That love can never be taken from you."

"That sounds like something she would say," Jenny said, sniffling. "She'd always be talking about Jesus loving this or that lost soul." Her eyes glistened, but she had no more tears to shed.

"Remember her words and cherish them," Rachel encouraged.

"But it hurts!" Tearless sobs shook Jenny's slender figure.

Rachel's mothering instincts kicked in again and she let the sobbing teen lean heavily upon her.

Lord, I don't understand, but I know You can ease Jenny's pain. Please cloak her in perfect peace.

Chapter 13:
Rough Tip Off

J. Edgar Hoover Building, FBI Headquarters
Washington, D.C.

Early Friday morning, "Wahoo! We got 'em!" ripped through the normal hum of activity in the FBI's D.C. headquarters.

Ann Davidson hugged the wall to keep from being run over by stampeding agents, George Baker and Lyle Vice. A fresh cup of coffee wavered precariously in her hand.

What the—

Clamping down on several half-baked comments, Ann hurriedly followed them to the small conference room. Her high-heeled shoes clicked the cadence of her frantic pace.

"Hey, Davidson, you're slipping these days," Agent Baker joked.

She coolly arched an eyebrow. "What do you mean by—" she began.

Just then, ADIC Lance Morgan entered and a hush descended over the peanut gallery. "Agents, my savings account is missing $4.97," he said grimly. "Whoever is behind all of this is getting on my nerves, and I want him taken out now!"

And we're going to do that how?

George Baker's cocky smile did little to improve Ann's mood.

"A CART guy found this in his e-mail yesterday." Baker triumphantly waved a piece of paper. Clearing his throat, he read the note aloud, "'Wallet feeling a little light these days?' The origin was well-hidden, but my guy's good. He tracked it to an abandoned building in Manhattan."

Something about the situation bothered Ann, but everyone else was ecstatic over the news. Of course, Patrick wasn't in the room to share her doubts. She frowned in concentration.

"Aww, cheer up, Davidson. You can crack the next case," said Baker, mistaking her frown for disappointment. He draped a comforting arm around her.

The fact that he thought she was upset because someone else solved the case offended her. Ann didn't trust herself with words yet, so she merely stood still, looking annoyed until he finally lifted his heavy arm off her shoulders.

Is it over? It sure doesn't feel over.

"Why play with us?" Ann finally asked, breaking the jubilant mood.

Her colleagues and boss quieted.

"The son of a monkey's uncle overplayed his hand," Baker said. "Come on, Ann. What's the big deal? It happens all the time."

Ann respected Baker's enthusiasm, but she found him a bit reckless at times and way too trusting of the bad guys to behave normally.

"It's a setup," said Patrick, coming through the doorway, his stride even and sure.

Ann smiled. *The cavalry's here!*

"What makes you say that?" asked AD Morgan.

"Sir, this guy's too good to let an e-mail foil him," said Patrick politely.

"If he wanted to gloat, he could have done it from any public library and we'd have little chance of tracing it back to him," Ann added. "Besides, I think there's a team involved, and they probably wouldn't take too kindly to someone giving away their hideout. If somebody's leaving us a clear trail to follow, he's probably got some sort of motive we've not predicted yet."

"Hey! My CART buddy worked hard for that info," said Baker.

Worked hard as in opened his email and printed it out? If that's working hard, I am in the wrong branch of this organization.

The others considered the Duncan-Davidson logic for a moment but then seemed to dismiss it. Only Hank Klipper agreed with them.

Even AD Morgan looked ready to bust down Manhattan doors. "I've contacted the NYPD," he said, breaking the mounting tension. "They'll have their SWAT guys ready to go when you get there."

Agent Baker gave another joyful whoop, albeit a somewhat subdued one, as he was in AD Morgan's presence.

"How are we getting there, sir?" asked Agent Klipper.

"Oh, I don't think all of you need to go," Morgan pointed out.

At this news, Agent Baker's face fell like a little boy denied pre-dinner cookies.

The assistant director thought for a moment. Muttering, "One and a half ought to cover it," Morgan studied the agents in the room.

Ann didn't know if she liked his tone.

"Baker?" Morgan asked.

"Yes, sir," said the young agent. His head snapped up as hope glimmered in his eyes.

"You're traveling with them," he said pointing to Ann and Patrick. "Agent Duncan has seniority, but I want you to mind them both, Baker."

"Yes, sir!" George repeated, eager to participate in the raid.

***

Parker's Base of Operations
New York City, New York

Ann was grateful they had caught a flight from Regan National up to LaGuardia. The thought of a five-plus hour car ride trapped with Agent Baker hadn't exactly thrilled her. Though only a few years younger, Baker possessed the temperament of a small child.

Did he have to send Baker? Ann would have been much happier being stuck with Agent Vice. *At least Vice wouldn't make me feel like I'm babysitting.*

Her partner gave her a knowing smile. His eyes laughed at her thoughts. It was comforting to know he understood.

"SWAT guys go in first. We're just here as spectators," Ann reminded.

"Yes, Mother," Baker said brightly, face pressed against the window for a better view of the city.

Rolling her eyes, Ann shot a quick prayer heavenward. *Lord, protect us today.* She couldn't shake the foreboding feeling that made her stomach uneasy.

"We're here," said Patrick. He helped her from the taxi.

"Thank you," said Ann, happy to stretch her long legs and not be squished between the two men. She had traded her pumps for comfortable flats that were more raid-friendly.

An hour later most of the excitement was over, the SWAT teams had broken down doors and scared the senses out of about thirty young people, most of whom loudly proclaimed their innocence. Backup trucks were called so the prisoners could be hauled away to temporary homes courtesy of the NYPD. Only after a careful sweep did the police let the three FBI agents tour the facilities.

Agent Baker stopped in the main

computer room and started admiring each of the fine toys therein. Agents Duncan and Davidson exchanged knowing glances and left Baker alone, sure he wouldn't miss them at all.

The sprawling ten-story building made a lovely hideout. It covered most of a whole block. One section still had a decrepit pool. An exercise room had been refurbished, and the new equipment still shone with manufacturing polish. The top five floors were abandoned, but the other floors were divided into small apartments. There was a cafeteria, kitchen, laundry room, generator room, and even an entertainment room complete with three pool tables.

Ann and Patrick separated to search the third floor. After about ten minutes, Ann looked for her partner so they could return to the main entrance. "Patrick?" she called. "Agent Duncan?" She got a funny feeling, and her left hand crept toward her gun. Willing her nerves to be still, Ann drew the weapon. Its coolness and weight reassured her.

After searching several more rooms, she returned to the second floor. "Patrick?" Ann called again before lapsing into uneasy silence. Turning a corner, she saw a body lying on the floor, visible by dim light. Her breath caught in her throat.

Patrick!

The creepy feeling returned full force. Someone was watching. Before she could move, the cold muzzle of a gun lightly tapped the back of her neck. Chills raced up and down her spine, and her mouth suddenly went dry.

I'm dead, Ann thought dully, surprised that the thought didn't upset her more. She wanted to curse herself for falling into the trap, but her mind went blank. Luckily, breathing's an ingrained thing.

"Agent Davidson, I need to talk to you," said the man with the gun.

Ann briefly considered spinning to face him but didn't relish being shot in the neck at point-blank range. She briefly bit her bottom lip, and said, "I can safely say you have my full attention, sir."

"Put your gun in your right hand and slowly pass it to me over your shoulder."

Easy on the trigger, easy on the trigger.

Having no choice, Ann followed the directives. Her empty hands fell uneasily at her sides. Strangely, she found the fact that the gun wasn't wavering comforting.

"I need you to save Rachel for me," the man whispered. "My family is being held in South Dakota."

"Dr. Collins?"

"Yes. You've got to trust me. Take this photo. There are coordinates on the back." His voice was low and urgent.

Something slipped into Ann's left hand. She held it tightly but didn't dare look at it.

"Convince the Bureau to take out this compound but be careful. There are a lot of potential hostages there, including my wife and children. There's an Alabama address on the back as well. Have someone watch the lady at that address."

"How can I trust you?" Ann asked.

"You have access to fancy computers. Use them. Check the satellite feeds. The man you want is a small-time smuggler who switched gears. If you want more information, look up the names Jonathan Parker and Paul Morton in the army database. You won't find anything until you call Fort Drum and have them do a manual search." Dr. Collins was quiet for a moment.

Ann held her breath.

"I'm a hacker, Agent Davidson. I wanted

out of that life, but an old friend forced me back in. Save my family, and I promise I'll fix the bank accounts."

Ann's head spun from all the information being spat at her. She feared her mind would suddenly blank on everything.

Dr. Collins shook her left shoulder, and the gun lost contact with her neck for a second before gently bouncing back into position.

"Do you understand?"

Inhaling a steadying breath, Ann said, "Yes. Get people to South Dakota to rescue Rachel, the kids, and the other hostages, check satellite feeds for smugglers, send someone to Alabama, and search Fort Drum's records."

"Correct. Tell only people you trust implicitly. Now, I hope you have a good memory, and I'm sorry."

Ann felt fingers close on pressure points in her neck.

Upon awakening, she found the photo and an unloaded handgun inches from her face. She was surprised to find her own gun already in its holster. She picked up the other gun, popped the magazine back into place, and hastily tucked the satellite photo into her knee-high sock, just behind her left calf. Dr. Collins had trusted her enough to leave the evidence, and she was going to make sure that it got put to good use.

Minutes later, Ann entered the computer lab where she and Patrick had left Agent Baker. *Oh, we're a lovely lot,* she thought.

Looking paler than usual, Patrick absently rubbed at his neck. Agent Baker held an ice pack over the right side of his head. His tie was askew, and he looked decidedly grouchy. Ann didn't know much about Chris Collins, but she admired his skill at rendering people unconscious. She smiled ruefully.

"What are you so happy about?" snapped Baker.

"We're alive," she replied pleasantly. "A fact I very much doubted a half-hour ago."

"What happened?" Patrick asked, staring hard at Ann.

She handed Patrick his gun and gave him a look that said: *I'll explain everything later.*

***

Ann's Apartment
Alexandria, Virginia
By the time they were back in the D.C. area,

the regular work day had long since expired. Ann casually asked Patrick to join her for dinner. With a knowing nod, he accepted, and they managed to ditch Agent Baker.

Safely tucked in her apartment, Ann peeled the photo away from her suffering lower leg. "Do you have any idea how uncomfortable a photo can be if it's stuck in a knee-high sock for more than five minutes?"

From Patrick's expression, he clearly didn't know how to answer her.

Waking from a nap, Danny realized people were home and let loose a string of excited barks.

"Umm, I'm not sure," Patrick said awkwardly over the din.

Men! They have no idea.

Patrick's deep blue eyes widened when she handed him the satellite photo, but before he could get a good look she snatched it back.

"Hey!"

"Sorry, I didn't get to look at it," said Ann, turning the photo so they could examine the picture together. It showed a rectangular compound with several tiny figures holding guns. Three white trucks in the center of the picture looked like they were being loaded or unloaded. "Smugglers," she murmured.

"What?"

"First, I want to hear your story. Then, I'll tell you mine." Ann walked to the kitchen, hopped the dog gate, and began refrigerator rummaging. "Make yourself comfortable."

"Uh, dog," Patrick said hesitantly.

Ann looked at Patrick, noted his expression, and followed his finger to the corner where Danny had dashed after greeting her. She made a face. "Yeah, um, just watch where you step when you come in," she said, gathering paper towels to sop up the spreading yellow pool appearing beneath her dog. "Sometimes, he gets a little excited." The paper towel wad in her hand soaked through and she had to get more. "And sometimes he gets a lot excited."

"I see." Patrick entered carefully, settled himself at the tiny table, and studied the photo.

After disposing of the dirty paper towels, Ann washed her hands and continued her quest for dinner fixings. "Hmmm, not much here." She closed the refrigerator, crossed her arms, and leaned back against it. "What do you feel like tonight? There's macaroni and cheese, hot dogs, questionable leftovers, or I can order a pizza or something."

"Questionable leftovers?" Patrick asked dubiously.

"Not recommended. I'd hate to see the headline 'Agent kills partner with rotten tofu.'"

Patrick made a gagging noise. "You eat that stuff?" he asked, scrunching his face.

She laughed. "Why do you think it's rotting?"

"Always knew you were a smart woman," Patrick commented. He turned the photo over. "There's something written here."

"Pizza it is," Ann said cheerfully, not wanting to explain just yet. "What would you like on it?"

"Anchovies and mushrooms, please."

They'd been partners long enough for her to know the answer, but she figured there was always the odd chance that his pizza preference would someday resemble a sane person's. It was Ann's turn to make a grossed-out face. She called the local pizzeria and ordered a large pie with half anchovies and mushrooms and half pepperoni. "It'll be about a half-hour; their 'twenty minutes' always are," she reported, returning her cell phone to its home at her waist.

"Good, because you have a whole lot of explaining to do," Patrick said, nodding to a chair.

"Would you like something to drink?"

"Water."

Ann filled two glasses with filtered water. She had expected as much. Her partner was strange. He always asked for plain water without ice or lemon or anything.

"You first," Ann insisted, handing him a glass. "It will be much quicker anyway."

"Someone snuck up behind me and knocked me out."

Short and to the point; can't complain about that.

"You don't have anything else to add?"

"Nope." Patrick glanced at the address on the photograph. "You going to explain this?" he asked, holding up the photo.

"My story starts and ends much the same as yours, but there's a whole lot of in between," Ann said, feeling Patrick's analytical eyes studying her expressions. "Dr. Collins was the man who jumped us, only that's not his real name. He pulled your gun on me, and we had a nice chat. He gave four instructions. One, we need to check the satellite feed at those coordinates," she said, waving to the photo. "Two, we need to rescue Rachel, the two kids, and a bunch of other hostages from some place in South Dakota. Three, we need to protect a woman in Alabama. Four, if we doubt him, we should call Fort Drum and get the records for Jonathan Parker and Paul Morton."

"Tall order."

"'Tall' doesn't even begin to cover it," Ann said flatly.

They sat in moody silence, each lost in thought.

"Do you trust him?" Patrick asked at last.

Ann hesitated for a split-second. "I have no reason not to trust him, but we need to move fast."

"That instinct talk or head talk?"

"Both. Logic and instinct both tell me he's trustworthy but not the patient sort. I'm curious about him. He even promised to fix the bank accounts if we can save his family. That's quite a guarantee. Tomorrow, I want to check out the names he gave us."

"Anything else?"

Ann nodded. "At the airport, I asked Brad to check out all the Dr. Christopher Collins he could find. There are five in the U.S. and three in the UK. Of the U.S. names, one's retired and lives in Hawaii, two live somewhere on the west coast, the fourth's our boy, and the fifth lives in Mississippi. The strange thing is that there are no medical school records for Christopher Collins number four."

"Interesting."

"Very. I talked to his co-workers at the hospital, and they all say he's a wonderful doctor."

"I don't think he could fake it."

"I don't either," Ann agreed. She finished her glass of water, fed Danny a belated dinner, and rummaged about in her cupboards for table setting things. Catching Patrick's amused look, she asked, "What?"

He gestured to the knives and forks in her hands.

"Oh." She traded the silverware and dinner plates for paper plates and extra napkins.

"Maybe he has the license under a different name."

The suggestion made perfect sense to

Ann. "That's it! Patrick, you're a genius. I'll bet it's either Paul Morton or Jonathan Parker."

Patrick nodded solemn agreement.

They traded theories about how exactly the two cases fit together until the apartment's buzzer rang.

"Ah, dinner. Be right back." Ann grabbed her purse, left her apartment, flew down the flight of stairs, and opened the front door.

"That's $18.50," said the freckle-faced pizza guy.

Thanking the pizza delivery boy, Ann handed him $23.00.

"Oh, and a man said you'd give me an extra twenty dollars if I gave you this," the kid said, holding up a white envelope.

Ann narrowed her eyes at the boy and frowned. "What did the man look like?"

The youth smiled, showing his braces. "He said you'd ask that and told me to tell you to quit being suspicious and take the darn message." The kid seemed to enjoy his messenger job.

"Didn't your mother ever tell you to avoid strangers," Ann muttered, searching her purse for the extra money.

Highway robbery.

The boy made no comment but grinned again, knowing she was going to give him twenty dollars for the letter.

Holding a piping hot pizza in one hand, purse in the other, and a plain, business-sized envelope clenched between her teeth, Ann returned to her apartment. Before she reached the door, it swung open and she nearly crashed into her partner. She gave a muffled cry of alarm as Patrick grabbed her arm and hauled her back into the apartment so she wouldn't take the stairs head-first.

He wore a sheepish grin and held his Glock 22 in his right hand. "Whoa! Sorry about that."

Ann steadied herself with Patrick's help. Thankfully, Danny was asleep and couldn't add excitement to her life. She stood in the sitting room with her hands and mouth full, looking dazed.

Patrick closed the door. Chuckling, he returned the handgun to his shoulder holster.

Ann spat the envelope at him, and he caught it deftly. "What's with scaring the heck out of me?" she demanded with mock crossness. She smiled to counter the tone.

"What else are partners for? Besides, you

made me nervous by not coming back right away. What's this?" He let the slightly damp envelope dangle between his thumb and forefinger.

"Bonus," Ann said, climbing the kitchen hurdle and lifting the pizza high so she wouldn't drop it.

Full attention on the mysterious envelope, Patrick forgot all about the dog gate. He tripped and went sprawling. The noise of his ungraceful entrance woke Danny who barked like he needed to scare off an invading army.

Ann assumed Patrick was all right because he rolled to his knees in front of the refrigerator. She moved to soothe Danny.

"I'm fine," Patrick said dryly.

"You're lucky your gun didn't discharge," Ann pointed out.

"Spent so much time resting today, I figured I could do with a little exercise."

"Oh, I think you've had enough excitement," she commented. She kissed Danny on the head then looked at Patrick.

The questioning slant of his eyebrows, told Ann he couldn't decide who she was talking to so she smiled to let him know the comment had been meant for him.

Patrick just stared.

Ann blushed before saying, "Wash your hands before eating. You *know* what's been all over this floor." She tried not to laugh but knew her eyes were betraying the sentiment.

They had a relatively peaceful meal. Ann ate the two pepperoni pieces that hadn't come remotely close to touching the mushrooms or anchovies. She even cut off the tips of her slices and gave them to Patrick.

"They're that bad, huh."

"Yup. Fungus and fish don't belong on pizza."

When they were finished, Patrick eyed the envelope. "So, are you going to open it?"

"Sure. Paid good money for it," Ann said lightly. She plucked the envelope off the table and ripped it open. "'Please hurry. Events are in motion for Rachel and the kids to escape on Monday night.'" Grim awareness of the danger replaced Ann's jovial mood.

"We have some planning to do," Patrick said.

"Indeed we do," Ann said, silently thanking her partner for trusting Chris Collins.

Why do I trust that guy anyway?

Chapter 14:
Escape Plans

J. Edgar Hoover Building, FBI Headquarters
Washington, D.C.

Ann and Patrick spent all weekend planning for the coming rescue. Saturday around lunchtime, they cornered Agent George Baker in the office.

"Hey, Baker, there's a hot lead we need you to follow in Alabama," Ann said.

"Really?" Baker asked, puppy dog eager.

"Go to the address and protect the lady," Patrick instructed, handing Baker a slip of paper.

"Keep your distance, but we have reason to suspect that someone may have put out a hit on her," Ann explained.

In a matter of seconds, Baker's expression morphed from interested to elated to euphoric to disappointed and finally settled on confused. "Regency Retirement Village? That's it? I'm supposed to chase down a possible hit on a little old lady?" Baker asked dubiously. "That's a long way to go for some quality car time."

"That's all you need to know," Ann said.

It took a few minutes of browbeating, but finally Agent Baker took off for Alabama, grumbling about hating stakeouts.

Ann mentally checked "protect woman" off her list of things to accomplish before Monday night. "That went well," she commented, as they walked back to her office.

"You want the military?" Patrick asked, referring to the phone call that had to be made.

"No way. I don't want them biting *my* head off. Besides, you could use the practice with long, tedious conversations."

"Your concern is overwhelming." Patrick left her doorway to make the Fort Drum phone call from his office.

He'll do it! Ann silently cheered.

In her opinion, the difficult job had been left for her anyway. Gathering her courage, she made her own dreaded phone call. "Good morning, Mr. Morgan. This is Agent Davidson. Yes, sir … yes, I understand, but I need you to talk to the computer guys for me." She gave several uh-huhs at the appropriate intervals, letting her boss vent his displeasure at being called on a weekend. She played her best card. "Sir, I believe this could break the bank case wide open, but I need clearance to check satellite feeds over South Dakota." She spent the next several minutes begging and cajoling until finally the man gave up and promised to make a few phone calls. Grinning in satisfaction, Ann set her office phone down.

Patrick strolled into her office a few minutes later. "Collins is Jonathan Parker."

"What else did you find out?"

He tossed her a file. "The grumpy young man sent that over."

"Before or after you threatened to call his CO?"

"After," Patrick admitted. "Morton, Paul A. Earned fair marks and a reputation as a troublemaker at West Point. Assigned to Fort Drum; went AWOL within two months. Dishonorably discharged," said Patrick, quoting the file.

Wow, he never strings that many sentences together.

Now that they knew who they were dealing with, Ann felt a whole lot better about the case.

An hour later, she and Patrick sat in the computer lab watching Brad's hands fly over the keyboard.

"You're in, enjoy the view," said Brad Matthews, resident computer guru.

"Thank you," Ann said, speaking for herself and her partner.

"No problem. Let me know if you need anything else."

Ann and Patrick spent the next half-hour scrutinizing satellite screenshots. Finally, they printed the ten clearest pictures of the compound. Most of the images simply showed trucks coming and going, but several also featured men hauling crates around and holding guns.

"Those are some heavy-duty guns," Ann commented.

Patrick agreed. "Yes, but it's still going to be a hard sell."

"Even after we tell them about the hostages?"

"Especially if we tell them that."

"I suppose they don't want another Waco," Ann commented. "But we're running out of options. Who do we have the best chance with? ATF—I mean ATFE? That name change thing still bothers me by the way. Where was I?"

"Starting government alphabet soup," Patrick prompted. His lips twitched upward in a tiny smile.

"Right. Do we have the best chance with the ATFE people, our own guys, or the local cops? We could just send out Stanley County's finest with their popguns against that." Ann gestured to a picture of a man cradling a wicked-looking automatic rifle.

"ATFE might be our best bet, but we've got next to no proof," Patrick mused.

Tightening the view on the current picture, Ann frowned in concentration. She centered on the gun and studied it. "Does that look like an AK-101 to you?"

Her partner leaned over her shoulder to take a closer look. "Mmm … AK something or other anyway."

"I'm going to do some research," said Ann.

"Checking on the LEO's out there?" Patrick asked, referring to the local law enforcement officers.

"Precisely."

"Good luck with that," said Patrick, leaving to make some phone calls.

Ann set to work looking up what law enforcement resources Stanley County already had in place. The results were rather depressing, but at least she found the number for the sheriff's office. The number of highway patrol troopers looked insanely low to cover such a wide area.

Patrick appeared at his customary spot in Ann's doorway, his deep blue eyes alive with amusement. "I take it you aren't happy with the information you're getting."

"You might say that," Ann muttered. She dialed a number she'd gotten from her search. When a man answered she asked, "May I speak with Sheriff Heckle please? Oh, hello sheriff. Special Agent Davidson, FBI. Listen, I was just wondering how many deputies you have and what your areas of jurisdictions are. I see … thank you … you've been most helpful. Yes, have a nice day." She slammed the phone down and glared at it. "I'm going to call the—"

"Don't bother," said Patrick calmly.

"What?"

"FBI South Dakota field office, right?"

Patrick grinned sympathetically, as Ann's curt nod confirmed it. "Don't bother; it doesn't exist."

Ann groaned and sank back into her chair. "Now, I know the bad guys are out there. There's hardly anyone else in that entire blasted state! It's perfect for a smuggling operation."

"There's a Resident Agency in Rapid City and another in Pierre,
but they both say they're a bit understaffed."

"Dare I ask how many people work there?" Ann asked tentatively. She squared her shoulders, as if bracing against Patrick's unspoken answer. "Okay, so our options are convince the Rapid City or Pierre guys to go on a field trip or call in the ATFE." She picked up her office phone and held it out until he accepted it. "Good luck," she said, rising from her chair to give him a reassuring pat on the shoulder. "I'll go get us lunch while you do the grunt work."

Patrick had already called the Rapid City people, but there were still plenty of Alcohol, Tobacco, Firearms, and Explosives guys left to badger. Settling behind Ann's desk, he started dialing.

***

Corra Compound
Stanley County, South Dakota

Rachel Collins spent Friday comforting Jenny Hapler who was still reeling from losing her mother. On Saturday, Rachel didn't have to work so she spent a few of the early morning hours with her children. After that, she acquired a few extra sweet rolls from the kitchen and went to the clinic.

"Good morning, Mrs. Jenson. I came by to see the patient. How is she?"

"About as well as can be expected, I suppose," Megan said.

"Why don't you go visit your children?" Rachel suggested, holding out a smuggled sweet roll.

Megan's eyes lit with mirth. "You're just trying to get rid of me."

"You work too hard. Take some time off; doctor's orders."

"Yes, ma'am." Pleased, Megan bolted for the door.

Rachel felt guilty for not spending every possible minute with her children, but she had a feeling Jenny needed her more at the moment.

"Doc?" asked Jenny sleepily.

"I'm here, Jenny," Rachel said. "I brought breakfast too. Or maybe we should just call it lunch." She handed the girl the other baked good and helped her sit up. "I'll go get some orange juice to go with that." She dashed from the room and returned with the drink. Then, she settled herself in the hard chair next to the bed and watched Jenny eat.

"Thank you for being so kind," Jenny said.

"You're welcome," replied Rachel. She said no more, having learned Jenny talked more if there was silence.

The day before, they had had some nice conversations about the girl's father, mother, and older step-brother. Jenny had eagerly spoken of the controversy surrounding her parent's interracial marriage.

"I think this was about my father's job," Jenny said out of the blue.

"Why do you say that?" asked Rachel, even as she thought, *I whole-heartedly agree with you on that.*

"He's important," Jenny said with a wan grin.

Rachel opened her mouth to comment,

but the words died on her lips when a man stumbled into the room. "Logan? What happened?" she asked standing up. "I'm sorry, Jenny, but I have to help him."

The girl looked disappointed but gave an understanding nod.

Logan Dales had seen better days. His forehead bled profusely, and he clutched his left ribs. His white cowboy hat look like it had been trampled. His tousled hair was covered in dirt, and his clothes were filthy. "I had to talk to ya," Logan muttered, letting Rachel help him to a cot.

Rachel chuckled at that and went to get a damp towel to wipe his hands and face before her examination. Upon returning, she said, "There are easier ways to get my attention."

"They'd get suspicious."

"Let me guess. You picked a fight with Jense so he'd beat you up and someone would send you here."

The look he gave her confirmed it.

Rachel shook her head, sighed, and whispered, "Let me clean you up a bit and then we can talk." She retrieved iodine, alcohol, a needle, and some thread from a storage cabinet. "This is going to sting," she warned.

A low moan escaped Logan when Rachel cleaned the cut above his eye.

"Sorry." Rachel placed a gauze pad on the cut and held it there for several seconds. When the blood stopped gushing, she swiftly stitched it a few times and put a fresh bandage over it for protection. "Now, take off your shirt."

"But there's a girl present," he protested, eyeing Jenny who was pretending to sleep.

"Oh, come now. Don't be shy. Here, sit up and turn your back to the girl. That's right, see no problem. I might have to tape those ribs for a few days." Rachel spoke soothingly as he carefully unbuttoned his shirt and took it off with a flourish.

"T-shirt too?"

"No, the thing's skin-tight. Besides, the fact that you can move your arms like that tells me you're faking anyway."

Smiling with much chagrin, Logan pulled his shirt back on and buttoned it. "You're right smart, ma'am."

"Thanks. I like to think so. Now, what did you want to say to me?"

Logan lowered his voice so Jenny

wouldn't overhear his words, and said, "Your husband's gonna send some friends out here to pick y'all up, but first, I gotta get ya away from here on Monday night. We'll hop in a truck and head east. They'll meet us before we reach Pierre."

Rachel's eyes brightened. "You really—"

"Shhhh!" Logan hissed. He inclined his head in Jenny's direction.

Dropping her voice to an excited whisper, Rachel asked, "You really talked to him?"

"Yes, ma'am, I did," Logan confirmed softly. "Monday night's gonna come up mighty quick. Rest up. I'll spring the kids, but then, we'll need to walk a ways afore we reach the truck I hid. Meet me here in the clinic at nine thirty."

Rachel gripped the young man's hand tightly and gave it a heartfelt squeeze. "Thank you, Logan." Her eyes flickered over to Jenny. "Can the Jenny and Jensons come too?" she asked with quiet urgency.

Logan shook his head vigorously and winced. "Sorry. Too many people'll just get us all caught. But don't worry. Your husband's sending FBI people out here to take care of the compound."

***

Parker's Base of Operations
New York City, New York
The bug Christopher Collins had planted in Agent Davidson's gun worked well. He smiled upon hearing them dispatch Agent Baker to Alabama. He felt better knowing his promise to the boy would be fulfilled.

"Thank you, Agent Davidson," Chris murmured. He had been worried he might have to take on the entire compound by himself. It wasn't high on his list of fun things to do, but he would have done it to save his family. He didn't want to increase their danger, hence his arrangements for them to leave before the government crashed in.

With his mind somewhat at ease, Chris finished cleaning his brand-new sniper rifle and made some travel arrangements. Before leaving the D.C. area, he sent an encrypted e-mail to Agent Davidson with some final details.

God, let me be in time!

Chapter 15:
Rescue

Ronald Reagan Washington National Airport
Arlington County, Virginia
Around midday on Monday, Ann and Patrick once again found themselves in an airport. Ann couldn't believe their luck. As soon as they had passed through the metal detectors, a commotion broke out behind them. Her hand clutched at the empty space where her gun should have been, but naturally, it wasn't there since they were in an airport. Seeing Patrick reach for his non-existent gun too, she didn't feel so silly.

A man holding a bag shouted at the security guards, screamed like a certified loon, and launched the black bag at the nearest guard. The make-shift battering ram slammed into the unfortunate guard, who promptly collapsed, momentarily blocking three other guards.

"Have you had your run today?" inquired

Ann.

"Not yet," Patrick answered.

By then, the maniac had reached them. He swung the bag about every which way to clear a path. Patrick ducked and leaned left. The bag came in low at Ann so she jumped. Both were momentarily off balance, but fortunately, they respectively avoided being brained or losing a kneecap to the infamous black backpack. They steadied each other and sprinted after the crazy man.

Why can't we have a normal day at the airport? Ann wondered as she ran.

Patrick caught the man first, but the slippery floor caused him and Crazy Man to land in a heap. The ensuing struggle spun them in a half-circle on the floor. The man managed to get on top and raised his backpack to drop on Patrick's head.

That's when Ann arrived and barreled into the crazy man's side with a strangled cry that sounded like "Aaaahlllllggggoafff." Her right foot caught Patrick's prone form, tripping her. She rolled once to avoid serious injury and landed on her back.

The guards ran up, and there was a brief struggle on her left. Ignoring them, she tucked her hands behind her head and crossed her feet.

Patrick walked over to her holding Crazy Man's false beard. Without looking, he chucked the beard at the guards who were currently hauling the guy away in handcuffs.

A guard carefully opened the backpack, peeked in, and muttered, "Rocks."

The guy's got a head full of those too, Ann fumed.

"Did I mention I hate airports?"

Patrick didn't answer, but he did help her to her feet. "Ann, I know you're a knockout but the literal part's a bit rough."

Ann just blinked at her partner. The comment was so far from the Patrick Duncan she knew, she might have put stock in alien abduction theories.

Tipping an invisible cap, Patrick affected a Southern accent, and said, "It's a mite dangerous, traveling with such a fine lady."

Laughing, Ann said, "I think I hit you too hard."

Patrick shrugged philosophically. "There are worse things in life."

Twenty minutes and a hundred questions later, Ann paced the waiting area. Security at the airport had tightened up wonderfully. At the rate security was going now Ann doubted the plane would leave for several hours. She watched a little girl being checked over with a security wand and shook her head in frustration.

"Relax," said Patrick, idly sipping a fresh coffee.

"I know, I know. Pacing will do me no good, but what else can I do?"

"We could wait for the next crazy guy with a bag of rocks," Patrick pointed out. "That could be fun."

"True ... Nice tackle."

"Charming scream."

"Thanks ... I think," they said simultaneously.

Well, that was slightly creepy.

The subsequent laughter eased the strange tension that had built up.

"We could also engage in idle chatter, if you like," Patrick offered, drinking more coffee.

"Oh and what would you suggest we talk about?"

"Anything."

"Well that narrows it down."

Nevertheless, Ann thought of various topics they could discuss.

"Tell me something about yourself," he prompted.

"Errr, okay …" Ann thought hard for several long seconds. "Did I ever tell you how I got my name?"

Patrick shook his head negative, lifted the cup to his lips, and gave her his undivided attention.

Ann refused to look away from his unnerving eyes. "The doctors told my parents I would be a boy. They'd planned to name me Julian after my grandfather. My mother was quite distraught for a few moments after she heard the news she had a daughter. She fainted—or so I'm told—but my father just shrugged, and said, 'Julie Ann it is.'"

"I guess your mother didn't protest too hard," Patrick commented.

"She was unconscious," Ann reminded with a shrug. "Anyway, the name stuck."

"Thanks for telling me."

Eventually, their plane was cleared to fly. They handed over their tickets and boarded with the other passengers.

"You look worried," Patrick said once they

were settled.

"I am," she admitted.

"Don't be." He impulsively took her hand and gave it a reassuring squeeze. "God is in control." With that, he buried his head under a magazine and went to sleep.

Ann smiled broadly, though he couldn't see it. Gradually, she relaxed enough to take a nap.

***

Corra Compound
Stanley County, South Dakota

Monday night at nine thirty, Rachel Collins waited anxiously for Logan Dales to arrive with her two children. Luckily for the sake of her nerves, Logan arrived on time.

"Mo—" Jason and Emily started to shout upon spotting her.

Logan's hands swiftly clapped over both young mouths.

"Shhhh! Hush, my loves, we have to be quiet now." Rachel cupped both of their chins and continued in a whisper, "We're going to play the quiet game until we get far away from here. Jay, you're a big boy. You can run with me. Em, Mr. Dales will have to carry you. I'll be right here the whole time."

The girl began crying, but Logan's hand muffled the sobs. He let go of Jason, scooped up Emily, and dashed away from Corra. Rachel grabbed Jason's hand and followed as fast as she could. Jason pumped his tiny legs full force to keep up.

We can't keep this up for long.

When they had gone about a mile, Logan slowed to a fast walk. Rachel gasped for breath and cast a longing look back toward the compound, feeling awful for leaving Jenny and the Jensons behind.

"Don't worry, ma'am. They'll be all right, but we won't be if we don't get far from here fast!" Logan shifted his grip on Emily and walked a little faster.

The child bawled, but since they were well out of hearing range of Corra, the noise didn't bother Rachel. Jason stumbled, and Rachel pulled him to his feet again.

"How far is it to the car?" Rachel asked.

"A few more minutes," Logan replied, not breaking stride.

"I'm tired!" Jason complained.

"I know, sweetie, but we've got to keep going."

O Lord, be our strength. We are weary,

and evil men hound us. Be our refuge.

"What we runnin' from?"

"Bad men, Jay. Bad men." Though feeling faint herself, Rachel picked her son up, shushing further questions. Fear kept her out-of-shape legs moving swiftly.

After another ten minutes of breathtaking travel, Logan and Rachel switched burdens.

"We'll be to the car soon," Logan promised.

Rachel sure hoped so. Her legs felt rubbery, and she had a monster adrenaline headache.

***

Near Corra Compound
Stanley County, South Dakota

"We'll make it," Patrick reassured for the twenty-first time. "Eat something."

Ann looked with distaste at the half-eaten chicken salad.

"It's soggy," she grumbled.

"Your fault. Besides, you need to keep up your strength."

She cast a grumpy look his way but reluctantly took a few extra bites of soggy salad.

"Are the SWAT guys standing by?"

"The ATFE has people ready to go at our word."

"Then, let's go."

After donning lightweight, black body armor, they headed out to the stakeout site. By 9:43 p.m., Ann began wondering if the plan would work. From beneath a camouflage blanket, she watched the abandoned car through a night vision scope.

Lord, everything's in Your hands. Please give us safety and success. Amen. Ann hoped Patrick would be praying too.

I wish the Pierre agents would show up soon.

Sheriff Heckle had driven them to the site. He was on the other side of the truck about a mile away. The mission was simple: escort the Collins family to safety. Nevertheless, Ann would have felt better knowing they had more backup than the elderly local sheriff. Feeling a tap on her shoulder, Ann glanced over at Patrick who frowned down at his cell phone.

Shielding the glowing screen, he showed her the text message: Car troubles will be late.

Ann grimaced. *Don't tell me the United States government can't afford working cars, even out here in the sticks!*

The full moon and warm night created an eerie atmosphere. Hearing footsteps, Ann squinted into the dim light. Seeing nothing, she thought, *Great, now I'm imagining things.*

Patrick touched her arm and repositioned the night vision gear.

A few seconds later, Ann spotted two figures approaching. She was about to go to them, when Patrick's hand gripped her arm firmly.

What?

Seeing the alert expression she had learned to never underestimate, Ann immediately stilled.

"Trouble," Patrick whispered.

Ann strained her ears and heard faint engine sounds.

"Run Rachel!" she murmured.

A truck rapidly approached the running figures. Someone stood in the sunroof holding a long, slender, heavy-looking object.

Ann gaped in disbelief, dropped the night vision scope, and scrambled to her feet.

"Down!" she yelled, madly waving her arms. "Get down!"

Patrick's shouts joined hers.

Together, they sprinted at the frozen figures. For the second time that day, Ann and Patrick took to the air. Sunroof man let a rocket fly. A young man carrying a boy stood dumbfounded to Rachel's left. Ann's right arm caught the guy's chest, just above the child's head, and hauled him to the ground. Meanwhile, Patrick pushed Rachel down. The rocket sailed over their heads and hit the escape vehicle.

"*That* is definitely illegal!" Ann exclaimed, once the waves of heat and noise had finished beating her senses about.

No longer needing to tread lightly, Patrick called in for backup. To make it easy, he sent the ATFE people a lovely picture of the burning jeep.

By the time he hit send, Ann was helping the young man and the boy get up. "Are you okay?"

Both looked very shaken but managed to nod.

"Are those the bad men, Momma?" asked the little boy. His voice was barely audible over the menacing thrum of approaching truck engines and the remaining ringing in Ann's ears.

"Yes, Jay," Rachel replied hoarsely.

"Just stay back," Ann barked to their charges. "Help's on the way."

"We've got to leave," Patrick said tightly.

It was too late. Three trucks formed a semicircle about thirty feet away. With the escape vehicle in flames and the sheriff's car a mile away, the fugitives and agents were out of luck. The truck headlights cast a comforting, yet deadly, pool of light.

A frantic visual scan of the area revealed only scruffy grassland, darkness, and more scruffy grassland. Desperate, Ann drew her handgun and side-stepped to place herself— and the bulletproof vest—between the bad guys and the young man.

If that rocket is any indication, we're in big trouble. I don't think the vest designers had that in mind.

Ann sensed Patrick move in front of Rachel. She would have loved to embrace her high school chum, but there was no time for greetings. Willing her knees to support her, Ann fought fierce instincts that said: run!

Rachel knelt, clutching her daughter tightly. Not a spark of recognition crossed her face.

Patrick said something to Rachel who waved to the boy. The kid practically flew into her arms. Then, Rachel and the children lay on the ground behind Patrick, making themselves small targets.

Good, stay there, Rachel.

"Get down," Ann ordered, hoping the man behind her would follow the directive.

"Any ideas?" inquired Patrick.

"Fresh out," Ann tossed back, her mind tracking several different plans.

Heart pounding, Ann clasped her right hand around the base of the gun to steady it while she considered their options. She and Patrick could make a stand while the other two ran. *That would work for about two seconds.* They could all run for it. *I'm not getting shot in the back!* They could open fire first and hope for the best. *I still don't want to die tonight.* They could try to talk some sense into the bad guys. *Uh-huh. Why don't we try tea and scones too!* She winced. *Hey, it keeps us alive for a few extra seconds.* For the best possible plan, it was pathetic.

"Keep them talking," she said tersely. Ann drew a breath and held it.

Most of the truck doors flew open, and

men lined up behind the open front doors. They leveled automatic rifles at the tiny band backlit by the smoldering former Jeep. Each truck also sported a spiffy sunroof with a guy holding a vicious-looking weapon. Two of the men held rifles and a third hefted the rocket launcher.

Ann's bad-guy count tallied nine rifles, one handgun, and a rocket launcher. Fully expecting them to just start blasting, Ann addressed the man standing behind the driver's door of the center truck. Releasing the breath, Ann asked, "Who are you? What are you doing here?"

"I've got more firepower than you do, so I get to ask the questions and set the terms," the man said calmly. He held his gun loosely in his left hand and casually leaned on the door he stood behind.

Several seconds passed.

"Special Agent Patrick Duncan, FBI."

Ann groaned inwardly, even as she agreed it was for the best.

"This is my partner, Special Agent Davidson." Patrick inclined his head in her general direction, keeping his gun steadily pointed at the leader.

A powerful flashlight suddenly lit Patrick's face then flicked over to catch Ann in the eyes. She blinked and squinted.

That hurt, she thought, trying to regain her vision.

"Meddling feds," the man muttered, throwing the flashlight onto the driver's seat.

"And who are you, sir?" asked Patrick.

"Jonathan Parker," the man said candidly.

Great, he's too willing to talk, that probably means we're dead.

"I think Paul Morton fits you better," Ann called loudly.

"Do you?" asked the man, sounding mildly surprised. "Drop your weapons and we can continue this pleasant conversation."

Though about as useful as a cap gun, the handgun made Ann feel safer.

The man sent a bullet over their heads, speeding up Ann's heart. Rachel yelped. The young man grunted. Patrick growled low in his throat.

"Next bullet drills a kid. Drop those guns!"

The man sounded stressed, and Ann decided not to push buttons. Gritting her teeth, she slowly stooped and placed the gun on the ground. Her phone vibrated at her belt. It lit up too.

"Answer it," the man ordered. "It's probably him."

Moving cautiously, Ann unfolded her phone. "Hello?"

"Put Paul on," commanded a man's voice.

She held her phone toward the man behind the car door. "The real Mr. Parker would like to speak with you."

"Bring me the phone."

"Why don't I just toss it to you?" Ann suggested hopefully.

"I'd rather you hand it to me in person."

Nine rifles, a handgun, and a rocket launcher added weight to his order.

Peachy. I'd much rather I didn't.

Scanning the hard expressions arrayed before her, Ann slowly stepped forward, trying to maintain her slippery courage. Her knees trembled, but she faked a look of grim determination. She stopped just out of Paul Morton's reach, leaned forward, and handed him the phone. Up close, she saw he was tall, muscular, and had cruel eyes. Ann backed up a step.

Paul clutched her phone in his right hand.

She took another step back.

"Wait," Paul said sharply, snapping his gun up until the muzzle came in line with her chest.

Not good.

Ann held another breath. His bossy attitude grated on her, but she didn't argue the issue.

He watched her closely. "Scared?" he asked, amused. An evil grin spread slowly across his face, and he raised his eyebrows. "Do you have any last words?"

God will have the last word, she thought automatically. Ann didn't realize she had also said the words out loud until she saw his strange expression.

Without further ado, he shot her.

Chapter 16:
When Bullets Fly

Near Corra Compound
Stanley County, South Dakota

The bulletproof vest did its job, but the blast knocked Ann flat and stole all the breath in her lungs. Scared, furious, and in pain, she thought, *Owww. Not nice.*

"Ann!" Patrick shouted running forward two steps.

"Back off!" Paul shouted.

Six rifles suddenly fixed on Ann's partner.

Once certain Patrick would say put, Paul casually called, "Mrs. Collins, please stand up."

No, Rachel! Stay down; it's the safest place.

"I insist." Malice filled Paul's voice.

Ann didn't have to look up to see the gun pointed at her face; she knew it was there.

Don't listen, don't listen, her mind chanted.

She shut her eyes tightly, waiting for another blast. The blast never came, so she

160

opened her eyes and drew in a painful breath.

Paul relaxed his grip on the gun, put the phone to his ear, and said, "Hey, old friend. It's been a long time, hasn't it?" There was silence for a moment. "You're threatening me?" Paul laughed deeply. "Jon, I have six hostages, including your wife and kids. Don't forget that." He listened again. "Hold on a minute," he said. Suddenly, a bullet slammed into the middle truck's front left tire.

Ann's already strained nerves frayed some more.

Slowly, the phone returned to Paul's ear. "Yes, I see your point." Paul sounded thoughtful but Ann's groundside vantage point denied her a good look at his expression. He chuckled again. "Can I keep the feds?" he asked, sounding like a little boy begging to keep a puppy.

I don't like the sound of that.

Paul grew serious again. "This is complicated, buddy. I'm going to put you on speaker here. There's probably a way we can all go home happy." He hit a button.

Jonathan Parker's voice rang out clearly. "I'm serious; you've got about thirty seconds to tell your men to back off. I want those rifles flung far."

"I'm not dying for you, Mr. Parker," one man said. He climbed into the truck on Ann's left, started the engine, and drove off. The passengers yelped, scrambled in, and held on for dear life. The man sitting on the sunroof cried out, flipped over the roof, and landed as an unconscious heap.

Ann didn't know if the man survived the fall. At the moment, she had more pressing issues to deal with, like breathing.

"Lousy help," Paul muttered. "All right, Johnny-boy, you've evened the odds a bit. But I still have your family, and you still have my money. I'm a reasonable man. Give me the codes, and you get all the hostages except the traitor and the G-man. What do you say?"

He got a pronounced click for an answer.

For the first time, Ann saw fear enter Paul Morton's eyes. The next instant a bullet struck the base of his neck, flinging his already lifeless body into the driver's seat. His gun flew from nerveless fingers and landed a few feet from her.

Then, everything happened at once. Morton's men shouted and turned their rifles on the hostages.

Adrenaline shocked Ann's body into action. Scooping up Morton's handgun, Ann dove under the open door and fired twice at the man in front of her. Then, rolling to her left, she aimed up at the man perched in the sunroof. She missed, but luckily, so did he. Bullets struck the ground near her head. Gritting her teeth and squinting against the dust raised by bullets, Ann fired three times. One shot missed; two didn't. She heard a flurry of additional shots; then, all was quiet. A quick glance at the other truck revealed no movement. Breathing hard, Ann struggled cautiously to her feet.

A pale young man stood across from her, frozen in position, his gun not quite in the firing position. For a timeless second, they just exchanged dazed stares. Ann's gun suddenly felt very heavy. She didn't know if she could pull it up in time. She didn't have to find out. The boy gulped, dropped the gun, and raised his hands.

"Step around the vehicle," Ann ordered, forcing her tongue to form the words. Heart pounding and head aching, she called out, "Patrick!"

"It's not over!" he shouted from

somewhere behind her.

Fear shot up her spine. Patrick had the uncanny ability to sense things like that. Knowing they didn't have much time, Ann motioned the young man forward.

"Turn around and kneel down. I'm going to cuff you. Then, I want you to lie still while the rest of this plays out," she said tightly. "I'll try to protect you as best I can."

He complied with wide eyes.

Before she could reach for the cuffs to restrain the kid, Ann heard Rachel say, "No, Jay! Em, stay there. Stay down, baby."

"Rachel! Get down!" Patrick shouted, running full tilt toward Ann's friend.

Handcuffs completely forgotten, Ann's head snapped up as the air filled with danger. She knew there was precious little she could do but watch Rachel tackle the boy to the ground.

God, protect them.

Patrick dove at the girl. A distant flash preceded the thunderous crack of a gunshot. The bullet pierced the girl's back and flung her forward into Patrick whose body jerked as the bullet struck him too.

"No!"

Armor piercing bullet, Ann thought numbly, her throat hoarse from her strangled cry. Without thinking, she emptied the rest of the bullets in Morton's handgun at the source of the last shot. Even after the gun was empty she pulled the trigger another half-dozen times. She became aware of another gun, a much bigger gun than her own, chattering away. Knees weak and head swimming, she struggled to snap her body into action.

The boy she had forgotten to handcuff stood next to her with a large rifle. When the gun was empty, the boy turned to her with tears streaming down his pale face. The gun slipped from his fingers. He turned around and knelt down.

Mutely, Ann cuffed him and laid him on his stomach in case the gun battle wasn't over yet.

Forgetting her own pain, she rushed to her downed partner.

"Patrick? Patrick?" Her voice trembled as she called his name. "Patrick, don't die … not yet. Please, not yet," Ann rambled. She dropped Morton's empty handgun next to Patrick, whipped off her light jacket and used it to form a pillow for her partner. She pressed her hands firmly over the bullet hole. The pressure seemed to increase the bleeding, so she released it, letting the tight constriction of his bulletproof vest work to slow the loss of blood.

Patrick groaned and snapped his eyes open.

"Ann? How is she?" Without waiting for a reply, he passed out.

The brief question did wonders for Ann's optimism. She swiped at hot tears with her forearm, trying not to get her partner's blood all over her face. Spotting her dazed friend standing on the other side of Patrick, Ann called, "Rachel! Rachel, are you okay?" Her friend didn't answer. Then, Ann noticed that Rachel was staring at the small figure draped across Patrick's stomach. As gently as possible, Ann moved the girl's tiny body off of Patrick and checked for signs of life. A weak pulse met her fingers.

A child's wail pierced her shock enough so she could speak.

"She's alive," said Ann tightly.

"Help her!" Rachel begged, her voice barely more than a whisper. She sank to the ground next to the girl and gathered the sobbing boy into her arms.

Ann didn't blame him. The only reason she didn't join him was that her emotions were already too strung out. She was functioning purely on instinct now. Her throat burned with rising bile and her stomach heaved. Not knowing what else to do, Ann pressed her right hand over the gaping hole in the child's side. She couldn't even give the girl her shirt since it was trapped beneath a bulletproof vest. Emily would bleed out by the time Ann worked through half the straps to remove the vest. She could steal back the jacket she'd tucked under Patrick's head, but the material wasn't exactly ideal for stanching blood.

"Rachel!" A man Ann recognized as Jonathan Parker rushed up clutching a deadly sniper rifle. He dropped the gun, wrapped his arms around Rachel, and gently cradled her and the boy. His eyes never left the tiny figure Ann knelt beside.

For several minutes, only choked sobs broke the stillness of the early summer night.

A breeze ruffled Ann's honey brown hair, and her senses returned.

We've got to get out of here!

She hesitated, torn between staying with

the child and getting her phone to call 911. Spotting Patrick's phone, Ann leaned over to retrieve it from the case clipped to his belt while still keeping pressure on Emily's wound.

Sheriff Heckle lumbered up just as she started dialing 911.

"I already called for backup," the sheriff announced, softening his normally gruff voice. The man reminded her of a plush teddy bear. He moved to the girl's side and took over the task of trying to stop the bleeding.

Yeah, so did we several minutes ago.

Ann gulped but couldn't find words. She wanted to help with either patient, but she didn't want to do anything that would make Patrick's wound worse. As Sheriff Heckle tended to the girl, Ann felt helpless.

Father, spare them, she thought, thinking of her partner and the little girl.

Ann felt Sheriff Clayton Heckle's sympathetic gaze as she waited by her unconscious partner for a full five minutes. Suddenly, she remembered the sniper. She needed to do something about him. Grimly, Ann wiped her bloody hands on her pants and grabbed Patrick's handgun which lay uselessly next to him. A quick check told her the gun still held six bullets.

"Where are you going?" asked Sheriff Heckle.

Ann knew she should answer the man, but she couldn't find any words, let alone the right ones. Ignoring protesting muscles, she raced to Morton's truck and retrieved her phone and the flashlight that had rolled to the floor. She shuddered at the gruesome sight of Morton's body. Steeling herself for the task ahead, Ann stopped long enough to pick up her own gun and tuck it into its holster before trudging toward the place where the last shot had come from.

What will you do when you get there? She swept the question from her mind, tightened her grip on Patrick's gun, and marched grimly onward.

Using the powerful flashlight from Paul Morton's truck, Ann quickly found the sniper lying on the ground behind his gun. Distantly, she heard the reassuring thump-thump of helicopter blades. She ignored it, letting anger fuel the rest of the journey to the sniper's side.

Ann flipped the man over and checked for a pulse. He groaned just as she found a faint indication of life. A second later, she had the gun's muzzle pressed firmly over the sniper's heart. It took all of Ann's willpower not to pull the trigger.

"Do you like my handiwork?" asked the sniper weakly. A pleased grin crossed his bearded face. "How is the child?"

"Why?" Ann croaked.

Why shoot a child?

Anger coursed through her like a spreading fire. "Why?" she demanded again, louder this time. Ann dropped the flashlight and gripped the gun with both hands. "Tell me why you fired! The fight was over!"

The sniper glared at her, and said, "Shoot me."

Ann's trigger finger itched to comply.

You can't. It would be wrong.

Studying the man's hardened expression, Ann felt a strange rush of cooling pity sweep through her.

Save him! That thought set off an epic battle of wills between Ann's heart and mind. Her heart wanted to reach past the man's anger and contempt and her head wanted to let him rot for the evil things he'd done. She felt the lesson of Jonah press upon her. He'd been sent to a completely wicked city to redeem them. Ann's heart finally won the fight and began racing with a new purpose.

God, give me strength.

A shiver ran down her spine at being so close to blatant evil.

The man's cold eyes met Ann's as he said, "Orders … just orders." The sniper began breathing in short, shallow gasps and blood oozed out of three bullet holes in his left shoulder.

A glance at the sniper rifle remains told her where most of the other bullets had gone.

Coming to a decision, Ann tucked Patrick's gun into the space at the small of her back. "You don't deserve to be saved, but neither does anybody else. Call out to the Lord to save your soul."

The sniper laughed again, weaker this time. "You a preacher?"

"No, just a messenger," Ann replied. "God always wants a repentant heart."

The man shook his head slowly. "I won't be a last-minute crawler. Go to—"

"Don't let your pride doom you," Ann interrupted. "I'd love to tell you all the facts concerning God's grace and love for all

Julie C. Gilbert

sinners. But there's no time!" Impulsively, she leaned forward and grasped his dusty hand. The day's events tried to render her unconsciousness, but she fought the weariness.

No! Not yet. She said a quick, silent prayer for the dying man as her eyes held his.

He glared at her until his body shuddered and became lifeless.

"So that's that," Ann whispered sadly. She picked up the flashlight, dragged herself to her feet for the umpteenth time that day, and slowly walked back to the lit area.

Sheriff Heckle waved her over to the place where Patrick had fallen. "They're flying your friend, her children, and your partner to St. Mary's Healthcare Center," he said hesitantly, as if speaking too loudly would break some spell. "The ATFE guys are here to take over, so I'll drive you to the hospital when you're ready."

Ann didn't really feel like talking, but she figured she owed the man an explanation for her odd behavior. "Thank you, sheriff." She paused to gather her thoughts.

Before she could say anything, Sheriff Heckle said, "There's a towel and a water

172

bottle in my truck. You can use them to clean off some of the blood on the way."

A wave of despair and worry crashed over Ann. She nodded her thanks, afraid that speaking would shatter her composure. Her expression betrayed her feelings anyway.

"Everything will be all right, ma'am. I'm sorry about your partner," Sheriff Heckle said, trying to soften his gruff voice.

As she climbed into the sheriff's truck, Ann thought, *Don't die, Emily! Your mother needs you. Patrick, please, please live! I need you.*

Chapter 17:
A New Race

St. Mary's Healthcare Center
Pierre, South Dakota

Upon reaching the hospital, Ann thanked Sheriff Heckle again and wandered a bit before a distracted nurse directed her to the waiting room. She hurried there, fearing exhaustion and worry would cause her to collapse in the middle of the blindingly white corridors. The hospital waiting room was full of hard chairs and old magazines. A modern painting meant to cheer the room lent a sterile chill to the atmosphere. Ann shuddered.

Rachel sat in a hard chair, and Jon stood in the far corner. "Ann?" Rachel asked, bewildered.

"I'm here, Rachel," she replied.

The two friends embraced tightly, causing Ann to wince.

Feeling the bulletproof vest, Rachel stiffened, looked down, and immediately spotted the bullet hole. She stumbled back a step, horror crossing her face. "You've been shot!"

Grateful no one besides Jon was in the room, Ann hastily said, "It's not bad. The vest did its job—"

"You've been shot," Rachel repeated, stunned. A dozen emotions swept across her face before a cool, professional expression took over. "Come," said Rachel, latching onto Ann's sleeve and hauling her through the heavy double doors.

Barely having the strength to stumble after her friend, Ann figured it best not to protest. She had no idea where they were going, but Rachel obviously did. Finally, they reached an empty examining room and Rachel waved Ann in.

"Hey! You can't go in there!" shouted a flustered nurse, rising from her seat behind a massive desk.

"I'm a doctor!" Rachel yelled, spinning to face the nurse.

Ann didn't envy the nurse tonight. *Never mess with a woman whose child is in danger*, Ann thought as she leaned against the wall.

"My daughter and her partner are in surgery, my son is being examined by a shrink, and I'm going crazy sitting in that blasted waiting room!" Rachel continued at the top of her lungs.

Rachel's eyes looked ready to launch from her head, and her flailing arms made Ann mighty glad her part of the wall was well out of her friend's reach. Ann craned her neck curiously and caught the *Lady,* **you** *need a shrink* expression on the nurse's face.

"Calm down, ma'am!" the woman commanded. The nurse motioned for some others to help her.

I think I'm going to faint.

"Is there a problem here?" inquired a male nurse. He walked up behind the nurse accosting Rachel. His dark skin made him stand out starkly against the white walls. Muscles rippled through his thin scrubs.

Blast, I hate fainting.

Ann's breaths grew shallow, and her eyes closed for a second.

"Of course, there's a problem!" Rachel snapped. "Everyone here is too busy questioning me to notice that my friend's been shot!" Her hand flew to her head and gripped at it like she had a really bad headache.

Ann felt herself falling and noted it with a

sort of clinical detachment.

The male nurse, who had stepped forward to prevent Rachel from hurting the other nurse, herself, or anyone else, saw Ann pitch forward and moved to catch her. "Whoa! Hang on, ma'am; you'll be just fine," said the man.

Ann felt herself being gently lifted up. Breathing was an effort now. Voices faded in and out. Darkness washed over her vision from all sides.

"Get that vest off of her!" came Rachel's irate voice. "Hang on, Ann!"

Ann's eyelids were so very heavy. Sleep sounded like a wonderful idea.

***

Since all the doctors and most of the nurses were busy, Rachel Collins took it upon herself to care for her friend. The work allowed her to relegate the day's terrible events to the back of her mind. For now, all that mattered was Ann's health.

Thanking the male nurse who laid Ann on the nearest bed, Rachel promptly shooed him from the room. A young nurse who had followed them into the room insisted on staying and helping. Rachel didn't have the time or energy to argue so she let her stay. "Help me get her vest off," she instructed.

Together, the two women removed the shoulder holster with Ann's gun and the other gun Ann had tucked into the back of her pants. The nurse eyed the weapons nervously. Then, they tackled the clasps that held the Kevlar vest tight around Ann's body. They worked swiftly and silently.

Rachel feared to look once the vest and Ann's shirt were removed because she couldn't determine how far the bullet had penetrated the armor. She had seen wounds before, but she didn't know how she would react to a bullet in her friend. Her mind flashed to that awful moment when the man had shot Ann in the chest. Rachel shivered at the thought of the man releasing the bullet at a slightly different angle into her friend's face or neck. Valuing Ann's life more than her own reaction, Rachel looked and saw a nasty bruise stretched across the lower right ribs.

"She'll be all right," Rachel said, even as she worried about internal bleeding.

She didn't like the fact that Ann had passed out. It could mean nothing more than that a very long, awful day had completely sapped Ann's energy, but a whole host of scarier options floated around Rachel's mind.

Once they had done all they could for Ann, including taping the wounded ribs so they wouldn't move, Rachel smiled her thanks to the young nurse. "What's your name?" she asked, allowing herself to be led to the other bed.

"Lori Hewer, but you can call me Nurse Lori or just plain Lori." The nurse bustled about gathering instruments. Efficiently, she checked Rachel's pupil reactions, temperature, pulse, and blood pressure. The nurse frowned at the blood pressure reading but quickly recovered her nurse-smile.

Rachel responded with a half-smile. "Blood pressure a little high, Nurse Lori?"

"Out the roof," the nurse replied. "You about broke my machine. What happened out there?"

A guarded look washed over Rachel.

"Never mind. Don't worry about anything right now," Nurse Lori added quickly. She patted Rachel's arm. "Will you be okay for a moment?"

Rachel nodded, already drifting off.

"All right, I'm sure Dr. Verni would like

you to sleep some. Goodnight."
***

Most of America slept peacefully that summer night. Absolutely nothing compared to the chaos that swept through St. Mary's Healthcare Center. Staff doctors worked throughout the night, and additional doctors were called in to attend the wounded and dying casualties of the Stanley County mini-war.

Dr. Verni had never heard of such an incident in the hospital's long history. They were used to car accidents and diseases, maybe single gunshot incidents, not multiple D.O.A.'s and gunshot wounds galore. Two children, one traumatized and the other in serious condition, were given immediate care. Two young men had been brought in, examined, released, and hauled off to jail. One man had died en route, five had come in body bags, and four more were in critical condition. A woman with bruised ribs and a thoroughly ticked off woman suffering from shock were sleeping. One healthy man submitted to a brief examination, answered some general questions, and spent the night pacing, impatient for news of his daughter. The police wanted to question the man further but let him be for the moment, which Dr. Verni thought a wise move.

The man looks frazzled, Dr. Verni thought as he bustled about his tasks. The short, balding pudgy, doctor practically glowed with restless energy. When it came down to it, he could bark orders better than a seasoned army commander.

Just when the head doctor thought everything was settling down, a new wave of government people swept in, escorting another man with a bullet in his arm. They milled about getting in the way, so Dr. Verni had them kindly tossed into the waiting room.

Dr. Armstrong and Dr. Joler spent hours trying to save the little girl. When Dr. Verni saw the expression on Dr. Armstrong's usually stoic face, he knew the worst had happened. The child had died. He grieved briefly for the family he would have to notify. Slowly, pondering his words, he headed to the waiting room. A thought came to him, and he quickened his pace. There was precious little time to lose.

He found the girl's father first and asked him the question.

The tired, dazed man closed his eyes and thought for a long moment. Finally, he said, "I'll say 'yes' as long as my wife's okay with it."

"Thank you, sir," Dr. Verni said hastily. With that, he raced from the room.

A quick investigation and a frantic jog down familiar, pristine halls brought him to the room where the two women slept. He felt guilty about waking them, but he forged ahead knowing that many lives were at stake.

Reaching the room, Dr. Verni glanced back and forth between the two women. Either one could be the mother. The lady with honey colored hair on his left stirred so he decided to question her first. Dr. Verni noticed her ribs were taped so he gently but firmly shook her, calling out, "Madam, I insist you wake at once! Please, do wake. This is most important!"

She moaned to protest the rude awakening.

Dr. Verni would not be put off from his task. "Madam, please! I must ask you something!"

She moaned again and woke up. Eyes flying open in alarm, the woman's left hand shot toward her right side where a gun would be if she had a holster strapped there. "What?" she demanded, half sitting up and then sinking down against the thin hospital pillow.

"I'm sorry, ma'am, but I had to wake you. I am Dr. Verni. Are you the mother of the little girl who was brought in tonight with a gunshot wound? I'm sorry to have to tell you this but—"

He cut himself off as understanding dawned behind the young woman's pale blue eyes. Tears spilled down her smooth cheeks and she bit her lower lip to keep it from trembling. Mutely, she shook her head.

"I see," Dr. Verni said disappointed. "I won't disturb you further. I'll just wake the other young lady and leave you in peace."

"Wait!" she cried, freezing him mid-stride. She made a weak attempt to get up, winced, clutched her right side, gritted her teeth, and finally sat up.

Confused, he turned back to her.

"Please," the woman pleaded. "Let me tell her. She's my friend."

Dr. Verni thought a moment then nodded. He didn't think the young woman was up to the task, but a friend was a far better choice than a stranger to break such heart-wrenching news. His old but strong arms helped the woman disentangle herself from the hospital sheets and climb out of the bed. He kept his arms firmly around her shoulders while they covered the space between the two beds. The woman could only manage a drunken stagger so it took them several more shuffle-steps than it should have. "Lean here for just a second and I'll get you a chair."

The woman followed the instruction, and when the hospital monstrosity gently bumped the back of her knees, she collapsed into it.

"Do hurry, please," Dr. Verni begged, when the woman paused to gather strength for the task. "I need to know if she'll consent to donating the child's organs. The father has already agreed, but we must receive the mother's permission as well. It's very important that we get the answer soon!"

***

Only vaguely aware of the excited doctor's babbling, Ann pushed thoughts of Patrick away. Worry would not help her accomplish the current task.

My turn to be strong for Rachel.

Ann could not and would not tolerate

anyone else breaking Rachel's heart with the news of Emily's death. She shut her eyes tightly for a second, trying desperately not to sob. Silent tears slipped out anyway.

If she waited too long, the elderly doctor would wake her friend as enthusiastically as he had awakened her and blurt the request. By this time, he shifted from foot to foot like a small child with a full bladder.

God, please give me the strength to do this. Help Rachel understand. Keep her spirit from shattering. May you be glorified through this tragedy.

After her short prayer, Ann took a deep, steadying breath and leaned forward. "Rachel," she called softly, touching her friend's arm.

She looked so peaceful sleeping.

Time is short!

"Rachel!" she called, louder this time. Ann picked up Rachel's right hand and squeezed hard. "Rachel, wake up!" More tears streamed as Ann gave up trying to hold them back. Though surrendering to the tears, Ann locked the sobs that would prevent her from delivering her weighty message deep inside an emotional wall built long ago through many horrors.

"Please hurry!" the doctor urged.

Ann shook her friend a bit more vigorously. Each movement caused pain through her right side. "Rachel, please, wake up!" She spoke in as soothing a tone as her parched mouth could manage. "Rach, I know a lot has happened today, but the doctor needs to ask you a question. Wake up."

Rachel moaned pitifully.

Ann steeled her heart as best she could and gently shook her friend. "Rachel!"

Slowly, Rachel squinted up at her. "Ann?" she mumbled, eyes half open. "Ann!" she cried, eyes now fully open. "You're—"

Ready for Rachel's attempt to rise, Dr. Verni firmly held her in place. "Calm down, Madam!"

"I'm fine, Rachel, but there's news—bad news."

Rachel's expression told Ann that her words were breaking through the sleep fog.

"Emily died, and—" Ann broke off as sobs rendered her voice box useless. She saw the doctor draw breath to ask his question and waved, indicating she needed more time. Ann swallowed half a dozen times to sink the mountain in her throat, took two shuddering breaths, stared directly in her friend's eyes, and picked up Rachel's right hand. "The doctor needs to know if you'll donate Emily's or- organs to other children who desperately need them," Ann said in a rush. She felt terrible, knowing that each word would knife right through her friend.

Rachel said nothing but returned Ann's fierce grip with all her might. Though it was painful, Ann let her friend squeeze her hand in a literal portrayal of the battle taking place within her. She saw in Rachel's eyes that something much fiercer than any physical test of strength was happening. Ann felt helpless but lent what strength she could to the struggle, knowing it was a scalding emotional fire that no parent should ever have to face. There was no helping the fact that it would destroy much of Rachel no matter what was done. Ann ached terribly over the whole situation. Rachel's only hope for emotional recovery was to grieve good, long, and well and then let go.

Many lives will be saved.

Ann kept the thought to herself, knowing it would mean nothing to Rachel right now.

She feared Rachel would go into complete shock and not be able to answer. She knew of her friend's deep inner strength, but she had never before seen her under such emotional pressure.

Rachel clenched her eyes against the pain and fought for words.

"Yes, doctor," she said at last.

Dr. Verni was out the door so fast that Ann felt the wind of his retreat.

Thoroughly worn out, Ann leaned forward and embraced Rachel. Their right arms remained locked together. The years that had separated them suddenly meant nothing. They were two friends sharing one pain. They wept until no more tears came. Bruised ribs and all,

Ann fell asleep with her head resting on her friend's bed.

Chapter 18:
Real and Realized Love

St. Mary's Healthcare Center
Pierre, South Dakota

Jonathan Parker's spirits sank lower with each passing second. His daughter lay dead, his career no longer existed, and he wasn't sure where he stood with his wife. Since sleep refused to come, he had a lot of time to think.

After about six hours of thought wrestling, Jon surrendered to the idea that he could not fix the problems on his own and committed his life to God. Folding his hands on his lap, Jon prayed that God would redeem his life and forgive his sins.

"God, I have run so far for so long I hardly remember how to be saved. Forgive my sins. Thank you for Rachel who has always been true to You first and me second. I didn't understand, but I think I'm beginning to. Help me make up for my sins. Thank you for the reminder that it's never too late for real love. Help Rachel to forgive me. I need her to understand me like You do ..." He prayed more in his heart.

Soon after, the elderly doctor returned. "I'm sorry for your loss, sir. On behalf of all those who will be saved, thank you," said Dr. Verni.

Jon listened torpidly.

"Can I speak to my wife?"

Dr. Verni gave him a sympathetic look, but said, "It's almost six o'clock, and your wife has just gone to sleep again. I don't want to disturb her for a while. You look like you could use some rest yourself. Try to get a few hours of sleep. I'll have one of the nurses set you up in an empty room. You can see your wife later in the afternoon."

Jon followed Dr. Verni who introduced him to Nurse Lori Hewer. In no time, Jon settled onto a hospital bed. Bits of dirt fell out of his blond hair onto the clean white pillow case, but he didn't care. He feared he wouldn't be able to sleep, but the conversation with God had lifted much weight from his weary spirit and exhaustion caught up with him as soon as his head hit the pillow.

Several hours later, Jon woke up feeling much better. He bolted down some nasty hospital food Nurse Lori Hewer brought and asked to see his wife. The nurse escorted him to a room down the hall and motioned for him to go in. Thanking her, Jon stared through the small window in the door, afraid to enter. A thousand anxious thoughts clamored for attention. He swallowed hard and pushed the feelings aside.

Rachel was awake and staring at nothing. She didn't react to his sudden presence in her hospital room.

"Hello, Rachel," Jon said, honestly not knowing where to start.

After several seconds of blank staring, recognition slowly dawned behind Rachel's tired eyes. "Chris," she mumbled. Confusion, then horror, then more confusion crossed her face. "You're not Chris, are you? There never was a Chris. He was just a dream," she went on. Fresh tears pooled in her eyes.

Rushing over, Jon sat on the edge of his wife's bed and picked up her hand. It felt cold. He bit back sobs building in his chest. "Rachel, I am so sorry. So very sorry. For everything."

"Tell me everything," she whispered with a mixture of love and pain.

Nodding slowly, he cleared his throat,

and said, "My name is Jonathan Parker. Most of what I've told you about myself has been true, but I left out key parts of my past." As he talked, his story unfolded easier. After all, this was the woman he had known for over a decade and with whom he had shared the last six years of his life. "I've always enjoyed fiddling with computers. As a child and then as a teenager, I became a decent hacker. I spent three months in juvenile detention for breaking the security codes of a pharmaceutical company. I swore I'd never be caught again.

"My parents split when I was sixteen. I lived with my mother, but she couldn't handle me and two jobs. I had to get away, so I created a false background story and joined the army. I was trained as a sniper, and I loved it. I became good friends with Paul Morton. Eventually, he taught me how to make quick, easy money through smuggling. Soon after we went into business though, I met you."

Up to this point, Jon's voice had been bland and informative, now it softened. "I fell in love and decided I wanted to change. I ran from my past, modifying records and files as needed. I wasn't a medical student at the time, but you were and I figured I needed to impress you. I forged undergrad info, recommendations, and other papers to get into medical school. I really did attend medical school, but my license says my real name." There was no note of pride in his voice, only regret. "I love you, Rachel. That won't ever change. Can you forgive the mistakes I've made? Do—do *we* still have a chance?"

A few tears slipped out of Rachel's eyes and made their way slowly down her face. She waited several moments to compose her reply. "Chris, I—I mean Jon, I fell in love with a good man not his name, and I still see that good man. I've spent a lot of time begging the Lord for guidance. It was my mistake to ignore the Bible's command to not be yoked unequally, but I was so in love that nothing could change that."

"I'm sorry I deceived you, Rachel, but you won't have to worry about being unequally yoked. I—I've changed. Again. This whole disastrous week ripped apart my old life. Little by little, over the long hours I waited for news of you, the Lord broke my spirit. This morning, when I finally accepted Him, I felt

Him rebuilding me from the inside out. Even Emily's death seemed more ... bearable."

Rachel nodded silent understanding.

Jon was encouraged by the love in her eyes. *It will be a long road back to where our marriage was.* Suddenly, a thought struck Jon and he gasped.

"What is it?" Rachel asked, bracing for more bad news.

Jon smiled, stood, and knelt beside Rachel's bed, gazing up into her red-rimmed eyes. "You married the wrong man, Rachel." He cast his gaze about the room and spotted his own wedding band. Clearing his throat, he asked, "Rachel Collins, will you marry me?"

Relief washed over her features.

"Yes, Jonathan Parker, I will marry you ... again. I still love you."

He slipped his too-big ring onto her finger.

Now, they were both crying, but for a brief moment, their tears were not of heartache but joy. Soon, the ache of loss would set in again, but at least, they would face the uncertain future together.

***

Ann woke up surrounded by people. Odd

hospital smells stung her nose, but she imagined smelling something warm and good too. She didn't have much time to think about it though because her family crowded close. Her eyes snapped open and got big.

A chorus of different variations of "She's finally awake," rang out.

"Mom? Dad? What time is it?" Ann asked, slightly confused. She didn't remember being moved to her own room, but other memories—darker ones—flashed through her mind. She sat up. The sudden movement caused a burning sensation in her right side. Her father and little sister each caught a shoulder and eased her back onto the bed.

"Down, girl!" scolded her little sister, Joy.

"Whoa! Easy does it. The police say you've had a busy night," Able Davidson said, smiling easily.

Ann loved her father's ability to shake off scares. She was grateful to have inherited some of that ability to roll with tough situations.

"It's well past time to wake up, though it looks like you could use some more beauty rest," said Joy. Hair clips, pins, and a brush magically appeared in her hands, and she set about ordering Ann's tangled hair.

"I'm fine," Ann mumbled, smiling faintly at the pampering. Her eyes silently begged her mother for understanding, but Carol Davidson looked too stricken to speak.

That's probably a good thing.

Ann loved her mother just as much as she loved her father, but she wished her mother would be a little more approving of her career.

"How's Patrick?" Ann asked, noticing the others for the first time.

"He's weak, but he woke up long enough to ask for you," replied Patrick's mother.

Ann couldn't pin down the emotion she heard, and she was thoroughly confused as to why her partner would want to speak with her when he had his family present. She tried to climb out of the bed.

The woman gave her a "hold on" wave and smiled gently. Her dark brown hair was just like Patrick's, but her eyes were a stunning shade of green instead of deep blue.

"We've met a few times before, but I'm not sure you remember me." She stepped forward and held out a hand for Ann to shake. "I'm Patrick's mother, Victoria." After a brief handshake, she waved to the men standing to her left. "This is my husband, Marcus, and our other son, Preston."

The two men nodded shyly, and Ann noticed that they both had eyes like Patrick.

"Dr. Anderson said he'd stop by when Patrick wakes up again," said Victoria.

"The nurse brought your lunch while you slept," Joy noted, pointing with distaste at the colorful, scary looking mush on a small green tray.

Suddenly, Ann realized she was ravenous. Her father took the tray out of reach before she could study the contents more closely. She looked confused.

"You're really going to eat that crap?" her little brother asked bluntly, receiving a glare from their mother. Nicholas Davidson's spirits would not be vanquished by a mere glare; he grinned impishly at Ann. "Why not try this?" he asked, pulling a bag from behind his back.

"Don't worry, it's safe and store fresh," her father assured.

Joy grabbed the bag from Nick and insisted on spoon feeding Ann the delicious chicken soup.

For a time, Ann focused on enjoying the

food, but she knew she'd have to broach the uncomfortable subject eventually. "How did you know?" Ann asked at last, not daring to look her mother in the eye.

"It was all over the news! Big shootout in South Dakota!" Nick said enthusiastically.

Ann winced. *That's not exactly the best way they could have found out, but the damage is done.*

"Oh, and your boss called," Nick added.

"Before or after?" Ann demanded.

"After," Nick replied with an easy shrug. His posture made him look a lot like their father.

Ann shook her head and groaned softly.

"Hey, I saw it first!" Nick said proudly. He was all right as far as little brothers go, but he had a carelessness streak that could hurt others.

Poor mom.

Ann could just picture the whole discovery debacle.

"Julie Ann, I ..." her mother couldn't finish the thought.

Flashing an uneasy smile, Ann switched the subject. "How'd you all manage to get out here?"

"Skipped school," Nick said.

"Skipped class," Joy threw in a split second later.

"Skipped work," Ann's parents said simultaneously.

Everyone smiled, and some of the tension dissipated.

"Agent Davidson? Are you up for a short visit with Agent Duncan?" asked a tall, lanky man wearing a white lab coat.

"Of course. I'll be right along," Ann said, feeling stronger already.

The two families were left to chat by themselves as Ann followed Dr. Anderson to Patrick's room which was next to the critical care unit.

"He's stable but weak so don't stay too long," the doctor said in a stern but kindly manner.

Ann cautiously entered Patrick's room. It was identical to other hospital rooms, save for the presence of a lot more monitoring equipment.

A very pale Patrick lay on the hospital bed with the adjustable back raised so he was sort of sitting up. Grinning, he affected his atrocious Southern accent, "I told ya it'd be a mite dangerous traveling with such a fine lady." He held out a hand toward her.

"I'm glad you're feeling better," Ann said. The words were inadequate to summarizing her relief. A huge burden lifted off her soul, making her realize how much she had worried. She walked over to his hospital bed intending to clasp his proffered hand, but when she got there, she impulsively leaned over to kiss his cheek.

Patrick responded automatically by turning his head and capturing her lips with his own. "Wow," he said after the kiss. "If that's the kind of greeting I get, shoot me any day," he joked. He sobered almost immediately. "I heard Emily didn't make it," he said, eyes watering. "I tried, Ann—I tried." A distant look crossed his handsome face.

"I know," Ann whispered. Her face still close to his, she cupped his head in her hands and met his eyes. "God knows, too."

"I love you, Ann," Patrick blurted.

Ann didn't know what to make of that statement. Her heart wanted to agree with him, but her analytical mind started picking the short statement apart.

Sensing her hesitation, Patrick said,

"Almost dying makes one think awfully hard. I've always been too afraid or too busy to fall in love. For years, I tried to deny what my heart and eyes told me: I had a beautiful, God-fearing woman as a partner and if I tried, she might be more ... could we be more, Ann?" he asked, baring his soul.

Stunned, yet in a lot of ways not surprised, Ann studied Patrick for several long moments. Her heart and mind raced, performing myriad calculations. Finally, she nodded and kissed him again. "I'd like that," she murmured.

He was almost shy now.

"I—I prayed about it."

"Perfect way to start, Patrick." After a moment's silence, Ann remembered his family was waiting. "Oh, your family's here to see you. You saw them earlier but only long enough to ask to see me." Concern furrowed her brows as she asked, "Are you strong enough to see them again?"

He just looked at her with "yes" written on his face.

Chapter 19:
New Priorities and New Life

Hapler Residence
Grandview, Illinois

Six o'clock Wednesday morning, Senator Orion Hapler watched the breaking news bulletin with detached interest. Still reeling from his wife's murder and distraught over his daughter's kidnapping, he had taken yesterday off, barricaded himself in his room, and refused to speak to anyone. Today, he had a bunch of rescheduled meetings that suddenly seemed trivial.

"Senator Hapler, Mr. Lanes is on line three," said his aide, Erik Fenning brusquely.

The senator ignored Mr. Fenning, his attention instead locked on the TV. He hit the mute button, turning the sound back on.

"—following Monday night's deadly South Dakota shootout. The raid on Morton's hideout lead to the rescue of many, including Jenny Hapler, daughter of Illinois senator Orion Hapler, who has been missing since last

Tuesday. Our reporters have been unable to reach Senator—"

Orion didn't bother listening to anymore. He grabbed his cell phone and started furiously pressing buttons.

Why didn't anyone tell me? Heads will roll!

He wanted information, and he wanted it five minutes ago.

"Sir, what do I tell Mr. Lanes?" Erik asked frantically.

"Tell him I'm not meeting with him today. If he doesn't like it, he can stuff his big fat check in his big fat mouth," Hapler shot back. "I'm going to see my daughter!"

Erik automatically reworded the senator's statements.

"I'm terribly sorry, Mr. Lanes, but Senator Hapler apologizes profusely that he cannot make today's meeting … I know, sir. But he has pressing family matters to attend to … I understand. Thank you for your patience … I'll be sure to tell him that, sir."

***

St. Mary's Healthcare Center
Pierre, South Dakota

Rachel pondered the news she had just

received. It should have been happy news, but fear sucked all the joy from it.

Jonathan Parker strolled into her room. As soon as he saw her face, he frowned and rushed to her side.

"Chris! Jon! Whoever you are!" Rachel cried. If she had been standing, she might have collapsed to her knees.

"It'll take time. What is it, my love?"

Tears of uncertainty streamed down Rachel's face, and it took a few minutes before she found the strength to speak. "I'm pregnant again." Her voice trembled with fear as her mind flashed to Emily.

Jon wrapped her in a warm hug. When he finally pulled back, he searched her face and noticed the fresh pain. "It'll be all right, Rach. God will be with us." The words sounded hollow to him, but he had her attention. "I ... don't think I'm the best person to be talking to here. Would you like me to get your friend? I think she's just about to check out."

Rachel shook her head and swiped at the tears with both palms. "No, you and I need to talk about this. I—I'm not sure I can do this, Jon."

"I'm sorry, Rachel, but we sort of don't have a choice," Jon answered, tilting his head to the side. "Just wait, Rach. We'll never forget Emily, but God will fill our empty hearts and this new baby will fill our empty arms." Jon's left hand slapped his forehead. "We still have Jason too!" His expression said he felt guilty for forgetting his son.

The barest shadow of a smile touched Rachel's lips. "Don't worry. He's okay. Ann and Nurse Lori have been bringing me regular reports."

She settled back against the pillows feeling drained. Taking the hint, Jon gently kissed her cheek and promised to return in a few hours.

***

Wednesday morning, Ann felt ready to face the world again. Eager to escape, she choked down the bland hospital food. She had tried to check out the night before, but Dr. Verni had taken one look at her and ordered another night of hospital observations.

Ann's family had stayed an hour longer than normal visiting hours making sure she was comfortable and generally spoiling her endlessly. Joy—with the aid of her bottomless purse—made Ann the best-looking patient the hospital had seen in years. Meanwhile, her mother had fretted, her father silently lent the support of his smile, and Nick babbled about hockey games, hot girls, sweet cars, and three dozen other random subjects. They left just in time to catch a late flight back home to Pennsylvania so they could get to Wednesday obligations.

Their willingness to drop everything and come to her touched Ann. She smiled at the memories. She had managed to see Patrick and Rachel a few times and even gotten to spend some time with Jason. Ann's thoughts wandered to Patrick. She wondered how long he would be stuck in the hospital. As she thought, Ann prayed for everyone touched by the Collins case.

I've got work to do!

Ann smiled and mentally set goals for the day. This case warranted way more than the usual end-of-case paperwork.

After a quick shower, Ann dressed in comfortable clothes from the travel bag her parents had picked up from Sheriff Heckle's office. Monday night, Patrick and Ann had been so late that they had not taken the time to check into hotel rooms.

Striding from the room, Ann practically barreled into her boss. "Mr. Morgan!" she exclaimed, jumping back a bit.

Yikes.

"What are you doing out here, sir?" Ann asked, unsure whether to be worried or pleased.

"Relax, Agent Davidson. I got word that two of my best were out here in the sticks getting shot at while working on the biggest case in the Bureau's recent history, so I figured it was time I got out of my office." His dark eyes twinkled, and he set her at ease with a smile.

Shyly returning the smile, Ann said, "I'll have a report ready in an—"

Lance Morgan held up both hands to ward off her rush of words. "It's all right. I want a thorough report, but take your time. I just talked to Agent Duncan. Looks like you two will be sitting the sidelines for a while. Don't worry, there are plenty of cases that just need a good bit of brain power, and knowing you two, I expect a full recovery will come much faster than anyone anticipates."

Ann noted his expression and picked up

on his inflection as he said "you two."

"Oh, and I hear that you two might be more than just partners soon," Morgan said casually, taking a sudden interest in his fingernails.

"Patrick told you? What did he tell you, sir?" The second question came out so fast it was barely understandable. Ann blushed.

Her boss chuckled. The pleasant, rumbling sound filled the hallway.

"Just that his near-death experience had given him new priorities, and that he'd taken an interest in a very special lady. It didn't take long to figure out whom he was referring to. Don't forget that I direct a bunch of glorified detectives. Heck, I used to be one, long ago." He leaned forward conspiratorially. "Besides, it doesn't take a whole lot to read a man in love. I should know. Can't hardly think straight when I get to thinking about my wife."

Ann wasn't sure what expression she had on her face, but whatever it was, it set the usually stern-faced assistant director into fits of laughter.

"You're a very popular lady, Agent Davidson," said Mr. Morgan. "There's a young man in Sheriff Heckle's jail requesting to speak with you, and a young woman here who wants to talk to someone who knows what went on Monday night."

"Do you know where I can find her?" asked Ann.

"I'll let her father take you to her," Morgan said, nodding over her shoulder.

Ann turned and saw Illinois Senator Orion Hapler striding down the hallway.

Her boss walked up and greeted the senator like an old friend. They returned to her, and Mr. Morgan said, "Senator Hapler, allow me to introduce Special Agent Julie Ann Davidson. She was involved in the Stanley County shootout. If anyone can explain this mess, it's her."

"It's a pleasure to meet you, sir," Ann said, shaking the senator's hand. "I'm sorry the circumstances aren't more pleasant."

She bid Mr. Morgan goodbye, but before she was out of earshot, he called, "Watch out for the reporters. They're waiting like a pack of hounds for anyone involved."

"Thank you, sir. I'll keep that in mind."

As they walked down the hallway, the senator filled Ann in on the short version of his side of the story. "So, I flew out here to find my daughter," he finished.

"I really think you want to talk to my friend Rachel, but I'm not sure she's ready for questions yet. I'll tell you what I know."

"I'd appreciate it."

Ann understood the man's curiosity, especially since his child was dragged into the mess. Anxious though she was to get back to her investigation, Ann patiently stood by and watched the happy father-daughter reunion. Then, she explained as much as she could and finished by saying, "I'll contact you once I've written my report. By then, I'll probably have a better idea of what went on."

"Thank you." As Ann turned to leave, Senator Hapler asked, "Agent Davidson, why did they take Jenny?"

Ann faced the senator again and regarded his statement with curiosity. "They didn't contact you?"

"Not a word."

"I imagine it's because of the hype about that satellite expansion bill you've been pushing for," she answered thoughtfully. Ann frowned and thought for another few seconds. Pieces of the puzzle clicked together in her head. "Mr. Morton was heavily involved in smuggling. Additional satellite activity would have endangered his supply lanes. From what little I know of him, sir, I believe Jenny would have been returned safely as long as the expansion bill failed." Ann had the pleasure of seeing Senator Hapler's remaining worry lines melt away.

He turned his attention back to his daughter, and Ann took the opportunity to leave.

***

County Jail
Fort Pierre, South Dakota

"If he gives you any problems, just holler and I'll be back in a hurry to box his ears," Sheriff Heckle promised.

Ann grinned at the bulky sheriff's retreating form and sat in a chair outside an old-fashioned jail cell. Then, she studied the tall, broad, mid-twenties young man inside the jail cell. His shaggy blond hair and troubled green eyes made him look younger.

"What's your name?" asked Ann.

"Thomas Randle," he answered, avoiding her eyes.

"I was told you wanted to see me," Ann said, attempting to get him to speak. She recognized him as the boy who had surrendered in the middle of the fight and even shot at the sniper.

"I did," Thomas said softly, finally meeting her eyes. "I have to ask you something, agent." His pale, haggard face spoke of very little sleep since his arrest.

"Yes?" Ann prompted, keeping her tone friendly. She leaned forward to hear him.

"I see that night in my dreams," he whispered in a haunted voice. "I go over what happened time and again, and it makes no sense. What protects you?" Randle's tone held genuine awe.

The question took Ann by surprise, but she began to understand. "Tell me what you saw." She leaned back and listened raptly as the boy's story unfolded.

"I've worked for Mr. Parker for several years. See, I was orphaned at age ten, and I hated staying with my Aunt Holly. I ran away and drifted about for a few months. Anyway, I got into drug dealing, got caught, and spent some time in prison. Guess you might say I'm a regular sob story," he said bitterly. "Monday night, Jense came tearing into the barracks cursing and shouting for us to get to the trucks. So, we did. You know most of the rest of it. The other guy called, there was a standoff, somebody shot Mr. Parker …"

"Then what happened?"

Thomas shrugged a bit. "After that shot, the government man dove for his gun and came up shooting. He hit several of the guys in the other truck. I was in the back of Mr. Parker's truck. I raised my gun to shoot your partner, but then, I heard your shots at Dillan and Jense." His voice strengthened as he got to his main point. He took a deep breath and let it out. "Ma'am, something powerful protected you that night. I took dozens of shots at you from point-blank range. I've been firing a gun for as long as I can recall. Do you remember me staring at you, all scared-like?"

Ann nodded her head affirmatively.

"I'm a good shot," the young man insisted. "It's like something physically shook the gun so I couldn't shoot straight!"

Shaken, Ann thought back to that night. So much had happened at once. She remembered rolling left to avoid the shots from the roof. Carefully replaying the scene, moment by moment, she recalled struggling to her feet and hearing a man's shout of surprised pain. Bullets had been flying everywhere. Now that she thought of it, a lot of shots had come from behind her. She had spun around and found herself starring into the young man's frightened eyes.

Thank you, Father, for the protection and this opportunity.

Rarely did Ann ever encounter someone begging to be told about God. "Thomas, God protected me that night," she said. "I guess it wasn't my time to die," Ann added, shrugging.

I guess I'll know it when the time comes.

Her breath hitched at that thought, causing a sharp pain of protest from her injured ribs. Pushing the discomfort aside, Ann asked, "Have you heard the good news of Jesus Christ's life and sacrifice for sinners?"

The young man nodded, a dubious expression coming over his face. "Sure, Aunt Holly talked about Jesus all the time. She reminded me that every bad thing I did nailed Christ to the cross again." His eyes hardened at the bad memory.

No wonder he never wanted to believe!

"Thomas, God loves you," Ann said quietly. "Christ's death, all those years ago, was in part *for* you. He died for the sins of mankind, but he also rose again so we could inherit God's gift of salvation. It was an act of love, not condemnation." Ann could tell she was confusing the young man. So, she did about the stupidest thing one can do while visiting a prisoner. She held her hand through the bars, palm down and waited for him to tentatively take her hand. "God's always reaching out to you. Simply grasp His hand."

"I don't understand."

Ann considered her words carefully. "Tell Him you accept Christ's sacrifice in place of your sins and ask for forgiveness and guidance. Don't worry; it will make sense someday. Let me find you a Bible and someone to help you understand it. Write me any questions you want. I'll do what I can to answer them." With one last, reassuring squeeze, Ann released the young man's hand.

"All right, but please, don't forget me!"

"I won't," Ann promised. She had a lot more to say but needed to get back to the hospital, so she took her leave.

As she pulled away from the county jail, Ann thought, *God can give you true peace, Thomas. I hope you'll understand this someday.*

215

Chapter 20:
Ten and Countless

St. Mary's Healthcare Center
Pierre, South Dakota

The next few hours were a whirlwind of investigating and visiting. Ann finished her final report for AD Morgan, did some side research, and had a long conversation with Patrick. By late Wednesday night, Ann had everything in place. She needed to return to Washington, D.C. soon, so she figured there was no better time than the present to lift Rachel's spirits.

Father, please let things go well tonight.

She offered up the brief prayer just as she entered Patrick's room followed closely by Mr. Parker. "Are you ready?"

Still extremely weak from being shot, Patrick had been denied the request for a move up to Rachel's room for the presentation, but Jonathan Parker had come to arrange for a laptop and webcam to be set up.

"Get me out of here!" Patrick cried, upon seeing the pair enter his room.

"Patience," Ann said, kissing his nose. "If you're a good boy, I might let you help with the presentation." She handed him a folder to look over while Jon handled the computer setup.

"How are you feeling, Agent Duncan?" asked Jon, shaking Patrick's hand.

"Just Patrick."

"Patrick it is. I don't know what this is all about, but Agent Davidson was rather insistent you somehow be present when she gives Rachel some news." Jon fiddled with the bed controls until Patrick was in a semi-sitting position.

"Ann, if you please. There's no need to be all formal here, Mr. Parker."

"Well, more than two can play that game," said Jon, turning to address Ann. "Please, call me Jon."

"As you wish," Ann answered.

Turning back to Patrick, Jon explained, "Since the doctors wouldn't budge on the issue of moving you, I volunteered to help. I synced this laptop with one we'll open in Rachel's room so you can see what's going on."

"Thanks," said Patrick. "Still wish I could join you."

"Cheer up," said Ann. She picked up his hand and gave it a friendly squeeze. "I'll be back down as soon as the presentation's over.

"I'll hold you to that," said Patrick, looking tired.

Leaning closer, Ann whispered, "Try not to pass out just yet."

When the computer was all set up, Ann and Jon bid Patrick a temporary farewell and hustled up to Rachel's room.

Barging through the door, Jon swept in and moved to Rachel's side. "Hi again, Patrick," said Jon, waving to the laptop sitting on the end table on the opposite side of the bed. He nodded at the laptop and then at Ann. "Patrick, Ann, it is my great pleasure to introduce my wife, Rachel Parker."

Ann rushed to her friend's side. "Oh, Rachel—when?"

"About two hours ago," answered Jon. "There's more news ..." He looked to Rachel expectantly.

Rachel's serious expression slowly melted into a slightly hopeful expression. "We're going to have another baby."

Hearty congratulations went around.

And here I came to bring lots of news, Ann thought wryly. She cast a quick glance at the laptop and caught Patrick's slight nod.

"Well, we also have an announcement to make," said Ann.

"I suckered her into marrying me," Patrick blurted from the laptop.

Everyone laughed. It was a wonderful change from the constant gloom that had prevailed the last couple of days. Congratulations went the other way.

"Where's the ring?" Rachel demanded. She cast a critical gaze between the laptop and her friend.

"It's in the mail," quipped Patrick.

Smiling, Ann said, "I gave him a short extension on the ring part since it's kind of hard to shop from a hospital."

"Not with the convenience of the internet these days," teased Rachel, motioning to the laptop carrying the live feed of Patrick at that very second.

"She even let me propose without the one-knee bit," said Patrick.

"I didn't want to have to haul you off the ground if you passed out," said Ann, shrugging.

Smiling at that, Rachel asked, "When's the wedding?"

"As soon as possible," answered Patrick, half-wistful and half-joking.

"We talked about it at length this afternoon. We'll probably get married in a few months. There's so much to think about, not the least of which is what happens afterwards ..." Ann trailed off as the other guests arrived.

As Dr. Verni, Dr. Anderson, Dr. Joler, and Dr. Armstrong crowded into the room, Ann said, "But enough about us, let's talk about you guys."

Jon perched on the bed next to Rachel. Ann motioned one doctor to stand by the laptop. Then, she positioned Dr. Verni and the two others on the opposite side, to the right of Rachel and Jon.

I sure hope there isn't a hospital emergency; most of the doctors are here.

"What's going on?" Rachel demanded.

"An information session," Ann replied. "Patrick, would you like to do the honors?"

He shook his head negative. "You did the hard work; I only claim the last one."

Ann launched into her report. "Rachel,

Jon, I know Emily's death is a terrible blow for you. It hit the rest of us hard and we barely knew her." She felt tears forming. "I hope that what we say tonight will bring you a measure of peace. In short, I want you to know just how many lives your daughter touched. I'll start and then let the doctors have their say.

"I count myself among the first to be touched by this case. When the sniper took that last shot, I emptied my gun in his direction. One of the guys who attacked us also turned a gun on the sniper. After cuffing the young man, I checked on Emily and Patrick. Feeling helpless, I went to find the sniper. I was furious, wanting nothing more than to blow the man into eternity. But God helped me fight my feelings. He also worked in the life of the young man who had turned the gun on the sniper. I had a nice chat with him this morning, and while he didn't immediately accept Christ, I think he's searching hard." Tears burned in her eyes. Unable to speak further, Ann waved to the short woman with auburn hair massed atop her head in a disheveled bun.

Dr. Joler's voice sounded like flowing gravel, but her words were soothing. "We donated the child's organs to other young people across the country. One kidney went to Jordan Basil in Tolstoy, South Dakota. The left lung was damaged, but there was enough healthy tissue for a successful transplant. Sasha Washington in Florence, South Carolina received the lungs. Her lungs had been failing rapidly and it is believed that her life was spared by a matter of days, maybe even hours." Dr. Joler handed two pictures to Rachel and Jon.

Next, Dr. Armstrong gave his news. For a big man, he had a surprisingly gentle voice. "Skin went to Jessica Richter of Louisville, Kentucky. The corneas went to Maybelle Thatcher in Carroll, Iowa."

It was Dr. Anderson's turn. He straightened his shoulders, and said, "The liver was received by Jonathan Driver of Des Moines, Iowa. The other kidney went to Sarah Weller of Pea Ridge, Arkansas."

"By my count, Jon's conversion makes nine people positively impacted by the tragedy," said Ann.

"Where did her heart go?" asked Rachel in a whisper.

"It stayed right here," Patrick replied.

"It stayed here," Ann echoed, forcing the words through a closing throat.

"Come on in!" Patrick yelled.

Nurse Lori Hewer walked in cradling a computer tablet. "This is Christopher," she announced, handing the screen to Rachel. The irony of the name was not lost on the group. Leaning over and tipping the screen so she could peer into it, Nurse Lori said, "Chris, these are the people I told you about. These are Emily's parents. Emily was the little girl who gave you her heart—" Lori stopped to sob, releasing her hold on the tablet.

Ann couldn't see the screen, but she'd seen the boy as Nurse Lori entered. He couldn't have been more than four-years-old.

"Thank you," Lori said in a trembling voice. She could say no more so Dr. Verni took up her tale.

As usual, Dr. Verni spoke rapidly. "Lori's husband Steve couldn't make it tonight, but he also sends his deepest gratitude. Christopher has been my patient since his birth. He's had a heart defect all his life. His heart was simply too weak to pump blood constantly. Often, it would stall and skip. We were worried that time was running out." He paused as emotion locked his throat. "We did everything in our power to get him to the top of the national heart donor's list. Over a year passed with no donors, then all of a sudden there were two available hearts. However, due to Christopher's blood type of AB+, the hearts would not have been compatible with his body, and then, Monday happened. Emily was AB$^+$, and her heart was perfectly suited in every way for young Chris." Dr. Verni pointed to the computer now held equally between Rachel and Jon.

"That makes ten," Ann noted. "You are aware of the reporters who have been lurking around, right?"

Jon and Rachel nodded.

"Your story has generated a large response. Emails and comments have come in from all over the country. I've read only a few of them, but Patrick's read a lot of them. He's going to share some of his favorites now."

Patrick read through several short printouts from the file she'd compiled at his request.

Ann was too busy watching Jon and Rachel to hear the letters.

This is the turning point.

Thus far, Rachel had cried silently, now she bawled openly. Jon's face was a mask as he listened to Patrick. He wrapped Rachel in his arms and sobbed softly into her hair.

There's nothing more that can be done tonight.

Ann quickly herded the doctors and Nurse Lori to the door. Then, she returned for Patrick's laptop. He had stopped reading. They exchanged a hopeful glance before she closed the laptop and moved toward the door.

"Wait!" Rachel called out in a strangled voice. "Thank you."

Smiling from ear to ear, Ann nodded acknowledgement to her friend and left to visit her fiancé.

You're welcome, my friends. Lean on the Lord and He will help you heal.

Epilogue:

As it turns out, Agent George Baker didn't miss the action after all. While on duty protecting Mrs. Dales of Huntsville, Alabama, he caught two burglars trying to enter a neighbor's apartment. Poor Baker surprised the two young men, sparking a scuffle that landed him in Crestwood Medical Center with a fractured arm.

Logan Dales came through the Stanley County shootout with a bullet wound in his arm, but he counted himself fortunate anyway. With a glowing statement from Rachel Parker about how helpful Dales had been, the District Attorney decided to cut him a deal.

Jonathan Parker worked for a week with a team of FBI computer experts until they fixed all the bank accounts. Fortunately, Jon had kept good records. Unfortunately, greedy people made false missing money claims for several weeks. Parker's work impressed the powers that be so much that they offered him an IT job. He consulted his wife, accepted the position, and moved his family to Kensington, Maryland. They kept in touch with the Longs for a while but eventually drifted away.

Once he finally straightened out most of the legal mess he'd made, Jon wrote his mother the following letter:

Mom,

I'm back. So much has happened since I left. I'm sorry if this letter hurts you, but you deserve to know what I've made of my life. Mostly, I've made mistakes. I have so much that should be said in person, but I thought you should at least see my wife and children. Emily's gone now. It's my fault. My mistakes and lies caused all this pain, but unfortunately, the pain is also felt by my wife and son.

Rachel has been more gracious to me than I deserve. Losing Emily has destroyed something between us. I don't know what will grow in its place, but I'm hoping it will be special. Please, forgive me.

Your loving son,

Jon

After the move, Mrs. Rachel Parker and her husband started the Emily Adele Collins Fund to raise money for families whose children need expensive surgery. The tragedy made Rachel reprioritize. She continued medical work in a volunteer capacity and spent more time with her family.

Thomas Randle spent many years in prison. Agent Davidson delivered the promised Bible which became his light and hope in that dark place. He freely shared that light with all who would listen. During his prison stint, he earned his high school diploma and a ministry degree. No one truly knows how many hardened men he saved through his ministry.

Thursday morning, Agent Davidson returned to work, and her stubborn partner came back three weeks later. Even as he brought them the toughest cases, AD Morgan practically handcuffed the pair to their desks.

Three months later, they were fully back in business handling all sorts of cases as Special Agents Duncan and Duncan.

THE END

Heartfelt Cases
Book 2: The Kiverson Case

By Julie C. Gilbert

Table of Contents:

Prologue:

Kiverson Residence
Vienna, VA
Five years ago

"The only thing you kids need to know is to protect the family," Asan Kiverson said. His gaze bore into each of his children.

Kevin, the eldest, returned his gaze steadily.

Angela, the middle child, nodded hesitantly, so Asan gave her a reassuring smile.

His smile faded when he looked at his youngest child. "What's the matter, Benjamin? Don't you believe me?"

"Yes, Papa," the boy murmured.

"That's my boy. You can choose your own path, but always remember the family protects its own. One day, perhaps you kids will be called upon to protect the family."

Chapter 1:
Charismatic Criminals

J. Edgar Hoover Building, FBI Headquarters
Washington, D.C.

It started on a perfectly normal, summer Wednesday. Special Agent Julie Ann Duncan sat in her new, yet still cramped, office and studied Patrick's collection of Kiverson files. She should be working on the Drier case, but the Kiversons were so much more interesting. She bit her lower lip and absently swiped at a few strands of honey colored hair that had fallen on her face.

Smugglers, thieves, drug dealers, murders, terrorists, and con artists—that is one heck of a family tree!

"Nice family," commented Special Agent Patrick Duncan. "Well-rounded."

Ann—as she was known to everybody except her mother—glanced up to find her husband leaning in his usual spot against her doorframe. "We've been up against some weirdos before but these people top the chart!" Ann bent her head again to look at the diagram.

"Well, let's go round some of 'em up," Patrick said casually.

Head whipping up, Ann's pale blue eyes met his. It never ceased to amaze her how their boss, Assistant Director Lance Morgan, allowed them to work each other's cases, but she couldn't imagine a better partner than Patrick. He'd already been an FBI hotshot when she'd been a fresh face. His uncanny instincts paired beautifully with her sharp eye for detail.

"You've got enough evidence for a warrant?" Ann asked, clearly surprised.

"Is there anything our good buddy Jon can't do?" Patrick asked with a twinkle in his eyes. The deep blue cast of his eyes contrasted nicely with his dark brown hair.

"Cook."

Those chicken breasts were like lemon flavored rocks.

"Agreed."

The things you endure for friendship.

Rachel and Julie Ann had been friends since high school. Rachel had even dubbed her just plain Ann. A harrowing case had brought them together again a couple of years ago. After that case, Jonathan Parker had accepted a job as an FBI computer expert.

"Jon gave us enough to take out this family branch anyway," Patrick said, tossing Ann a file. "He used one of the oldest techniques on the books."

Snatching the file out of the air, Ann asked, "What's that?"

"Follow the money, honey," Patrick said.

Ann grinned and swiveled her chair to grab her purse. "Well, what are we waiting for?" she asked, half rising from her chair.

Patrick waved for her to sit again. "Relax. We've still got time until the SWAT guys finish their primping."

"Let me guess. They wanted an extra hour to run simulations, and you wanted a good excuse to come and see me."

"Guilty," Patrick said, abandoning his doorway post and moving to stand behind her chair.

"Sounds good to me," Ann said. "And while you're back there, why don't you make yourself useful?"

Grumbling good-naturedly, Patrick

massaged her shoulders. Ann was surprised at how many tiny knots crackled under his fingers.

Unfortunately, her mind was preoccupied with case questions, so she couldn't concentrate on how good the massage felt. "Ouch!"

Patrick halted immediately. "Sorry."

"No, no, don't stop. It's the good sort of pain."

"Good pain? I thought pain was a bad thing." When she didn't respond, Patrick took up the massage again.

"Charismatic, aren't they," Ann mused after a few moments. She picked up a pencil and rolled it between her fingers, an old habit that meant she was deep in thought, thoroughly bored, worried sick, or some combination thereof.

"They are indeed. They attract quite a following," Patrick noted, resting his hands on her back and leaning over her shoulder to read the articles she'd spread on her desk.

I can see that, Ann thought as she skimmed a newspaper article on the arrest of James Kiverson, patriarch of the notorious family.

After an intense five-year investigation, Interpol had finally trapped Mr. Kiverson in Italy. He had been extradited to the U.S. to stand trial for drug trafficking and supporting terrorists. The picture next to the article showed a small mob holding up support signs welcoming James Kiverson home.

The FBI had people frantically gathering evidence to bring down the rest of the family for crimes ranging from fraud to murder. Jon's ingenious linkage of the recent rash of bank robberies to Asan Kiverson was the first breakthrough in over three months.

"Are we going to have any trouble?" Ann wondered, as she scanned another article which featured the San Diego riot that had occurred when Kiverson supporters had picked a fight with James Kiverson's escorts.

"I hope not."

"Why are people so enamored with them?" Ann inquired, genuinely mystified.

"They make good antiheroes."

Ann nodded reluctant agreement.

"Antiheroes, right. Like Asan's brother, Jack, who ordered the Chicago gang massacre or Jack's son, Derrick, murderer of the Claytonsville Cop Killer. Ah, this is confusing!"

Many of the Kiverson crimes were against other criminals. Some people cheered the family while simultaneously condemning law enforcement agencies for failing to keep the streets safe. Ann's mind wandered to some of the news specials where celebrities and common folks alike had voiced their support of the family.

They have no idea how many disasters are averted every day.

"Murderers vs. murderers," Patrick said in a far-away voice that indicated he didn't quite get the whole picture either.

"I think they redefined the term 'street justice.'"

"Not good."

Ann touched his right hand which still rested on her shoulder and squeezed it. "That's why they hire people like us." She let a long, slow breath hiss through her teeth. "One thing's for sure, Patrick, we'll never run out of crimes to solve."

Chapter 2:
Take Down

Kiverson Residence
Vienna, Virginia

Within the hour, Ann and Patrick Duncan stood ready to participate in the Kiverson raid.

Lord, please keep the teams safe today.

Ann had done this kind of thing many times, but each new experience struck her as a heady mix of danger and excitement. She adjusted a strap on her bulletproof vest and wished someone would invent lighter body armor for summer raids.

"Nervous?" asked Patrick. He wiped sweat from his brow with a white handkerchief.

"Slightly," Ann answered. Her mind flew to the first take down after the Collins case, when they'd started the tradition. She hoped this one would go as smoothly as that one.

"At least we've got the odds on our side," Patrick said.

"We don't need odds, only God," she

finished. About two years ago, they had been involved in a shootout in Stanley County, South Dakota. Greatly outnumbered and outgunned, they had both been shot and lived to tell the tale. Since then, they reminded themselves of God's sovereignty and protection before every raid.

We're alive only by the grace of God.

As she waited, Ann studied the Kiverson's spacious house. Sunlight bouncing off multiple windows made the house look like an alien. Ann's mind ticked through the targets again. She didn't like there being so many targets. It was difficult enough to apprehend one suspect, let alone five. Asan and Amelia were the primary targets, but they had three children who were wanted for questioning: Kevin age 25, Angela age 18, and Benjamin age 16. Ann knew some mafia families passed on the proclivity to commit crimes like other people passed on bad hair, but the Kiversons were in a league of their own.

Strange and sad situation. I wonder what will happen to the children.

She didn't have time to conjure an answer. Patrick gave the "go" signal, and the heavily armed SWAT teams swept through the building with Ann and Patrick on their heels. Both agents held handguns at the ready. Crashing doors, shouting voices, and pounding footsteps made an intense racket.

Instinctively, they split up with Patrick following Alpha Team, and Ann trailing Bravo Team.

Patrick's team found their quarry first, but Asan Kiverson refused to go down easily. A short but vicious fistfight broke out. They rolled several times, making it impossible for Alpha Team members to get a clear shot off. They traded a flurry of shoulder and chest blows before Patrick's left fist finally connected with Asan's nose, stunning the man long enough for the rest of the team to pounce.

When Asan was safely handcuffed, Patrick asked, "Where are your children, Mr. Kiverson?" He frowned and wiped blood from his hands onto his handkerchief, hoping for—but not really expecting to get—an answer from the big man.

Blood seeped out of Asan's nose as he glared up at Patrick. "They left. You'll never catch them, you—"

"Get him out to the car," Patrick said, cutting the man off. He ignored the hatred boiling out of Asan Kiverson's eyes. "Henderson, please inform Mr. Kiverson of his Miranda rights."

"Yes, sir," said the young agent. He and a buddy plucked Asan off the ground and escorted him toward the door. "You have the right to remain silent. You have …"

As Henderson droned through the Miranda rights, Patrick contemplated his handkerchief and wondered if it was worth saving. Deeming it a lost cause, Patrick went to find the restroom where he could toss the handkerchief and thoroughly wash his hands. "That could have gone better."

While Patrick and his team tussled with Asan, Ann and Bravo Team swept through the rooms upstairs. After four bedrooms, they found Amelia frantically searching a cluttered storage box. The Bravo Team men pointed rifles at her and shouted orders.

"Freeze!"

"Stop!"

"Don't move!"

Amelia seized a small, silver object from the box and twisted her head to face them with a wild look in her eyes. Her triumphant grin chilled Ann.

"No!"

The shout came from Ann as she launched herself at the woman. Ann landed on top of the Amelia's back and desperately tried to pin her arms to the hardwood floor. She had to prevent the razor clutched in the woman's right hand from touching anything. A brief, frantic struggle ensued. The smooth, wooden floor made it difficult for either woman to get a good grip. The Bravo Team members were about to enter the fray when Amelia's elbow struck Ann's jaw. Momentarily stunned, Ann's hold on Mrs. Kiverson slipped. Tasting blood, Ann knew what would come next, but no words would come.

Without hesitation, the woman raked the razor down her own left palm.

As Amelia Kiverson fell limp beneath her, Ann groaned and rolled off the woman. Salty blood from her bitten tongue added to her misery.

With her last scrap of strength, the woman rolled onto her right side to face Ann.

"Why?" Ann asked, her voice a hoarse whisper.

"You'll never put us in jail," Amelia declared with her dying breath.

Ann could only blink helplessly as the fast acting poison killed her prisoner.

Why? The question cruelly repeated in her head.

"Are you all right, Agent Duncan?" one of the Bravo guys asked, helping her up.

Ann glanced at him before letting her eyes return to Amelia's body. "I'll be fine in a moment, thanks, Victor. Why don't you guys sweep the other rooms again? I don't want any more surprises."

Could I have done something differently?

Once alone, Ann leaned her forehead against the window and mentally replayed the scene. Dust kicked up by the fight stung her eyes, making it easy for tears to come. This wasn't the first time a raid had gone sour, but it still hurt. The knowledge that she had tried to prevent the woman's suicide failed tosoothe her. Ann gritted her teeth, squeezed her eyes shut, closed her fists in frustration, and hit the wall below the window. Ann knew she ought to help Bravo Team search the rest of the house for the children, but she instinctively knew it was already too late.

Five minutes later, she met up with Patrick and his team.

"We missed them," Patrick said, confirming her sinking feeling.

"Amelia's dead. She killed herself with a poisoned razor." Ann spoke without much emotion, but her eyes said much more. "I couldn't stop her. I should have, but I couldn't."

Patrick drew her into a hug and spoke softly into her hair. "You did your best."

Irrational anger blossomed within Ann. "My best wasn't good enough," she snapped, pulling back to look into his eyes. "We didn't even find the children." Her tone added: we should be better than this.

"We'll find them, Ann," Patrick assured, knowing her anger wasn't directed at him. "It's only a matter of time."

"I don't doubt that, Patrick," Ann said wearily, allowing her head to rest against his chest. "I just wonder how long it will take, and how many will die before this is over."

Chapter 3:
Secondary Targets

Kiverson Residence
Vienna, Virginia

"Get out of here!" his mother had ordered.

"Aren't you coming?" Benjamin Kiverson had asked. He wanted to ask more, but further questions died inside him.

"Not this time, baby," his mother had said with a strained smile. *"Go with Kevin and Angela. Hide in the woods. The feds won't look there."*

Fifteen minutes later, Benjamin lay in the woods behind his house watching government agents mill about. In his hands, he cradled a tablet linked to hidden cameras located around the house. He switched from one camera to another, frantically searching for his mother. When he found her, he exclaimed, "There she is!" He pointed to the screen and tried to keep his voice low as he continued, "She's in the spare room rummaging through the old chest."

Benjamin's older brother and sister knelt beside him. Angela peered over his shoulder and squinted at the screen while Kevin watched the house with a pair of binoculars.

A man's leg suddenly filled the screen.

Ben grunted and Angela cursed.

"One of those jerks is blocking the camera," Angela complained.

A moment later the man moved allowing Ben a clear view of the struggle unfolding in the spare room. His mother's right elbow struck the other woman's jaw, stunning her.

Yes! cheered Ben. The joy collapsed into painful panic when Ben saw the tiny object clutched in his mother's hand.

Her expression clearly spoke her intentions.

No! Don't do it!

Shock and dread rendered Ben completely helpless as his mother raked a poisoned razor over her left palm. His black eyes stung with unshed tears. He held his breath and used the discomfort of his aching lungs to control the urge to sob. He would mourn his mother later in private, but if he broke down now, the government agents might hear him and find them.

A low growl escaped his brother. Then, Kevin's expression cleared, becoming less concerned and more calculating. "I'll kill them," Kevin declared. "They'll suffer first then die."

A glance at Angela showed tears flowing freely down her cheeks. She looked ready to pass out. "No, Kevin. Please, don't." Her expression added a dozen fears to her statement.

"I'm not going after them now," Kevin said with disdain. He glared at Angela before turning his attention back to the tablet. "Revenge comes later."

Ben exchanged a worried look with Angela. Kevin had uttered similar threats against others, *dead* others. He shuddered at the thought of his brother as a murderer.

Ben remembered his father's words concerning Grandfather's arrest, *"Arrest is a minor setback. Nothing can destroy this family."*

What would Father say of Mother's death?

"Payback isn't the answer, Kevin," Angela whispered fiercely.

"Payback's the *only* answer," Kevin

retorted.

"We've got bigger things to worry about right now," Angela insisted. She swiped at her tears and glared at the screen Ben held. Her dark eyes bore into the machine so much so that Ben thought it might explode in his hands.

"Let me handle it," responded Kevin. "As soon as they leave, we'll go to the safe house and regroup."

Ignoring the rest of their conversation, Ben fiddled with the tablet's controls. He switched to several different room cameras until he saw a man with dark brown hair talking to the woman who had fought his mother. From their dark suits, Ben guessed they were government agents. The woman's suit was smudged with dust and grime. Kevin gripped Ben's shoulder reassuringly and stared at the screen. Ben shifted uncomfortably and stole a glance at his brother's hardened expression.

"What will you do?" Ben asked, fearing his brother's answer.

"I told you. Kill them."

"It won't—" Angela began.

"I didn't ask for your opinion," said Kevin

in a cool, even tone. "Help or don't, but don't advise."

Shifting to a more comfortable position, Ben flipped from room to room again so they could watch the careless search.

Get out of my house!

His teeth clenched hard enough to give him a headache. He hated the invasion as much as his siblings, but he didn't think revenge would help. He had always been an outcast in his family. The clandestine meetings and mysterious influxes of cash bothered him enough to avoid "family" business, but he still loved his family.

Angela and Kevin left shortly after the government people. Ben told them he wanted some time alone, and Angela promised to return for him later.

Once alone, Ben leaned back against a tree trunk to think. *Dad's on his way to jail. Kevin's about to snap. Angela's going to withdraw. Mom killed herself.*

The last thought clobbered Ben like a falling brick, hitting him so sharply that a few stinging tears fell.

Why, mom?

It made no sense. Ben saw no reason for

his mother to commit suicide over the threat of arrest. Ben knew his mother had spent some time in prison as a teenager and vowed to never go there again, but he couldn't fathom any place being so awful that death was a better choice.

Who can I talk to? Angela? She probably wants to be alone too. Ben had always been closer to Angela than Kevin, partly because of the smaller age gap and partly because Kevin actively pushed people away.

What should I do?

The obvious answer was to join his siblings at the second house. Wanting to avoid that as long as possible, Ben replayed the invasion scenes again and again. Hating it but needing to see it, he watched his mother's death three more times.

The woman tried to save her.

The realization sucked the moisture from Ben's throat. He watched the incident twice more to be sure and concluded that the government lady had tried to wrestle the weapon away. Ben sprang to his feet and paused.

I don't owe the government anything.

They had invaded his home, arrested his

father, and let his mother die.

The woman tried to save Mom.

Ben sat down, leaned against the tree again, and sighed, resigned to spending the night thinking in circles.

Kevin doesn't make idle threats.

Chapter 4:
Case Closed

J. Edgar Hoover Building, FBI Headquarters
Washington, D.C.

The day after the Kiverson raid, Ann Duncan tried to ignore thoughts of the warm, welcoming sunshine waiting beyond the office walls. Instead, she confined herself to her office and wrote the report. As she signed the report with a flourish, she thought, *Case closed*, and waited for the emotional click releasing her to relax.

It didn't come.

She couldn't shake the feeling that this case would come back to haunt her. For some reason not locating the secondary targets bothered her. The Kiverson children had only been wanted for questioning. Jon's evidence had specifically implicated Asan in the bank robberies. Even his wife would have been cleared in a few hours. Ann scowled at the memory of Amelia's suicide.

How could any mother do such a thing?

"Cheer up," Patrick called.

Ann grunted and rubbed her forehead before looking up at her husband. "I know. I know. I can't change the past. I should let it go. Move on. Et cetera."

Sure wish I could change the past.

"It's all true. You know what you should do?"

"What's that?" Ann asked.

"You should let me hand in your report then join me for a long walk to get lunch."

Ann forced a smile and held the packet of papers out to her husband. "Sure. It's a date."

It's not our most romantic case-closed celebration, but I'll take what I can get.

"Be right back," Patrick said, adding the papers to his own.

While waiting for Patrick to return, Ann prayed. *Father, please help me get past this woman's death. Be with her family. Lord, please bring them comfort over the loss of their wife and mother. Thank you for being in control. Help me trust You more. Amen.*

She closed her eyes as she prayed, leaning forward and bowing her head. When she finished, she saw Patrick at his usual doorway post smiling at her.

"I love that you're always ready to pray."

"I hate asking for help, but if I've got to ask for help it might as well be from the One who can make a difference."

"You're good for me," said Patrick, walking over and pulling her out of her seat for a quick kiss. "A gift from the Holy One," he added, settling his arms around her waist.

"The Lord has been good to us," Ann agreed. Glancing at her open door, Ann nestled her head against his chest and closed her eyes contentedly. "I love you, Patrick."

The embrace lasted until Patrick's stomach rumbled a lunchtime alarm. "Uh, honey, we'd better go if we want lunch."

"Thinking with your stomach again, love?" Ann asked, pulling away and grinning. She stood on tiptoes and kissed his nose. "Very well. Off to lunch with you. I know you skipped breakfast."

"I was late," Patrick argued lamely.

"Excuses, excuses. Grown men ought to know better."

"Yes, dear." Patrick tried and failed to set his expression to contrite. "Shall we see what culinary wonders we can scare up?" He offered his elbow in an exaggerated, courtly gesture.

Rolling her eyes, Ann grabbed her purse and suit jacket. Then, she took the proffered elbow and let him escort her to a fabulous lunch of street vendor hotdogs. Ann put mustard on hers. Patrick piled sauerkraut, onions, relish, mustard, and ketchup on his two hotdogs. Next, they strolled through the streets surrounding the FBI building, finally getting to enjoy the sunshine and gentle breeze.

Ann bit into her lunch and savored the contrast between sweet meat and tangy mustard. "Can you even taste the hotdog?"

"That's the point," Patrick replied.

"I see." Ann chuckled and took another bite.

They walked past the U.S. Navy Memorial and casually waved to Mrs. Briant and her three little boys.

I could set a clock by that woman.

Having finished lunch, they paused by a garbage can, wiped their hands on flimsy white napkins, and threw out the wrappers. Suddenly, a creepy feeling seized Ann.

Patrick knelt to retie his shoes.

Am I imagining things?

"Young man, coppery hair, forty feet behind and left," Patrick said softly, standing again.

How does he do that?

He reached for her hand, and they walked on as soon as their fingers were entwined. Patrick's casual gait gave nothing away, but his grip belied the tension mounting inside him.

Ann stole a peek at their tail. There wasn't much extraordinary about the young man, but if his red hair didn't make him stand out, his posture did. He stood ramrod straight and glared lightning bolts at them. She couldn't tell much about his face, aside from the very nasty looks he was giving them. "Have you seen him before?"

Blast it. You ruined a perfectly peaceful lunch.

"He's too far away to see much of his features," Patrick replied, glancing back. "I don't think he's going to do anything besides watch. Shall we give him something to watch?"

Responding to Patrick's impish tone, Ann reached up and pulled his head down for an exaggerated kiss.

Watch that, creepy man.

Now, they had many people watching. A nearby male jogger whistled. Two old ladies gawked. A woman with a stroller walked by quickly, trying not to stare. Ann felt better about the whole situation.

"Maybe we should pick up tails more often."

"I'll consider it," Patrick said, glancing surreptitiously back again. "We scared him off though."

They finished their walk around Ford's Theatre and returned to the office.

***

Pennsylvania Avenue
Washington, D.C.

Kevin Kiverson knew the agents had spotted him, but he didn't care. The more he could upset them, the better.

Look over your shoulders. Wonder where I am and what I plan to do. Fear me. Fear your own shadows. Let the fear consume you. When you're half-mad with the fear, I'll kill you. He clenched his teeth when they taunted him with a kiss. *My mother is dead, my father is in prison, and you mock me. You don't care about consequences, but you will. I promise. In the end, you will care.*

With this silent declaration of war, Kevin spun on his heel and stalked off in the opposite direction.

Should I let Angela and Ben help?

Ben would argue against retribution, and Angela always had a soft spot for their kid brother. It would be her undoing. Kevin shook his head in disgust. If he was going to get his revenge, he would have to plan carefully. He would also need help. Uncle Hiram came to mind.

Yes, Uncle Hiram will help me.

"I'll make them pay, Father," Kevin vowed under his breath.

Chapter 5:
Exciting Outing

Duncan Residence
Kensington, Maryland

On Saturday, Ann listened to the coffeemaker work its magic and considered Thursday's mysterious tail.

Who was he?

She figured it must be work related, but since she and Patrick had either worked or consulted on dozens of cases throughout their careers, it was hard to pin down the exact case. She jumped when warm arms wrapped around her waist.

"Less work, more play, doctor's orders," Patrick said. He settled his chin on her shoulder and waved a sticky note in front of her.

Ann plucked the note from his left hand and laughed as she read the same message. "When did she call?" Ann asked, referring to her best friend, Rachel Parker, who worked part time as a physician at a clinic so she could spend the majority of her time with her two boys.

"Last night, when you were showering," answered Patrick. "She wanted confirmation that the child swap was still on."

"She thought we'd cancel?" Ann didn't attempt to hide her incredulity.

"Well, work is unpredictable," he reminded.

"True."

"Since we're still on, I'll go collect the strapping young man," Patrick said. His voice contained a tender quality that always touched Ann's heart and made her smile.

While Patrick went to collect Joseph Cale, Ann fed their Golden Retriever, Danny, a permanent resident to the spacious kitchen. The dog's imprisonment owed partly to their nearly constant absence and partly to the presence of an eight-month-old baby.

At least the kitchen's bigger than the one in my old apartment, Ann thought, attempting to assuage her guilty conscience. They had moved into their new home about a year ago. Ann fondly remembered the chaotic days of moving in and fixing up the house. It had been the good, exciting sort of chaos, not the nail-biting stuff she dealt with these days.

Ann fixed two travel mugs of coffee, light with sugar for her and black for Patrick. When he failed to return, she slipped back to the baby's room to see what kept her husband. Spotting Patrick making faces at the sleepy baby cuddled in his arms, Ann paused on the threshold and leaned on the doorway wishing she had a camcorder. A few years ago, she never would have imagined Patrick Duncan cooing at a baby, let alone *their* baby.

"Let's greet the momma," Patrick said to the baby, walking toward Ann. "Hi, Momma," he said, holding the child out to her.

Joseph presented quite a sight. He had his mother's soft light brown hair and his father's deep blue eyes. At the moment, his fine baby hair flew every which way. His eyes and fists were clenched shut, his legs pumped furiously, and he made fussing noises.

"Patrick! Don't torture the poor child," Ann scolded, snatching the boy from the air. She propped him on her left hip and slipped her right arm around Patrick's waist. "Daddies are rough, aren't they, sweets?" She murmured at her son before kissing his damp forehead.

"Would you listen to us," Patrick said, amused.

"Yep, the sound of proud parents."

They watched Joseph for a few perfect minutes. Ann's left arm began to ache, but she didn't want to disturb the moment.

"We'd better get going," Patrick said at last.

Ann glanced at her watch.

Yikes! We're late again.

***

Parker Residence
Kensington, Maryland

Twenty minutes later, the Duncan family arrived at the Parker home.

Seven-year-old Jason Parker answered the door before they could even ring the bell. "Hiya!" he greeted. He spun around and announced their presence at the top of his lungs. "Mom! Aunt Ann and Uncle Patrick are here!"

Wincing at the volume, Ann looked at Patrick who, much to her amusement, had anticipated the boy's summoning method. Patrick had pressed Joseph's left ear against his chest and covered the baby's other ear with his right hand.

"I used to do that," he admitted by way of explanation.

Ann shook her head in amazement. She'd always known Patrick as the quiet sort. Since their marriage almost two years ago, he had opened up some, but she couldn't picture him as a loud, crazy child.

Before Ann could ponder that thought long, Jason's younger brother, Andrew, toddled up with Rachel lumbering a few steps behind.

"I see I planned too much extra time," said Rachel.

Ann hugged her very pregnant friend. "How are you?" she asked, concern in her eyes.

"Tired," Rachel answered. "These two are driving me crazy."

As if prompted by the challenge, Andrew swatted his brother, squealed, and fled. Jason took up the chase, and the boys circled their mother twice. Then, Andrew wisely held his arms up to Rachel. With practiced ease, she swung the child up to her side.

"Jason, what did I say about chasing your brother?"

"He hit me," said Jason, the picture of

righteous indignation. "I can't take that from him." He gave his brother a scathing look.

In return, the toddler stuck his tongue out and leapt from his mother's arms. Luckily, Ann stepped forward and turned with the child as he flew past, yanking him from flight and easing him to the ground. Andrew's move had surprised Jason whose eyes widened as he ducked behind Patrick.

"Easy there," Ann said, holding the youngster back.

"You see what I mean?" Rachel asked in a world-weary tone.

"He's just got too much energy," Patrick pointed out.

"Tell me about it. I don't even know where he gets it. His father's so—"

"Whipped? Love struck? Tell me, my love, what am I?" asked Jonathan Parker. He came up behind Rachel, took her shoulders in his hands, and rested his left cheek on her right shoulder. His blond hair must have tickled her ear for she pulled away, chuckling.

"Daddy!" Andrew shouted in Ann's ear.

She flinched and shifted her grip so Andrew wouldn't dive from her arms.

Jon stepped around Rachel, and took

Ann's squirming charge. "Settle down, Andy," he said quietly and firmly.

Immediately and miraculously, the boy listened. Ann and Patrick exchanged impressed glances.

"You're good with children, anyway," Rachel answered.

"So, Rachel, are you ready for a simple day with a sweet baby?" asked Ann, marveling at how well her son could sleep.

"Absolutely," Rachel declared, opening her arms to receive the slumbering bundle. "Are you ready for a chaotic day of chasing boys?"

A very good question, Ann thought.

"We can handle it," Patrick said, squaring his shoulders bravely.

Ann kissed Joseph's fuzzy head, bid her friends goodbye, and herded her two godsons out the door.

"What we doing today?" asked Jason. He bounced on the balls of his feet.

"It's a surprise," Patrick replied. He adjusted the baby's car seat to accommodate Andrew. In moments, he had the toddler safely strapped in.

Ann took the passenger seat and Jason

sat behind her. Then, without further ado, they set off on their outing.

***

Montgomery Mall
Bethesda, Maryland

Two hours later, they sat in a crowded food court people watching.

Perfect way to spend a Saturday, thought Patrick, senses alert for trouble. Most trouble came from the Parker boys. Even after three different toy stores, an hour in Play Town, and a long lunch, the boys brimmed with energy.

"Don't you dare," Ann said, catching Jason's contemplative stare at the last of the cold fries.

He gave her an innocent look but ruined it with a guilty grin.

"Food is for eating, not throwing," said Ann.

"Now what?" asked Patrick, calmly gathering the trash for disposal to remove the throwing temptation. "Want to split up?"

"Sure," Ann replied. "I promised Rachel I'd find new shoes for Andy. It might be easier if I took him by himself."

"That's fine. We can find something for men to do, right Jay?"

266

"Right, Uncle Patrick." Jason jumped up, took Patrick's hand, and tugged him away.

"Why don't we meet back here in an hour?" Patrick called to Ann who was still sitting at the table with Andrew.

She waved in acknowledgement.

"Where are we going?" Patrick asked, once they were alone.

"Candy store," Jason answered. He stopped suddenly. "Can I get some candy, Uncle Patrick?"

"I don't know, Jay. We just finished lunch."

"Pleeeeeeeeeeease."

"Well, I guess it couldn't hurt to see what they have," Patrick said.

Jason whooped, knowing that meant *yes*.

Minutes later, they left the candy store with a heavy bag of assorted goodies. Patrick practiced excuses for spoiling the boy. *He looked at me with big, sad eyes!*

Aw, you're just going soft, he told himself, picking out a strange, yellow gummy thing Jason had insisted on.

Jason's smile displayed bits of partially chewed gummies. "Thanks, Uncle Patrick."

"You're welcome," Patrick said

distractedly, as his agent-sense told him something was amiss. "Jay, go sit on that bench and don't move, got that?"

Catching the serious tone, Jason shrugged and did as he was told. He wondered what could have Uncle Patrick so worried. Sad he understood, but not worried. His mother was often sad. She tried to hide it behind smiles, but Jason knew she sometimes cried in her room. He also knew why she cried because he still had nightmares of Emily's death. He missed having a sister. Andrew was okay, but he sure could be a pain. Jason sat on the bench munching candy and watched Uncle Patrick pace.

Patrick instinctively knew something would happen soon, but he couldn't guess what. *Something* could be almost anything. Patrick paid special attention to the nearby women's clothing store. He observed several customers. One young woman with red hair spoke with a clerk about a shirt. An older lady weighed down with heavy looking bags pretended to examine a rack of designer jeans. A pair of jeans disappeared into a shopping bag.

Patrick blinked and watched as more

shirts and pants disappearing into the bags.

Shoplifter.

Wearing his impatient-man-waiting-for-wife expression, Patrick paced in front of the store. He had done it enough times to make the act believable. He nearly choked on suppressed laughter when the "elderly lady" made a very unladylike move to adjust the back of her stockings. Patrick shook his head. Though stooped, the tall man was definitely hard-pressed to pull off the elderly woman look.

As "she" strode from the store, Patrick casually stepped in front of him. "Excuse me, ma'am, but I was wondering if—" Nearing the end of his sentence, Patrick started to panic. He really had no legitimate reason to accost a woman.

A few patrons watched the scene unfold, and a collective gasp spread through the crowd as the man straightened and swung two shopping bags at Patrick's head.

Ducking, Patrick said, "I mean you no harm, ma'am."

The man decided a confrontation wasn't worth it. Clutching his bags tightly in one hand, he took off with Patrick in hot pursuit.

The man was a surprisingly good sprinter, but he slowed himself by pausing to chuck pieces of his costume at Patrick. They didn't get more than forty feet before a security officer stepped in the man's way and was promptly flattened. Patrick tackled the young Hispanic man.

Deftly plucking cuffs from the moaning mall cop, Patrick secured the man's hands behind his back. "Who was your partner?"

"You do find ways to liven a day, don't you?" a woman called out dryly. "Patrick, meet Jill Kiverson."

Patrick's head whipped toward his wife. She ambled up slowly hand-in-hand with a wide-eyed young Andrew. Her other hand held a bag with the distinctive, shoebox outline, and her eyes guarded the young red-haired woman who had been distracting the store employee.

Talented woman, this wife of mine.

"Kiverson? Haven't we run into enough of them lately?"

"More than our fair share," Ann agreed.

"You mean you two are the d—"

A sharp "ahem" from Ann silenced the young woman. "There are children present."

Three more security officers showed up fashionably late. They looked almost afraid to approach Ann and Patrick.

"What's going on here?" asked a young man. He drew his shoulders back importantly.

It was a comical attempt at appearing intimidating, but Patrick decided not to point that out. All of the guards had their hands on their stun guns.

"This loco man attacked me!" exclaimed the prisoner.

"Roy, this stuff is from Jenny's Designers," said the sole woman security officer.

"That's right! I caught this man trying to steal from that—"

Patrick cut him off with a laugh.

"Liar!" shouted Jason, running up. He looked apologetically at Patrick. "Sorry, Uncle Patrick." He turned back to the man on the floor. "You and the red-haired lady are bad! I saw her talk a lot while you stole things."

The crowd chuckled at Jason's enthusiasm.

"Couldn't have said it better myself," said Ann.

"And you are?" the first guard prompted.

"Special Agent Duncan, FBI. This is my husband, Patrick, ... also Special Agent Duncan," Ann explained awkwardly.

At that, there was a collective "oh" from the crowd.

You'd think they'd never met government agents.

"Uh. Um. Could you ..." the security guard stammered.

"Sure." Patrick smiled and slowly reached into his pocket for his ID badge. "Not the best picture of me, but it's me."

Once satisfied, the officers left, taking both prisoners with them to wait for the police.

When they had gone, Ann frowned and said, "That girl's no more than fifteen."

***

Bethesda Police Department
Bethesda, Maryland

"I met the people who killed your mother," Jill Kiverson whispered into the phone. "I've got their names."

"How did you end up in jail?" Kevin demanded.

"Dad sent me over to deliver some cash. I went by your house, but only Ben was there.

I left the money with him and went for a walk. I ran into an old friend who needed a small favor. It was a simple plan. I just had to distract some bimbos for a few minutes."

"Simple," Kevin scoffed.

"Save the sermon and get me out of here!"

"Tell me the names."

"No way. You'll go on your crazy quest and leave me here. Stop by the jail and bail me out. Then I'll tell you their names."

Grumbling about stupid cousins, Kevin agreed to her terms.

Chapter 6:
Play the Game

Parker Residence to Duncan Residence
Kensington, Maryland

The Duncans and Parkers finished a lovely dinner of fried chicken, mixed vegetables, and what Jason called triple-whammy potatoes, mashed potatoes loaded with cheddar cheese, bacon, and garlic. Then, they listened to Jason recount the afternoon's adventures. The small audience wisely steered clear of the boy's flailing arms.

"Then the security guys came and swarmed over the whole lot and hauled 'em off to jail!" Jason finished, relishing the retelling.

"You're a hero," Ann whispered into her husband's ear.

"Yeah, heard that way, I impress me. You'd think I took on a whole gang with my bare fists," said Patrick. He bounced Joseph on his left knee and wiped away some drool making its way down the baby's chin.

Sunday flew by. Ann and Patrick attended church, ate lunch, put Joseph down for a nap, and settled down for a lazy afternoon. Patrick took Danny out for a walk. When he got back, he shared a chicken pot pie with Ann. They read the Bible together, prayed, watched their son sleep, and all around had a restful day.

Monday morning began like most other mornings. Ann and Patrick woke up slightly late and rushed to get ready. Ann made the coffee while Patrick packed Joseph's things. She felt a brief pang of jealousy for Rachel who stayed home with her two boys.

It must be nice.

Ann and Patrick had of course considered going to one incomeat least for Joseph's first few years, but after much prayer, they had agreed God had placed them both in the FBI for good reason. So, like every other workday morning, they took Joseph to work where he would spend the day being cared for by others.

At least we're near him in case of emergencies.

***

J. Edgar Hoover Building, FBI Headquarters

Washington, D.C.

The morning dragged by as Ann pored over cases, making little headway. As she hit the peak of the boredom, her phone rang.

Pinching the bridge of her nose to ease a headache, Ann sighed and picked up the phone. "Agent Duncan speaking, how may I help you?" Her attempt to keep her voice cheerful fell flat.

"You will pay for your crimes," said a sinister, electronic voice.

"You want to run that by me again? No, wait, I take it back. I don't want to know." She slammed down her receiver and glared at the thing.

"Whoa! Duncan's getting feisty," cracked Agent George Baker who was walking by her office.

Oh, shut up, she thought grumpily at Baker.

The office phone rang again, but she let it go to voicemail.

Her cell phone rang.

Ann looked down to see if her cell phone had identified the caller, but it came up name and number blocked. Instinctively knowing the caller would be the same, she picked up the phone. "Hello?"

"That wasn't nice, Agent Duncan," admonished the voice.

"Look, I really don't have time for crank calls."

"Make time!" the voice hissed.

Man or woman?

Somehow, Ann doubted the caller was a woman. She sighed again. "What do you want?" she asked, mentally kicking herself for talking to the idiot.

"I want you to pay for your crimes. So, you will play the game. My game."

"And if I don't?"

"You have no choice."

The caller hung up.

Such a nice guy.

Questions flooded Ann's mind. Who was the stranger on the phone? How did he get her number? Why did he call? Was the threat real? What were her supposed crimes?

Dear God, please be with the lunatic making these calls. If he intends harm, I pray for Your protection.

Part of her knew the guy intended harm.

***

No matter how long Patrick worked on the

paperwork pile, it never got smaller. His phone rang for the tenth time in the last half-hour.

I'm never going to finish this junk if that phone keeps ringing.

Grunting, Patrick cleared his throat and picked up the phone. "Agent Duncan speaking, can I help you?"

"Your wife said almost exactly the same thing," said a sinister voice.

"What does—ah, never mind," he muttered, slamming the phone down.

Seconds later his cell phone rang.

Name blocked, number blocked. Gee, I wonder who that could be.

Rolling his eyes, Patrick let it ring and wished he could turn off his cell and disconnect the office phone. However, a missed call made a pretty poor excuse for a slow emergency response time.

His cell beeped, announcing a text message. **Play the game**.

What does that mean?

Another beep heralded a second text message: **Answer phone**.

When the cell phone rang a few seconds later, Patrick hosted an internal debate over whether or not he should answer it.

Curiosity won.

"This had better be good," he muttered into the phone.

"Like I told your wife, you must pay for your crimes. I—"

"You know, there are mental health hotlines. Would you like one of those numbers?" Patrick held the phone away from his ear as an incoherent, strangled cry came from it. "Feel better?"

"Listen, you lousy—"

"Keep insulting me and I'm hanging up," Patrick said in a sing-song voice. "If you have something to say, get on with it."

"You two don't get it, do you?"

"You have yet to make any sense whatsoever, so I suppose you're right."

"You have blood on your hands, and I intend to cleanse you of it. You'll receive instructions in one hour."

"I love games, but I'm disinclined to play yours." He hung up.

I'd better tell Ann.

***

Ann abandoned the report she had been working on and rushed from her office. Two steps out her door, she ran straight into

Patrick.

"Ann! Just the woman I wanted to see," Patrick said, turning her around and steering her back into her office.

Agent Baker looked up from the boring file in his hands. Patrick Duncan never used a fake happy tone but that one was about as fake as they come. Baker's eyes widened even further when Patrick closed the door to Ann's office.

"Anybody else get the feeling those two are just plain weird?" Shaking his head, Baker went about his business.

Inside Ann's office, she was also perplexed by Patrick's odd behavior. She sat down behind her desk and waited for him to explain.

He leaned back on her door, which was now closed. "I don't want to worry you, but I just had a very strange phone conversation."

"Man with an electronic voice? Sinister? Arrogant?" she asked, sitting up straighter.

"Uh-huh."

"Not good," Ann said, wincing. "I was hoping it was some crackpot who'd gone off his meds."

"No such luck."

"Let me guess." Ann paused for dramatic effect and dropped her voice to a mysterious tone. "He said you must play the game."

"That's about the gist of it."

A glint came to her eye, and she gave him a wry smile. "Knowing you, you did exactly what I did."

"What's that?"

"Told him you weren't interested and hung up."

Patrick nodded, but before he could comment someone knocked on Ann's door.

"Come in," called Ann.

Jonathan Parker, computer expert and family friend, flung the door aside. "Good morning Agent Duncan." There was a definite bounce to his steps as he entered Ann's office. "Ah, and good morning to you too, Agent Duncan," he greeted, as Patrick stepped out from behind the door rubbing an arm. Jon's eyes laughed. Even after about two years, he still enjoyed teasing them.

"What do you want?" asked Ann. "You hardly ever come up out of that dungeon you call an office."

Jon quickly shut her office door. When he turned around again, he wore a serious expression.

"Out with it!" demanded Patrick. He walked behind Ann's desk, leaned against the back wall, and folded his arms across his chest.

"Look, I don't want to alarm either of you," said Jon, holding up his hands in a placating gesture. "Something weird happened this morning."

"Don't worry, Jon, the way our morning's going, we can handle weird," Ann said. She gestured for him to take a seat.

"What happened?" asked Jon, glancing back and forth between them.

"Strange phone calls," Patrick said. He didn't elaborate.

Jon gave an understanding nod. "Well, Rachel and I are always willing to listen as needed," he offered. He moved a pile of papers to the floor and sat on the chair in front of Ann's desk.

"Thanks. What news do you have for us?" Ann folded her hands, rested her elbows on the desk, and leaned forward.

"Noticing how easily I hacked into your files a few years back, I took the liberty of setting up a warning system should anyone else try to do the same. This morning, around 9:55, someone retrieved both of your personnel files."

"Do you know who it was?" asked Patrick.

"I'm working on that," Jon replied. "I would have told you sooner, but I got caught up in some other work."

"Don't worry about it. We appreciate your concern," Ann said, waving off the excuse before changing the subject. "Speaking of concern, how's Rachel?"

"Miserable," Jon answered with a half-grin. "I keep telling her it'll be over in a few days, but she only glares when I say things like that."

Poor Rachel.

Patrick's cell phone rang, and his expression said it must be their mysterious friend.

Chapter 7:
Proof and Pressure

J. Edgar Hoover Building, FBI Headquarters
Washington, D.C.

The three friends exchanged uneasy looks.

How do we handle this?

Ann gestured for Patrick to answer the phone.

"Speak," he ordered, pressing the speaker button.

"You are in a bad mood today, aren't you? That's a mistake—"

"No, my first mistake was answering your call. My continuing mistake is not hanging up!" Patrick said crossly.

Ann squeezed his hand and smiled encouragement.

Jon nodded goodbye and escaped the office. Ann mouthed thanks for his message.

"You have thirty seconds to ex—"

"You want proof. You've got it," the voice growled.

The line went dead.

"I'm not sure I handled that well," Patrick muttered, letting his eyes linger on his phone.

Ann's phone rang.

They exchanged perplexed looks.

"Hello?" Ann asked, trying to keep her voice from trembling.

"Somebody dies every day. I'm offering you the chance to be a hero and save a life. Play the game or live with the knowledge that they died because you didn't."

The caller hung up as soon as he finished.

Didn't what? Play his game? Or die?

"What'd he say?" Patrick's eyes reflected his concern.

She repeated the short message and added, "Patrick, we've got to stop this guy! He sounds crazy enough to be dangerous."

They spent the next half-hour discussing the specifics of their individual conversations with the man. At one point, Ann thought she heard a faint popping sound, but she paid it little mind. In the end, they concluded that the threat was real and turned their discussion to some other cases.

Ten minutes later, a commotion outside

Ann's office caught their attention. They locked gazes and dashed from the office.

Patrick snagged Agent George Baker's arm as he flew past. "What's going on?"

"They found a body dumped in an alley about a block from here. Some gangster kid, but the body had a note pinned to it." He paused to savor the moment. It wasn't very often that he had the pleasure of divulging information to either Agent Duncan.

"What did the note say?" Ann demanded, staring steadily at Agent Baker.

"It said, 'Tell the Feds to play the game,'" Baker said in a low, mysterious voice. His eyes danced with amusement. Seeing their serious expressions, he sobered. "I know, it sounds silly, but that was the message."

Ann and Patrick glanced at each other.

"Morgan's office," Patrick said.

Ann had already spun on her heel, headed for their destination. In seconds, they were gone.

Confused, Agent Baker shook his head and muttered, "They're getting weirder by the minute."

***

Ann and Patrick Duncan barreled through

Assistant Director in Charge Lance Morgan's outer office door like offensive linemen battling for a first down. The secretary, Ms. Klinger, looked up from her phone call, smiled tightly, and motioned for them to wait. They marched right past her desk. She stammered an excuse into the phone, put the person on hold, and leapt angrily from her chair.

The Duncans were faster.

Ann neatly positioned herself in front of the secretary. Patrick sidestepped both women and sailed through the door to the inner office. He paused inside before jogging to a place in front of Morgan's desk.

Mr. Morgan was also on the phone. The ADIC didn't look happy about being interrupted, but he merely raised his eyebrows at Patrick. "May I call you back, sir? I have an emergency to address. Thank you."

He hung up slowly.

By this time, Ann had joined the men in the office. The fuming secretary stood behind Ann, looking like she wanted to ring the neck she was breathing down. Fury locked the words inside her.

"It's all right, Ms. Klinger."

"Shall I call security, sir," she offered

through clenched teeth.

Ann glanced back and figured she could probably boil water if she bottled the fire behind the secretary's eyes.

"That won't be necessary," Mr. Morgan said to the secretary. His eyes darted between his two top agents. "I'm sure the Duncans have a good explanation."

The secretary left, leaving an outraged harrumph echoing about the room.

Silence reigned as Ann and Patrick endured their boss's scrutiny.

"You *do* have a good reason, don't you, Agent Duncan?"

"Yes, sir," they responded crisply.

He chuckled. "Have a seat then. We may have company in a few minutes, if Ms. Klinger gets nervous out there. Which of you wants to explain?"

"He will," Ann said pointing to Patrick.

"She will," Patrick said at the same time, pointing to Ann.

"Actually, we both had the same experience, so it's probably best if we explain the different parts of the story," said Ann.

Nodding sagely, Morgan folded his hands on his desk, leaned forward, and said, "Ladies first."

"Yes, sir. About an hour and a half ago, I received a call from a synthesized voice. Despite the filter, I believe the caller was male. He said, 'You will pay for your crimes,' and I hung up on him. He tried the office phone again, but when I ignored that, he called my cell phone."

"And you answered it?"

"Yes, sir. I told him I didn't have time for crank phone calls, and he said to make time. Then, he repeated that I had to pay for some crime and implied that he would force me to play a game."

Patrick explained his first conversation with the maniac. Then, they took turns explaining the second round of calls.

When they finished, the traces of impatience had melted from Lance Morgan's dark features. All concerned boss now, he asked, "Do you have any idea who it could be? Do you have any enemies?"

"A few," Patrick admitted.

"Dozens," Ann stated flatly.

"Heh, that's what you get for being good in this business," Mr. Morgan said with another chuckle. This one ended in a sigh. "I guess the big question is: how serious is this guy?"

"There's more," Patrick said.

"Agent Baker told us a body was found in an alley about a block from here," Ann explained.

"How is that related to the phone calls?"

"There was a note pinned to the body, sir. Agent Baker said it read 'Tell the Feds to play the game.' Just before this, Patrick and I had both expressed doubts about the man's sincerity," Ann said softly, looking guilty.

Morgan narrowed his eyes and shook his head. Pinning them each in place with a steely gaze, he said, "I don't want either of you blaming yourself for that body."

"But sir—" Ann began.

"It is *not* your fault!" Morgan stood up and looked out his window.

Silence fell as they each pondered the situation.

We don't know enough to do anything! Ann thought miserably.

Finally, Mr. Morgan turned away from the window. In a softer tone, he said, "Look, I know you're both upset about the calls. Return to your desks and try to get some work done. Go home if you have to, but I want to see you both tomorrow at 11 o'clock. By then, you should be thinking clearer. Oh, and before you stop by, have Brad Matthews or Jonathan Parker wire your phones for tracing."

"How should we respond to further calls?" Patrick asked.

Morgan hesitated. "I'm reluctant to tell you to cooperate, but for the moment we have little choice. Just be careful. Keep yourselves and others out of danger as best you can."

"Yes, sir," they chorused.

"I'll see if Jon can work up a quick tracer to back trace future calls," Patrick added.

"You do that. I'll see you tomorrow."

They filed out.

***

With considerable effort, Ann and Patrick put aside the disturbing calls and made some headway on paperwork for other cases. They discussed the Drier case, agreed on the conclusion, made some phone calls, and dispatched a team to pick up Louis Drier for white collar crimes against his business. Over all, it was a fairly productive day despite the stress.

They walked out of the building at 5:30. Patrick held the baby's empty carrier, and Ann

291

held the bundle of joy. As they approached their car, Ann felt like she was being watched again. She didn't want to alarm her husband, but she quickened her pace. They only passed one other couple along the way, tourists by the looks of them.

"I can't believe I allowed myself to be dragged out to see some stupid old tree!" the man complained.

"It's nature, my dear. You must learn to love it," said his wife.

The man's unenthusiastic response was lost because they passed the couple, thanks to Ann's frantic pace. When they reached the car, she hastily secured Joseph in his car seat. They climbed in, and she breathed an audible sigh of relief.

"You had a creepy feeling too?" Patrick asked, starting the car.

"Yes," Ann said with a small laugh. "I suppose we're getting jumpy."

"No, I think we are being watched again," said Patrick.

Ann didn't know whether to be pleased that her instincts weren't failing or upset because of the danger.

"This guy's putting pressure on us for

some reason, and I want to know why," Patrick said tightly. He pulled out of the parking space and began the drive home.

Ann's cell phone rang, and she forced down a groan of dismay. She breathed a sigh of relief when Jonathan Parker's name appeared. "Hi, Jon, what's up?" Her heart leapt at the news. "Really? We'll be right there." She hung up and faced her husband, her cheeks flushed with excitement. "To the hospital."

Patrick made a quick U-turn, and they were on their way to be with their friends.

Thoughts of the stressful day vanished like smoke in a stiff wind.

Chapter 8:
For Friends

Providence Hospital
Washington, D.C.

Concern for Rachel Parker cured Ann's current worries. The hospital waiting room was a tense place to be. Even the Parker boys sensed the somber mood. They sat quietly on the carpeted floor in the corner and played with the toys.

Ann held Joseph and watched Jon pace. Holding her sleeping child made her feel much better. Patrick had left to pick up some food. In the excitement of the moment, everybody—except the boys—had forgotten about dinner.

Patrick returned shortly before eight carrying several sacks of food. After a brief prayer, they ate, but Ann hardly tasted anything. She enjoyed watching the Parker boys eat though.

Children make things so lively.

The stockpile of napkins quickly dwindled as the meal was devoured. Ann grabbed one of the last three clean napkins and used it to clear gooey sauce from Andrew's beaming face.

Children are definitely messy.

Two hours after dinner, they still fidgeted in the hospital waiting room. Both boys slept by the toys. When a doctor came out, Ann, Patrick, and Jon stood automatically.

The doctor was distractedly reading a chart. "Mr. Parker?"

"Yes?"

They collectively held their breath. The last report had been that there were a few complications with the birthing.

The doctor smiled, "You have a beautiful baby girl, sir. And

Mrs. Parker is fine, but she's tired. You can see them now if—"

Jon was through the doors before the doctor could finish. Ann hesitated. She wanted Jon to have a moment alone with Rachel, before they barged in. "Let's wake the boys," Patrick suggested.

Five minutes later, the whole crowd trooped into Rachel's room.

"Mommy!" the boys shouted.

Ann and Patrick held them back so that

they wouldn't jump on Rachel in their excitement.

"Whoa! Calm down, boys. Your mother's had a rough night. Give her some room to breathe," Ann said in a rush.

"Gentle, now," Patrick warned.

The serious expressions returned to both young faces and they walked up to their mother like gentlemen.

"Hello, darlings."

"Hi, Momma," said Andrew. "You feeling better now that the baby's out of—of your tummy?"

His question made the adults laugh and earned him a dirty look from his brother.

"That's a dumb question. Of course, she's feeling better," Jason said with the authority of a second grader.

"Be nice," said their father, his attention fixed on his wife.

Ann handed Joseph to her husband and went over to her friend and the newest Parker. "Hey there," she said softly, smiling at Rachel and the newborn. She embraced her friend. "She's beautiful."

"You're a bad liar," Rachel scolded in a whisper.

In truth, the baby's face resembled an abused, overripe tomato.

Ann shrugged. "She will be beautiful."

"As long as she doesn't look like her father," Patrick said, looking critically at Jon.

Jonathan Parker couldn't speak. He had a dazed, silly smile plastered on his face. Try as he might, he couldn't hold back sentimental tears. He carefully picked up his daughter. Ann remembered the day Andy had been born. Jon had been joking and laughing the whole time. This time, he had a look of dumbstruck awe on his face. He held his baby girl like she was a fragile, priceless entity.

That she is: fragile, beautiful, priceless.

Patrick had worn a similar expression when first holding Joseph.

"What's her name?" asked Ann, realizing that they had never asked their friends what they intended to name their fourth child.

"Caitlyn Rose Parker," Rachel replied.

Ann sensed her friend's strength reserves waning. "Lovely name," she said merrily. "Well, I think it's time for me and the boys to leave."

No one moved.

"We'll be back tomorrow to drop them off

again," Ann asserted, taking charge. "Jon, I'll tell Mr. Morgan you're taking the day off. He'll understand."

He nodded, still wearing the silly grin.

"Ah, snap out of it man," Patrick said. "Kiss your wife, sons, and daughter goodnight, go home to rest, and come back to break down the hospital doors tomorrow morning."

"Patrick, I think we're escorting our good friend home tonight. His head's in a cloud, and I'd rather not have to scrape him off someone's bumper."

"At least someone knows what's going on," Rachel said hoarsely.

The entire group said their goodbyes to Rachel and Caitlyn Rose before Ann marched them all out of the room. "Goodnight, Rachel."

"Ann!"

"Yes?"

"Thanks."

Ann smiled again. "What are friends for, but to stand by hospital beds? Go to sleep now. I'll see you in the morning."

Chapter 9:
Clear Picture

Providence Hospital to FBI Headquarters Washington, D.C.

Tuesday morning, Ann and Patrick dropped the Parker boys off at the hospital. Ann hustled them to Rachel's room and found Jon already there. Quickly, she greeted the new baby again, kissed her friend hello and goodbye, and rushed back out to the car. Then, they sped off to work to face another day. With the goal of unmasking the mysterious caller, they spent the morning hours researching, making phone calls, and checking facts.

At precisely 11 o'clock, they were ushered into Lance Morgan's office by the stern-faced secretary.

After exchanging greetings, Ann surprised her boss, "I think I know who's behind this, but I still don't know what to do about him."

Mr. Morgan smiled and turned to Patrick, "I suppose you have the answer as well."

"I do," Patrick confirmed.

"And I doubt if you discussed this with each other yet. Am I correct?"

They nodded.

"Well then, here's a perfect opportunity for me to test you." Director Morgan's smile broadened as he rummaged through his spacious desk for two pieces of scrap paper. "Write down the perpetrator's name, fold it, and hand it back."

Ann took the piece of paper and did as instructed. Her husband did likewise, but he handed Morgan his scrap of paper much faster.

"Thank you ... and thank you. Now, let's see if the Duncan minds are as uncanny as I've come to expect them to be. We have one vote for K. Kiverson," he said, opening the first piece of paper. Next, he unfolded Ann's note. "And the second nominee is ... Kevin Kiverson."

Ann and Patrick exchanged amused looks.

Cheater, she thought, referring to his abbreviation.

"That's good enough for me," Morgan declared. "Now, tell me, how you came to the same conclusion."

"Do you want to go first, or shall I?" Ann asked.

"We probably have different reasons anyway," Patrick said, waving her on.

"True enough," Ann confirmed. She faced her boss again. "We can't be a hundred percent sure, but I'm convinced because of several things."

"Such as?" Morgan probed, waving for her to continue.

Ann ticked the items off as she spoke. "One, the caller's accusation got me thinking of every case that went wrong. The Kiverson raid definitely fits. I struggled with Amelia Kiverson right before she committed suicide with a poisoned razor. Someone could easily think I had been trying to kill Mrs. Kiverson rather than save her. Two, Brand Piearson— the gangster killed to give the FBI that note— had connections to the Kiverson family. Last month, he was arrested for drug trafficking. He cut a deal to testify against James and Asan Kiverson, provided the latter could be found. That was part of the reason for the raid, despite the fact that the official report only mentions the bank robberies. Three, the coroner told me Piearson's right hand was sliced by a razor, as if someone had shaken his hand with the blade fixed between his middle and ring fingers." She demonstrated with her hands. "Four, I did background checks on the Kiverson children and found out that Kevin has a history of mental instability."

Patrick picked up smoothly.

"My reasoning is similar to Ann's. The caller said I had blood on my hands. At first, I thought it was a figurative comment about culpability, but when I considered taking it literally, I remembered I got some of Asan's blood on my hands during the raid. Also, Piearson's murder fits as a Kiverson hit, and the three children escaped. Fourth, the Kiversons are high-tech and very paranoid. It doesn't stretch the imagination to think they might have electronic surveillance around their house. The team I dispatched to check out the possibility reported cameras in every room. Finally, Kevin's name came up twice in connection to local mental hospitals."

"Wow," Morgan commented. "I told you, you'd think clearer in the morning." A thoughtful expression crossed his face. "Most of your evidence suggests the Kiverson family, but all you've got on Kevin is a few extended vacations in the nut house. What else makes you think it's him?"

"Instinct," said Patrick.

"Gut feeling," said Ann a split second later. "Kevin's brother and sister aren't very good suspects in Piearson's murder. Piearson had very low regard for weak men and women in general. Benjamin Kiverson isn't exactly a street tough, and Piearson wouldn't have dealt with Angela." Ann handed her boss pictures of the young Kiversons.

"They wouldn't have the wrist power to make the blade penetrate Piearson's hand which was roughened from his job at the United Postal Service," Patrick said, continuing the logic. "His job allowed him to ship drug packages to various dealers around the country."

"You've certainly done your homework. That's a lot of circumstantial evidence against Kevin but not much physical evidence. What else did the coroner say? She didn't happen to mention they had Kevin's prints on the body, did she?" he asked, only half-joking.

"No such luck," Ann responded wistfully. "The forensic team found a few shirt fibers that didn't belong to the victim, but the victim's hands were clean. The initial cause of death was thought to be the gunshot to his face, but the medical examination picked up the poison."

Ann's cell phone rang. A quick peek confirmed that the name and number had been blocked.

"Is it him?" wondered Patrick.

Nodding, Ann asked, "How do you want us to handle this, sir?" She waved her phone.

"Play along," came the answer. "Did you get the tech boys to give your phones the royal treatment?"

"Brad did the honors since Jon was otherwise engaged. He should be standing by for the trace," Patrick said.

Never one to solely rely on something, AD Morgan pulled out a tiny digital recorder.

Patrick took the recorder from their boss and held it close to the receiver to catch every word.

On the fourth ring, Ann answered the phone. She held it out so Patrick and her boss could listen too. "Yes?"

"Greetings, Agent Duncan. Round One begins at noon which is very soon. It features three towheads and a gun. It's sure to be fun. It's a woman's job to kiss each head, lest they meet with chunks of lead. Head off on your own, and I mean truly alone, or risk my wrath crossing your path. I'll kill all three, just wait and see," said the same nasty voice that had haunted Ann's dreams the night before.

The click let her know the instructions had been delivered.

Ann sat stunned into silence but her thoughts raced. *Is this guy serious? Now, I know he's gone off the deep end.*

Patrick's phone rang. Grim faced, he picked it up and listened.

"What no snide comment? Well, that's good. Round Two begins at three. You'll find the first in a big old tree. This is not a job to handle by yourself for the next is on a high shelf. The last is sure to be a blast. To make each one stop, simply pop the top. Disappoint me and others may not see for a good long time, maybe permanently," said the man, ending with a derisive laugh.

click

They waited the appropriate thirty seconds, and predictably, Ann's phone rang. Patrick's one-sided conversation with the wacko gave her time to collect her thoughts. She knew she would have to speak fast and first if she wanted to get in a word.

On the third ring, she answered the phone, speaking quickly and clearly so there wouldn't be a misunderstanding.

"Listen up. We *never* agreed to play these games. I'm willing, but there are rules to everything. These are the ground rules. We will not do anything remotely illegal, immoral, unjust, or dangerous to anyone else. You got that?"

"Agent Duncan, you're purposefully twisting my words," said the eerie voice, managing to sound hurt even through the filtering. "Here I am trying to make you and your husband into heroes, and you battle me at every turn." He let out an exaggerated sigh. "Well, that makes the game more interesting, doesn't it? You threw off my train of thought, but luckily, I wrote the rounds down." The man cleared his throat. "Round Three touches only thee and perhaps Patrick too. What will draw a stare? A child lying there dead as can be for all to see."

click

The creep threatened Joey.

It would be a gross understatement to say Ann was livid. She nearly broke her phone by squeezing it too tightly.

Patrick's phone rang.

"How many rounds are there?" he shouted, also coping poorly with the threat against their son. He was standing now, holding his phone in a viselike grip and wishing it were Kevin's neck.

"Ah, finally, a reaction. Wonderful. Five, to answer your question. Oh, and do remind your wife that time is ticking on Round One. Round Four involves danger at your door. Find it fast for the fuse is not meant to last. I'm patriotic, not psychotic. Cut the cord the color of blood, or be blown to a little pile of crud."

click

Patrick sank into his chair.

You most certainly are psychotic! Ann thought.

Familiar with the drill by now, Ann answered her phone midway through the first ring.

"I'm listening," she said edgily.

"You enter Round Five, only if you're still alive. If I have my way, that won't be the way that you stay. You'll come to me. That I can guarantee. But since I'm a good sport, I'll make your death nice and short."

click

Ann slowly returned her phone to her belt and glanced at her watch. It read 11:47. She gasped.

"I know who he's talking about!" She bolted from her chair like she had been sitting on hot coals.

"Where are you going?" demanded Morgan.

"I'll explain later. I've got to get to the U.S. Navy Memorial right away! And Patrick—"

"Already contemplating trees, dear."

With a nod, Ann barreled out the door and raced for the stairs. An elevator might have been faster, but she couldn't afford a delay of any kind. Praying for the Lord to make her steps sure, Ann dashed down flight after flight of stairs and out onto the street. A glance at her watch told her time was ticking onward relentlessly. Panting hard, Ann ran on.

Lord, let me be on time!

Her heart thudded harder when she caught sight of Mrs. Briant and her three boys. Automatically, Ann's eyes scanned the nearby tall buildings. She knew it was futile. If Kevin or whomever he hired was a good sniper, he could be miles away and still make the shots as long as he had a clear line of sight to the victims.

Let him keep his word, she begged.

"Agent Duncan! What's the matter?" asked Mrs. Briant as Ann ran up.

"Hello, Agent Duncan," chorused the boys.

"Where's the other Agent Duncan?" asked Kyle, the youngest of the towheaded triplets.

Momentarily ignoring them, Ann said, "This is going to sound very strange." She paused for a few quick breaths. "But I need to kiss your boys on the head!" she finished, nearly fainting from the adrenaline rush.

Mrs. Briant shot Ann a puzzled look but nodded assent.

Ann quickly kissed each young head, starting from left to right. She could almost feel a menacing laser dot brush the back of her neck. By the time she kissed Ned's head, her watch said 11:59. She breathed a sigh of relief. "It's a game," she said trying to sound cheerful. "Uh, you'd better be moving along. Go straight home and avoid the memorial for a few days."

"What's wrong?" asked Mrs. Briant nervously. It didn't take a rocket scientist to figure out Ann was greatly disturbed.

"Ma'am, I owe you answers I cannot give at the moment," Ann said. She reached into her pocket and took out one of her cards. "Please call me in a week. I hope to have answers for you then."

I hope to be alive then.

Mrs. Briant was dying of curiosity, but she acquiesced to Ann's request. She waved her boys along.

Ann mustered a weak smile to their exuberant goodbyes. Once they disappeared from view, she sank to the ground to emotionally decompress and pray. A minute later, Ann forced herself to stand up so she could walk back to the office. Patrick would worry if she didn't get back soon, and she had no heart to use her phone at the moment.

She walked slowly and deliberately. As she walked past a garbage can, a bullet sent it crashing toward her.

A woman let out a bloodcurdling scream fit for any horror movie.

Ann's heart leapt into her throat as she

jumped. Her mouth went dry, and she shook her head. Her phone beeped. Reluctantly, she took it off her belt and read the message: **Cngrts U win rnd 1**.

Wordlessly, she put the phone back in its place as tears pooled in her eyes.

O God, help us catch Kevin. Thank you for protecting those little boys.

Chapter 10:
Round Two

"Sorry I'm late," Ann apologized, nearly collapsing when Patrick wrapped her in a tight hug.

"Are they all right?" Concern knit his brows together. His expression said he'd been about to place an All-Points Bulletin on her.

Still breathing hard, Ann held up her phone with Kevin's text message.

"That's my girl. Now, come sit down before you pass out," Patrick said.

They sat in the chairs facing Mr. Morgan's desk.

After giving Ann a chance to catch her breath, Morgan demanded, "What was that about?"

"Mrs. Briant always brings her triplets down to the Naval Memorial on Tuesdays and Thursdays. I don't know how Kevin knew her tradition, but she's been doing it ever since her husband died four years ago," Ann explained. "I followed Kevin's instructions. As soon as I'd kissed each boy on the head, I sent Mrs. Briant home. On my way back, a sniper shot a garbage can causing a raucous, but I left before the police arrived. I'll call them later and explain."

"Don't bother. I'll have Ms. Klinger fax the police an explanation," said Morgan.

"Was it a warning shot?" asked Patrick.

Ann shrugged. "He wanted to let me know he was watching."

"There wasn't any military training in Kevin's file, but he has a lot of connections," said Patrick.

"So, what about you? Have you made any progress on Round Two?" inquired Ann.

"Does he mean a real tree or a figurative tree?" wondered Morgan.

They considered the question carefully.

"Most of the old trees around here wouldn't affect many people," Ann pointed out.

Patrick looked thoughtful. "Ann, do you remember that conversation we overheard yesterday? The one between the two tourists."

Nodding slowly, Ann said, "I can't remember what they were talking about, but the man was complaining about something."

Patrick's eyes lit up, and he jumped from his chair for at least the third time that day. "He was complaining about being dragged out to see an old tree!"

Even in her distraught state, Ann had to smile at Patrick's remarkable memory.

You'd remember too if your nerves weren't scattered about the fifty states.

"There are a lot of museums around here," their boss warned.

Patrick waved the comment off. "Yes, but not many recently finished a display involving a Giant Redwood tree, complete with a thirty-nine-foot preserved sample."

"The National Museum of Natural History did though," Ann said, finishing his thought. "You'd better get over there. Do you want me to come?"

"Yes. He never said you couldn't come, and he did say the second whatever would be up high. Besides, I'll feel better knowing you're there."

They were on their way out the door.

"Be careful," said Morgan. "I'll have Ms.

Klinger call over to get you clearance, and I'll try to get the place evacuated."

Ann and Patrick both whirled and shouted, "No!"

"Sir, if Kevin gets word we've spoiled his fun, he may release whatever it is he's threatening," Ann said urgently.

"I don't think there will be too many people in the museum," Patrick added. "It's probably best if we don't tip our hand. Kevin's twisted, but he follows his own honor system."

"You've got until a quarter to three, and then I have the place emptied."

"If it gets that late, sir, I'll pull the fire alarm myself," Patrick promised.

Is that what he wants us to do?

Ann considered the awful possibility, imagining some toxic chemical spraying from the water spigots.

Before they exited, Morgan said, "Oh, and I'm assigning Agents Piker and Morrison to your case."

They paused again.

"Are you—" Ann began.

Morgan sat behind his desk and scribbled a note. "Uh-huh," he grunted. "Since you two don't have time to watch your back, I'm taking the liberty of having someone watch it for you."

They didn't answer.

There was no time to lose.

With hasty nods, the Duncans took off for the museum.

***

National Museum of Natural History Washington, D.C.

Five minutes and a brisk jog later, they strode up to the ticket counter.

The young woman behind the counter gave the two agents a look of awe mixed with fear, but she waved them through without a word of protest. "Do you need any help?"

"Yes, thank you," Ann replied. "Where is the Giant Redwood display?"

"Oh, that's easy. Follow this hallway to the end, you can't miss it. The Giant Redwood is one of our special exhibits so it's in one of the S.E. rooms," she said, pointing in the proper direction. Out of sheer habit, she handed Ann a map.

"We'll start there then," Patrick stated. "Thank you."

"Should we split up?"

"Not yet."

They ran the entire way. It didn't take long to find the first canister of Sorium gas, stuffed behind the Giant Redwood display. Patrick whistled softly. "That is some nasty stuff," he remarked, after reading the warning label. "But it makes no sense to 'pop the top.'"

"We are so out of our league," Ann muttered. "Hang on a minute." She picked up her cell and called Jon.

When he answered, she launched into her impromptu speech.

"Hi, Jon, sorry for bothering you on your day off, but I need you to give me the number of your friend over at Sprii Tech … uh-huh … thanks. I'll explain later, I promise. Kiss Caitlyn and Rachel for me. All right, thanks again, bye."

"Who are you calling?"

"Keith Grand," Ann replied, already dialing the number Jon had spouted off at her. She put the phone on speaker so Patrick could hear.

The picture display showed the chiseled features of a sandy-haired scientist.

"Hello, Mr. Grand? My name is Julie Ann Duncan—"

"One of Jon's FBI buddies, right?"

Smiling, Ann said, "Yes, and this is my husband, Patrick." She turned the phone so the camera could pick up Patrick's face as well. "We have a situation here that requires your expertise."

"Really?" Keith asked, eyebrows climbing his forehead. "What is it?"

Patrick gently took the phone from Ann. "It's a canister of Sorium gas, Mr. Grand. And it's stuffed behind a display in the National Museum of Natural History." He pointed the phone at the evil can. "Ah, there's not enough light. Hold on a minute." He pulled a penlight from his pocket.

"I'll hold that," Ann offered. She took the mini flashlight and shined it on the Sorium canister.

Patrick again focused the phone's camera on it.

Keith Grand shook his head and whistled softly. "That's not good."

"Our instructions were to 'pop the top,' does that make any sense to you?" Ann asked.

The phone was facing them again in time to see the scientist nod thoughtfully. "Let me see the container again."

They repeated the flashlight and phone

deal, making sure that the scientist got a good look at the canister.

Several "uh-huh" and "hmmms" followed. "Yes," Grand said finally. "The canister is pressurized. Air seeps in the side vent and becomes trapped in the smerik layer."

The what? Ann's brain fired the question, but she forced herself to concentrate on Keith's explanation.

"Pressure builds up until it reaches maximum capacity. Then, it explodes propelling the product out. Popping the top will release the pressure … uh, that is if you're early enough. It'll sound like opening a can of soda, but the Sorium gas itself should remain in the inner container."

"Thank you," Ann said.

They collectively held their breath as Patrick gingerly eased up the tab and yanked. As promised, it popped satisfactorily. They waited ten tense seconds. Since Ann and Patrick weren't blind yet, she figured they had gotten there in time.

Ann let her breath out in a whoosh. "How did you know?" she asked Mr. Grand.

"I read lots of magazines," he replied.

Oh, that's reassuring.

"And I know the guy who invented those canisters. They were originally designed to—"

"I'm sorry, sir, but we have two more canisters to find and disable," Patrick said, getting to his feet.

"Of course, don't let me keep you, agents. I was glad to help," Grand said good-naturedly.

They hastily said goodbye, and Patrick hung up. He handed Ann her phone and took back his flashlight. It was nearing 1:00 p.m. EST.

"Perhaps we should split up now," Ann suggested. "We've got two containers to find in less than two hours, and there are about a thousand spots he could have hidden them in."

Patrick nervously eyed a bunch of small children from a day care program. "You're right. Call me if you find any high shelves," he gave her a weak smile and trotted down the hall.

Where do I go, Lord? Help us find these last two canisters.

Not knowing what else to do, Ann wandered the museum. Along her way, she passed several small tour groups. She allowed herself to listen in on a few of the conversations. Most of them were irrelevant.

A tension-filled hour and a half passed, and Ann was no closer to finding another canister.

I hope Patrick's having better luck than I am.

More time slipped by. Then, as Ann passed the IMAX Theater for the third time, a conversation between two boys caught her attention. She abruptly stopped and listened hard.

"The movie was the best," claimed one boy.

"Notuhh. That exploding spore thing was cooler!" his friend declared.

Exploding spore thing?

Both boys wore loud, yellow, "summer camp" T-shirts. They started walking away. Ann followed, making no move to mask her approach. She tapped the second boy on the shoulder. He turned around and stared up at her with big brown eyes.

"Excuse me, but you said something about an 'exploding spore,' right?" she asked, trying to be calm. She bent down to look the child in the eyes.

Julie C. Gilbert

"Can I help you?" asked a woman, challenge clear in her voice.

Ann turned slowly and recoiled when she found a plump woman standing arms akimbo less than a foot away. Her glare reiterated the challenge that had been in her tone.

"Yes, I need to get to the exhibit this young man was talking about," Ann said, straightening and smiling in a disarming manner.

The woman's frosty gaze shifted to the youth behind Ann. "Bobby! What did I say on the bus about talking to strangers?"

"I didn't!" Bobby protested.

"He was talking to his friend," Ann added, trying to keep the peace.

"What were *you* doing eavesdropping on *my* students!" bellowed the woman. Tiny droplets of spit showered down on Ann.

So much for diplomacy.

By this time, all ten of the woman's charges huddled around them in a little circle.

I don't have time for this!

Ann's left hand automatically traveled to her temple to massage away a tension headache. Her right hand reached for her ID. "I am—"

"Well? Speak up!" the woman interrupted.

Ann's right hand clenched around her badge. She counted to five, then to fifteen, so she wouldn't lose her temper. "I apologize for the misunderstanding, Ms.—"

"Odderson," whispered a boy.

Ann smiled her thanks to the child. "I'm sorry, Ms. Odderson, but it's imperative that I get to the exhibit Bobby was referring to." She abandoned the ID for the moment and turned to address Bobby. "Can you remember where you saw the exploding spore thing?"

"That was down in the creepy section," said a girl.

"Melanie, not one more word!" cried the woman.

Ann got the impression that the children enjoyed tormenting their hard-handed keeper. *Why are all these children in day care?*

Of course, Ann knew the answer and felt immediate guilt over her own infant son being cared for by others. Pointedly ignoring the reddening woman at her side, Ann held her slightly mangled map out so Melanie could see it. "Can you point out the creepy section?"

"I can take you there," Melanie offered.

She took about two steps before the woman snatched her arm. "Ouch!"

"Ma'am, the sooner I—"

"Hey, what's that?" asked Bobby's companion.

"What's what?" Ann asked, turning to face the boy.

"On the back of your pants—"

"Jimmy!" exclaimed Ms. Odderson.

Ann's headache increased. She took a deep breath and sighed. "I suppose I'm not going to get anywhere until I introduce myself. My name is Special Agent Julie Ann Duncan. I work for the Federal Bureau of Investigation."

The announcement earned her a round of "Ooohhhhs."

"My dad says you're a bunch of lazy good for nothings," said one boy.

Ann chuckled at that pronouncement.

"I've never met an FBIer before," said Melanie.

The children were speaking over each other.

Ann shushed them by holding up her hands.

"Where's your badge?" demanded Bobby, once the din had subsided. "You can't be an agent if you don't have a badge."

This isn't going well. Kid, you've got a great future as a lawyer.

"You still haven't told us what that thing is," Jimmy reminded.

"That *thing*, Jimmy, is my gun, and yes, I have a badge. Tell you what. I'll make you a deal. I need someone to give me directions to the room with the exploding spores. When I come back, I'll answer any questions you want to throw at me," said Ann.

"Oh, come along then," grumbled Ms. Odderson. "We're going right past the room anyway." She turned and strode huffily away.

"Thank you," Ann said, genuinely relieved to finally be getting somewhere.

The woman led the troop on a whirlwind tour of the museum. They went down a flight of stairs and back to the Early Life displays. When they reached the threshold, the woman pursed her lips and pointed.

"Thank you again," Ann said, stepping forward.

"Can I see your badge?" begged Bobby.

I owe them that much.

"I guess I still need to prove who I am," Ann said with a grin. She fumbled in her suit jacket pocket, pulled out her ID badge, and let the children pass it around.

"Come children!" yelled Ms. Odderson, striding briskly away. The caretaker seemed in a greater hurry than Ann.

The children handed her the badge and thanked her.

Civic duty done, Ann tucked the badge away, pulled out her flashlight, and entered the dimly lit room. A full five minutes passed before she found another canister of Sorium hiding in one of the exploding spore pods meant to simulate early life spreading across the land. She reluctantly admitted Kevin had chosen an interesting spot to conceal a chemical that would blind everyone in the room.

The talking box accompanying the display ironically claimed, "This exhibit will open your eyes to the true origins of mankind."

Ann spent four minutes making certain the container was exactly the same as the last one. Once satisfied, she pulled the tab to disarm the thing. When the deed was done, she took several relaxing breaths. Then, she picked up her phone to call her husband. "Hi, Patrick, I found one of the canisters."

"I think I did too."

"You sound worried," she noted.

"Uh-huh, I'm considering how many museum employees I want to tick off for a hunch," Patrick replied.

"I see. Where are you?"

"In the Ice Age room."

"Okay, stay put. I'll be right there. They can yell at both of us for your hunch." Ann referenced the handy map and raced up to meet Patrick at the Ice Age display. "Oh …" was all she could say as she watched Patrick contemplate the fake ice shelf.

Well, Kevin did say shelf.

"Ann," Patrick said, dragging out her name. "Honey, I know you've always wanted to climb on a wooly mammoth."

"Patrick, tell me you're kidding," Ann pleaded, eyeing the brown monstrosity conveniently located two feet from the ice shelf they were trying to reach.

"Don't worry, my love. I've got it all planned out, and I'm fairly certain the last can is up there." He pointed to the far corner of the ice shelf.

"Can't we simply ask for a ladder?"

"There's no time," Patrick said patiently.

The crazy look in his eye said quite enough about his foolhardy plan. Nevertheless, he explained. "Climb onto my shoulders and pull yourself up. Once you're on top, it's a short leap to the other display."

How do I get myself into these crazy things?

They tried twice and failed. On the third attempt, Ann scrambled up onto the wooly mammoth. A shower of dust descended upon Patrick. Above him, Ann sneezed. "I don't think this thing's been vacuumed, cleaned, or otherwise touched for thirty years," she grumbled.

"Are you all right?"

"Fine. Peachy. Swell. But if I become allergic to dust, I'm holding you personally responsible."

"You do that, dear. I'll buy the Sudafed. Is it there?"

"Yup, it's tucked over in the far corner as you guessed."

"Good, now, hop on over to the ice shelf."

Oh, is that it? Ann thought sarcastically, trying to stand on the precarious display. She could almost swear the wooly mammoth was shifting on purpose. Her foot brushed something and she heard a loud groan of gears.

Oh, crud!

She barely had time to flatten herself on top of the display before it lifted itself up on hind legs. "Yaaahhhhh!"

The wooly mammoth let out a trumpeting noise, adding to the confusion.

Ann grasped the fake fur with every last scrap of her strength.

"Hang on Ann!" Patrick encouraged.

I'm trying!

The sound of running feet drew Ann's attention. She spared the two men in dark suits the briefest of glances, but her concentration remained fixed on clutching the rough fur.

Agents Mark Piker and Lionel Morrison stood in the entrance to the Ice Age room and gaped at Ann.

Wonderful timing.

"S-sorry we're late! Is there anything we can do?" asked Agent Piker, pushing his thick glasses back up the thin bridge of his nose.

Patrick ignored the newcomers. "There's a button by your left knee, shift forward and you should be able to hit it."

Ann moved her left knee trying to find the button she had stepped on earlier. Finally, she succeeded, and the display meekly returned to its proper standing position.

What idiot put the buck button on the back of this thing!

Shakily, Ann clambered to her feet again. "Okay, here I go." Looking carefully before she moved her feet, Ann took two unsure steps and launched herself at the next display. She landed with a loud "Ooaammph." Within seconds, her job was done. "Patrick—"

"I'm on it," said Agent Morrison. He had his cell phone to his ear. "Hello, yes, I'd like to request a ladder for the—um, where are we?" he asked Patrick.

"Ice Age room," Patrick replied.

Ann noticed him looking at his watch. She did likewise. Her watch said 2:57. She breathed a sigh of relief. They had cut it close, but they had reached all the canisters in time.

If Kevin was telling the truth, said Ann's pessimistic side. She cut off the self-argument in favor of listening to Agent Morrison acquire a ladder to rescue her from the dust-ridden shelf.

"Please deliver it to the Ice Age room," Morrison said. His tone suggested he was ordering pizza. "It's kinda hard to explain. Yes, I'll do that, thank you, sir." He looked up to where Ann was perched. "The maintenance man wanted me to inform you that the sign says 'no touching.'"

"I'll keep that in mind," Ann replied. She rubbed her sore arms.

"So, now what?" Morrison asked eagerly.

"Maybe you should call some hazmat guys to come and get these babies," Ann said, holding up the can so they could see it clearly.

"I'll take care of it," Agent Piker offered. Once he had finished with the hazardous material people, he asked, "So, how's it feel to be on top of the world?"

"Lovely," Ann responded.

"Lands sakes, lady, whatcha doing up there?" asked a grizzled old man carrying a ladder.

"It's a very long story, sir."

"Well, we best gitchya off there afore Wallace sees ya and pitches a fit," muttered the man.

The maintenance man, Patrick, and Morrison wrestled the cumbersome ladder into position.

Soon, Ann had her feet back on solid ground. "Thank you for the rescue."

"I've seen critters on that shelf before. Even rescued a kitten once. The little fellow came with the Egyptian exhibit and forgot to learn itself how to climb down. But this is the first time a grown woman's been shelved up there."

"First time for everything," Piker noted.

"Why is there an activation button on the back of the wooly mammoth?" asked Ann.

"Oh, they use to hire a feller to dress up like an early human. Neanderthal man or something. Anyway, he'd grunt and hit the button and old wooly would rear up and scare the youngins silly."

After thanking the man again for the rescue, Ann took Patrick's arm and steered him toward the main entrance so they could wait for the hazmat guys. She left the other two agents to fend off the talkative maintenance man.

Chapter 11:
Safe Haven

Duncan Residence
Kensington, Maryland

The Duncans spent the rest of the afternoon answering police questions. Finally, they were able to go home. Patrick fed Joseph mushy green stuff while Ann fixed dinner.

"It's been a long day," Ann commented.

"That's an understatement."

"I'll never be able to look at a museum the same way."

"How often do you get to ride on a wooly mammoth?" asked Patrick innocently.

Over shared chicken tetrazzini, they talked about the case until they grew sick of it and indulged in idle chatter. Ann jealously guarded her mushroom-free portion. They decided to turn in despite the early hour. After all, they had to be back at the office bright and early the next morning.

Ann chatted briefly with Rachel, who had finally come home from the hospital. Then,

Patrick spoke with Jon long enough to learn that Brad hadn't been able to trace the phone numbers because Kevin kept switching burner phones. Patrick then told Jon the latest case developments.

Ann awoke sometime later with a burning sensation deep inside. Initially, she thought it might be heartburn. She clicked on the lamp that occupied the small table next to the bed. Patrick stirred next to her and woke up.

"Sorry," Ann mumbled, thinking she had awakened him.

He shook his head to clear it.

"You didn't wake me, something else did, something strange."

"Like what?" Ann asked sleepily. Gazing into his anxious eyes, she grew more alert.

"Like something telling me you should take Joseph and leave," said Patrick.

Eyes widening, Ann muttered, "That's weird." She examined her own feelings.

The burning sensation seemed to say: *take Joseph to a safe haven.*

"Where should we go?"

"Think as you pack, honey," Patrick said, getting up.

"You're worried because of Kevin's Round

Three," Ann stated. "So, am I," she added a heartbeat later.

"He's been far too accurate with his games, and the third threatened Joseph," Patrick said, his jaw tight with anger.

"I'll get dressed. You pack his bag," Ann said. She pulled on jeans and a T-shirt, threw water on her face, brushed her teeth, and tied her honey-colored hair away from her face. As she read 4:32 off the clock, Ann determined to go to the safest place she knew, her parents' home. Somehow, she knew that she would have to get Joseph to safety on her own. Patrick needed to stay home. She didn't know why, but she didn't question her instincts.

"I don't know if Kevin's watching us, but I don't want you taking any risks. Go straight to your parent's house," Patrick instructed. "I'll let Mr. Morgan know what's going on." Patrick handed her a cup of coffee for the road.

Ann nodded and smiled, thankful they seemed to be on the same page. "I'll be back late tonight."

They shared a lingering kiss, and Ann walked out the door holding tightly to the baby and lugging a large bag of necessities.

Wide awake now, Patrick spent the

remaining time before work praying for Ann and Joseph.

***

Davidson Residence
Fairview, Pennsylvania
About five hours later, Ann turned into her parents' familiar driveway in western Pennsylvania. She had made good time despite the few stops along the way. She picked up Joseph's carrier and hauled it up the pleasant path leading to the front door. Her younger brother came charging out, and Ann neatly sidestepped to avoid a collision.

"Ann? What are you doing here?"

"Hi, Nick. I came to see—"

"Mom's going to be glad to see you. She's been driving me crazy. I have to go. I'm late again, but I'll catch you later," Nick babbled, rushing away.

"Bye, Nick," she murmured after him. "It was nice seeing you."

Nick had left the door ajar so Ann could easily have entered, but she felt it only right to knock since this wasn't her house anymore. She set the carrier down, knocked, and called out, "Mom! Mom, where are you?" Joseph began fussing. "Shhh, it's okay, sweetie.

336

Grandma and Grandpa are going to take care of you for a few days." Ann spoke tenderly, picked the boy up, and rocked him, cradling his soft head in her right hand.

"Julie Ann! Well, this is quite a surprise," said her mother sauntering up to the open door. She wore an expression Ann had come to recognize as a mixture of love, concern, and outright dread.

"Hi, Mom," she said, not knowing how to explain her presence.

"What brings you back out to the open country? Where's Patrick? Are you two all right?"

Her mother fired questions faster than Ann could track, just like old times. Carol Davidson was a wonderful woman and a caring mother, but she and Ann had seen things differently from day one. She was prone to worry, and Ann's job certainly hadn't eased her mind.

"Mom, I have a favor to ask of you and Dad," Ann began.

"Well, come in already. No use letting in all of nature while you're at it," her mother scolded. She shooed her away from the door and shut it. Then, she hustled Ann to the kitchen table. "Are you hungry?"

"A little," Ann said.

Her mother knew that meant, *"I'm starving."* Carol looked compassionately at her daughter and set about making some pancakes. She handed Ann a cup of coffee and waited for her to tell the story. Once breakfast was set out and prayed over, Carol fixed Ann with a questioning gaze. Joseph fell asleep, and Ann set the baby in his carrier. Carol held her questions, and they ate in silence.

"What's going on?" Carol finally demanded, worry turning her tone abrupt.

Ann tried to smile, but tears stung her eyes making the simple task a chore.

How much do I tell her?

"I—I need you and Daddy to take care of Joseph for a while," Ann whispered, trying to choke back sobs. She picked up her sleeping son and held him close. Something about her childhood home left an opening for a good cry. Here, in her safe haven, Ann finally lowered her defenses. "I—we need to concentrate on work for now," she said, letting the tears flow unchecked.

It was the truth, but not the whole truth.

Carol eased Joseph from Ann's tight grasp. Her eyes fired more questions. A brief flash of condemnation soon faded in favor of motherly concern.

Anger might be an improvement over worry. I'm sorry, Mom.

"Go get his things," Carol said.

Ann swiped at the tears and ran out to her car. She returned with the bag full of baby clothes, diapers, toys, and other odds and ends. "This should have everything he needs," she said, handing the bag to her mother.

She read: *He needs his mother more,* written on her mother's face. It stung, but she didn't have the heart to explain.

How would I begin to tell you there's a psychopath out to harm my son?

She wanted to keep her mother's scant peace of mind intact.

"Aren't you coming back in?"

Ann shook her head, stepped forward, and kissed her son goodbye. When she finally dared to meet her mother's gaze again, she said, "You were right, Mom. My job is dangerous."

"Oh, Julie Ann, I've been telling you—"

"Sssshhhh, Mom, please," Ann said,

embracing her mother. "I need you to not worry about me. Just take care of Joseph until—until we wrap up this case. It should only be a few days, but I'll feel better knowing he's safe."

"Of course, dear, you know he's always welcome here."

"Thank you." Ann bolted for her car before she lost her nerve. Lack of sleep and a heavy heart made her feel terrible, but she found comfort in the knowledge that Joseph was out of harm's way.

Is anywhere truly safe?

Chapter 12:
Danny Senses Danger

Duncan Residence
Kensington, Maryland

Distracted, Patrick got nowhere on his cases. He couldn't help worrying about Ann and Joseph. It felt like part of him was missing. He had lunch with Jon Parker in his office next to the computer labs.

"How are Rachel and the baby?" Patrick inquired.

"They're fine, but Andrew's driving Rachel crazy. How's Joey? And where's his gorgeous mother?" Jon returned. Catching Patrick's serious expression, he immediately sobered. "What is it?"

"We think Kevin Kiverson is behind the strange phone calls, and Ann and I spent yesterday playing his mind games."

"Go on," Jon said taking a drink of coffee and a few bites of his liverwurst, garlic, and cheese sandwich.

Patrick's stomach flipped at the sight of

the odd concoction. Nevertheless, he managed to down a few bites of his own boring ham-and-cheese-with-mustard sandwich. "He threatened Joseph."

"Not good," Jon commented.

"Yeah, not good. By the way, did you get a chance to listen to the audiofiles I left on your desk?"

"No, I forgot. Sorry," Jon said, looking guilty. "I tried those traces, but I didn't pay much attention to the conversations. I remember dumping them in here somewhere," he muttered, rummaging around his desk. "Ah, here they are. If you don't mind, I'll catch up now."

Patrick nodded.

They finished lunch while listening to the recorded phone conversations.

When the last message finished, Patrick said, "Ann took Joseph to her parents' house out in Fairview, PA."

"How long will she stay there?"

"She's coming right back. We've got to wrap up this case fast, but we wanted Joseph far away from that lunatic."

The two friends sat in silence for several minutes.

"Jon," Patrick began hesitantly.

"Yes?"

"If something—"

Jon waved him off. "Nothing's going to happen."

Despite the words, Patrick could tell his friend was shaken. "Please, Jon, pray for us. If something does happen, I want you to promise that Joseph will be cared for," Patrick said, his voice wavering. "Like I said, Ann took him to her parents. Their names are Carol and Able Davidson. I forget their address, but it shouldn't be hard for a talented hacker like you to find." He smiled weakly.

"I promise. Of course, I promise. You'll do the same for my children, right?"

"Definitely."

They sealed the deal with a handshake.

Patrick went home early, taking some files with him in the off chance that he had a moment to catch up. He knew it was a useless gesture.

Danny greeted him with a storm of barks.

"Hey, boy. Want to go for a walk?"

More enthusiastic barks answered him.

Patrick put a leash on the dog and grabbed a few plastic bags to take with him on their daily walk. When they returned half an hour later, Danny whined.

"What is it, Danny boy?" Feeling silly but not wanting to take any chances, Patrick drew his gun, entered the house, and searched the spacious ground floor before ascending the stairs to the second floor. They didn't actually use most of the unfinished upstairs rooms yet. Patrick eyed the scattered equipment. It had been far too long since they had had a free Saturday to paint or wallpaper.

Returning downstairs, Patrick found Danny pawing at the hall closet. A spreading yellow puddle under the dog announced his excitement. Patrick confined the dog to the kitchen, got some paper towels, and cleaned up the mess. Then, he considered the closet door, studying it from all directions. The fourth phone call ran through his mind.

Round Four involves danger at your door. Find it fast for the fuse is not meant to last. I'm patriotic, not psychotic. Cut the cord the color of blood or be blown to a little pile of crud.

On the bottom of the door, Patrick found a tripwire that would trigger an explosion.

Father, help me. I want to see Ann and

Joseph again.

Patrick carefully cut the wire. After double and triple checking to make certain that the wire he had cut was the only one, he eased the closet door open. Inside, he found a shoebox. Kevin was not a professional bomb maker, but Patrick believed the device would still do a decent amount of damage.

Three wires stuck out of the top. As promised, they were red, white, and blue. Without hesitation, Patrick snipped the red cord with his pocket knife. Nothing happened. Patrick held his breath a few seconds longer then relaxed marginally. Furious at having to play this stupid game, Patrick called the bomb squad to take the repulsive thing away.

Patrick couldn't shake the danger feeling.

That's odd.

He sat on the ground by the box and contemplated it. Then, he started pacing.

Fifteen minutes later, a man called out, "Agent Duncan?"

"Come on in. It's over there," he said pointing to the shoebox. "I didn't open it, so I don't even know if it's real."

"We'll handle it, sir," the bomb handler said. As he carefully examined the box, a second man walked in.

Patrick recognized him as Evan Turner.

Suddenly, Danny sent up a racket. "I'll be back," Patrick muttered. He went into the kitchen and found Danny dashing back and forth, crashing into cabinets and knocking over chairs. "What's gotten into you?" Patrick asked, perplexed by the dog's behavior. "Evan, could you come here a minute?" he called to the second bomb guy.

"Sure, Agent Duncan," the young man replied, strolling over.

"Dogs can sense danger, right?"

"Absolutely."

"I think we ought to search the kitchen."

Evan stared at him curiously but didn't argue.

In minutes, Patrick found another bomb. Only this time there was a slow-burning fuse to contend with. Using flowery oven mitts, he gingerly shoved his hands inside the cabinet, grabbed the bomb, and yanked out the fuse.

Evan's eyes bulged, and he paled upon seeing the black metal ball in Patrick's hands. "That thing's like an antique! May I?" He reached for the bomb.

Bomb loving weirdo, Patrick thought,

handing the scary contraption to Evan.

"Is it dangerous?"

"Heck, yeah! This baby can send shrapnel a hundred and fifty feet at speeds up to six—"

"Then, I want it out of my house," Patrick said firmly. "Take that other one with you, too."

"Don't worry, Agent Duncan, I know how to handle things like this," Evan insisted, nearly dropping the bomb in his excitement.

Eyes wide, Patrick hurried the two men out of his house. Once they were gone, he felt the foreboding sense slowly slip away. "I wish Ann were here." But he knew she wouldn't be back for another few hours.

He re-entered the kitchen and fixed himself a lonely dinner of leftover chicken tetrazzini. Eating the section that was totally mushroom free made him think of Ann. After the meal, Patrick sat by Danny and gave the dog an extra treat for sniffing out the danger. Finally, he settled down to have a deep conversation with God and wait for his wife to return.

Chapter 13:
Sold Out

Second Kiverson Residence
Chevy Chase, Maryland

Benjamin Kiverson had spent the last five days reflecting on his family and wrestling with questions of morality. He watched the recording of his mother's death more times than he cared to think about. The more he watched, the more he believed that the FBI woman had tried to save his mother. At one point, the picture showed a clear shot of the lady's distraught expression.

She looks like she really cares.

Despite being well-stocked, the second Kiverson home felt different. It wasn't home. Ben had quit school months ago or he might have pending finals to contend with. As it was, he battled boredom. He tried getting drunk to forget his problems, but only got sick. After finding him wasted, Angela locked him in his room and threatened to keep him there until he came to his senses. He couldn't sneak out even if he wanted to because his sister checked on him every half-hour. Knowing she acted out of affection didn't make the situation any easier to accept.

On Wednesday morning, Angela strolled into his room with a breakfast tray.

"Why don't you leave me alone?" Ben whined.

"Grow up, Ben," Angela replied. "I don't want you moping about for the rest of your life. You can join the family anytime, you know that."

"I don't want to! It's wrong!"

"Ssshhhh! Ben, it's me!" Angela glanced nervously at the door. "I understand your feelings, and I even sort of respect them. But you've got to keep those opinions to yourself. If Kevin finds out—"

"I'm not afraid of him."

"Maybe you should be," Angela snapped. She took a moment to compose herself, and said, "Look, whatever you do, be careful today."

How do you know? Ben asked the question with his eyes.

"You talk in your sleep," Angela said with

a forced smile. "I think you're an idiot, but I won't stop you."

"Thanks. I think."

Today, if his courage didn't fail, Ben would find the federal agents that had led the raid and warn them. After dressing, he gulped down his breakfast and took the dirty dishes down to the kitchen sink. As taught, he rinsed the glass and plate and set them in the dishwasher. Since that constituted the extent of his chores, he couldn't really complain.

After catching a cab to a place about a mile from his target, Ben walked the DC streets, letting his thoughts wander. His sister confused him. Angela could be extremely loving and gentle, but she worked for the family by organizing the drug trafficking branch.

Sometimes, she's as crazy as Kevin.

Ben knew he couldn't approach the FBI agents himself since they still wanted to question him. Still, they should know Kevin had pulled their files and might come after them. Kevin had several contacts in the city. Most Ben wouldn't trust as far as he could carry, but he knew a few of them.

He found Rat first.

The pale man about Kevin's age with dark, greasy hair and a winning smile spotted Ben quickly. "Whadda ya know, it's a Kiverson. What's up? Hey, sorry about your parents."

"Rat … um, hey. Would you do me a favor?"

"I am at the service of any Kiverson," said Rat, bowing gallantly.

"Thanks. I need you to get this letter to the FBI," Ben said, rushing so he wouldn't lose his nerve.

"Whoa! That's a tall order, Benny," Rat said, holding up both hands in protest. "But seeing as it's you, I shall do my best," Rat added. He snatched the letter and scurried away in the quick steps that had earned him his nickname.

Ben thought he would feel better, but somehow, he felt worse with the letter in Rat's hands.

***

Kevin's Car
Washington, D.C.
"Rat, why are you calling me?" demanded Kevin Kiverson.

"Would ya pay for information concerning wayward family members?" Rat asked in his oily, bouncing voice.

"Depends on the information quality," Kevin said, carefully not making any promises. "What are you talking about?"

"Your baby brother, Benny, just asked me to deliver a letter to the feds," Rat explained. "A letter! Who the heck writes letters these days? Am I right? It's a lovely, heartfelt letter about you and your plans for them."

"I thought he might do something like this," Kevin said darkly. "Where is he?"

"About a block from me."

"Bring him to the usual place. I'll handle him. You'll get paid when you deliver Ben," said Kevin.

"Right you are, K-man."

"And Rat?"

"Yes, my liege?"

"I want my brother alive."

***

Streets of Washington, D.C.

Ben never sensed a thing as two men snuck up behind him, slipped a hood over his head, tied his hands behind his back, and threw him into a trunk. Though nervous, he wasn't truly worried for his life. Although a first for him,

Angela had explained the procedure for secret meetings.

Where are we going? Who wants to talk to me?

A short ride later, Ben was lifted from the trunk and dumped onto the hard ground.

Someone yanked the stuffy hood from his head.

He blinked in midday sunlight.

A man's silhouette stood before him. "You're a fool, Ben," said his brother.

A foot connected with his stomach, and Ben groaned. Still tied, Ben was tossed into the back seat of his brother's nice car.

When they got back to the house, Kevin dragged him to the living room and threw him onto the couch.

"Why would you contact the feds?"

"You want to hurt them," Ben muttered.

"They killed mom and threw dad in prison! Don't you get that, Ben? Don't you want revenge?" Kevin's voice and temper rose with each word until he started punching. His right fist crashed into his brother's face, then his chest, neck, and shoulders. When that hand got tired, he used his left. Kevin stopped hitting Ben long enough to grasp his shirt, pull him close, and shout, "You're a disgrace!"

As Kevin flung him down and raised a fist to resume the beating, Angela burst on to the scene and threw herself between the brothers.

"Stop it!"

"Get out of the way. I'm not listening to you this time," Kevin growled. "He's got to be taught a lesson!"

"He's not your son!" she retorted. "He's our brother."

"He's my responsibility. Our parents aren't here because of *his* friends!"

"What friends?" Angela wondered.

Kevin shoved his right hand into his pants pocket and withdrew a crumpled letter. Thrusting the letter at Angela, he growled, "Read that and stay out of the way." He pushed her aside, but she stepped in again.

"You want revenge, right?" Angela asked, wielding the mangled letter like a dagger.

Kevin nodded.

"And I'll get it." He turned his blazing eyes from Benjamin to Angela. "Don't interfere in things you don't understand," he said, pointing a finger in her face. His anger abated over the course of the next few seconds. Finally, Kevin let his hands fall to his sides.

Glaring past Angela, Kevin muttered, "Take him to his room and keep him there."

"I'm sorry, Ben," Angela whispered. She untied his hands and helped him up to his room.

Ben saw tears in Angela's eyes, yet she followed Kevin's order and locked him in his room.

What's going to happen to me?

Chapter 14:
Simple Truth

Second Kiverson Residence
Chevy Chase, Maryland

Angela Kiverson knew the risk she was taking, but she had no choice. Kevin had gone to a meeting, leaving strict instructions regarding Ben, but he said nothing about restricting her movements. She swiftly searched his wreck of an office.

It's a wonder he finds anything in here.

Four minutes of diligent searching yielded the items she sought. She studied the papers carefully, memorizing the pertinent information.

I hope I'm not too late.

Kevin came home early, causing Angela to scrap her plans. Instead, she took food and water to Ben, frowning at the ugly bruises on his face. "What did I say about ticking Kevin off?"

"It wasn't a good idea," Benjamin supplied.

"Remember that," Angela muttered.

Why can't I have a normal family?

***

J. Edgar Hoover Building, FBI Headquarters to Duncan Residence
Washington, D.C. to Kensington, Maryland

Arriving back at the office late in the afternoon, Ann discovered that Patrick had already left for the day. Unable to face the thought of climbing into her car again, Ann barricaded herself in her office and waged a half-hearted war against some paperwork. Surprisingly, she immersed herself in the work so thoroughly that it was well past dinner time by the time she bothered looking at the clock again. Lightheaded with lack of food, Ann quit for the day and went to grab a quick, lonely meal at a diner.

When Ann finally pulled her car into the garage and entered the house, her arms felt empty without the baby. She found Patrick dozing on the living room floor, head tipped back and pillow clutched tightly to his chest. Papers surrounded him on the couch, floor, and coffee table.

You were lonely, too.

Ann smiled down at him. A wave of weariness swept over her. After clearing a spot next to him, she sat down, took away the pillow, and wrapped her empty arms around him. Instinctively, he drew her closer.

"Wake up, sleeping brute," Ann murmured, kissing Patrick's nose.

"Ann!" Patrick said, surprised to find her in his arms. He craned his neck back to see her better.

"Miss me?"

"You know I did," he replied.

"That's good to know." Ann planted a kiss on the tip of his nose.

"How did it go?"

"I told my mother as little as possible. I don't want her worrying," Ann reported. "I'll give my father a call to explain later."

"You want me to do that?" Patrick offered.

"Sure, thanks," Ann said, grinning. She found it highly comforting to know that the two men she loved and respected deeply had a good relationship. "I need a shower to wash off the road."

Patrick nodded, reluctantly released her, and unburied his cell phone to make the call.

"Hello, Mr. Davidson? Yes, it's Patrick. Ann thought one of us should explain Joseph's presence, but she didn't want to worry Mom. Our current case involves a man who threatened our son, so we thought he should stay with you for a few days … Yes, sir, we'll be careful. Thank you. Yes, you too. Goodbye."

Ann took a quick shower while her husband spoke with her father. Then, while Patrick took a shower, Ann had her quiet time. She began by reading Psalm 107. Verse 13 spoke deeply to her. She whispered the verse aloud, "Then they cried to the Lord in their trouble, and he saved them from their distress." Though the situation was different for the people the Psalmist spoke of, Ann knew the promise of God always being there was timeless.

God is forever.

Ann slipped from the couch to the floor and prayed.

Patrick came back with his dark brown hair still damp. He stood in the doorway and watched her. Deep in prayer, Ann's face lost the anxious expression, making it far more beautiful. Her peace made him happy.

A few minutes later, Ann looked up and noticed her husband. "Patrick, I just remembered something."

"What's that, love?" Patrick sat on the couch behind her and squeezed her shoulders.

Ann twisted her head around so she could look at him. "Do you remember the Dawson Case?"

"How could I forget?" he asked. "It was our first case that went very wrong. You were reeling for days after finding that boy's body." He moved back and to his right to make room for her on the couch. "I half-expected you to quit after that," Patrick murmured as Ann settled next to him and leaned back against his chest.

"I realized something during that case that I'm just remembering now." Ann adjusted Patrick's arms so that they were tucked under her own, coming together above her waist.

"Tell me," Patrick said.

"Life's fragile, but our days are numbered by God so we have no reason to fear."

"There's a poem that talks about us being in good hands," he said, even as she picked up his hands and studied them. "Would you like me to quote it for you?"

"Please do."
Patrick's voice was soft as he said:

"My days are numbered,
And I don't know that number.
But I thank my God for every breath,
For every moment He's seen fit to grant me.
This I do know: I'm in good hands.
My days are numbered,
And I don't know that number.
But I thank my God for every day
Of this life, I so oft take for granted.
This I do know: I'm in good hands.
My days are numbered,
And I don't know that number.
But I know God knows,
And that's a comfort in trying times.
This I do know: I'm in good hands."

"Thanks, Patrick," Ann said. She tilted her head up and left and added, "You'd make a good public speaker."

"Here I thought I made a halfway decent FBI agent, and you're telling me to quit my day job," said Patrick, lacing his voice with mock hurt.

"Would I do that?" Ann asked, feigning

innocence.

"Yes, you would, but what were we talking about?"

"Simple truths."

"Ah, yes, simple truths," said Patrick, now speaking into her hair. "You said God has numbered our days. And I said that we're in good hands." He tightened his hold on her then bent his head to whisper directly into her left ear. "Well, here's another truth. God has given you to me to treasure, and I will guard you with my life."

"I know. That's why I love you so much. I feel the same, and He's given us Joseph to love and protect as well."

"And we will," Patrick vowed.

Thoroughly exhausted, Ann and Patrick went to bed soon after their couch-side conversation. They both sensed that tomorrow would be a hectic day.

Chapter 15:
Less Subtle Sibling

Duncan Residence
Kensington, Maryland

Angela Kiverson knew her plan was dangerous, but it might save Ben and that made it worth trying.

Thinking, *Brothers are stupid*, she grabbed some cash and called a cab.

The driver nodded when she gave him the address, but he didn't say two words to her during the trip.

Angela didn't mind. She needed time to meditate on her plan anyway. She wanted to catch the agents before they left for work. Fingering the digital camera, Angela tapped the side of her purse to feel the gun, barely resisting the urge to reach in and touch the silencer.

Until a week ago, Angela was a typical, privileged teen beauty. She hung out with friends, lived and breathed by her phone, and generally ignored anyone who couldn't do something for her. She dressed fashionably and enjoyed the popularity attained by striking red hair, mysterious, dark eyes, and an attractive figure. Occasionally, she felt bad that her clothes and pricey car were bought with drug money, but she assured herself she wasn't hurting anyone. Then, the government agents had upended her life.

She loved her family and wasn't dumb enough to question them, but Ben was a different matter. Defying Kevin had landed Ben in deep trouble, and as his older sister, Angela felt obligated to protect him. This wasn't her original plan, but it would have to do.

The cab drew up to the indicated address, so Angela paid the driver and climbed out.

***

A quick, morning shower left Ann feeing refreshed and ready to face the world. She dressed quickly and started making breakfast. By the time Patrick stumbled into the kitchen, she had eggs and pancakes cooking and water boiling for coffee.

"Good morning."

"Morning," Patrick mumbled. "What's got

you so upbeat?"

"It's another day, we're still alive, Joseph's safe, the sun is shining, and last I checked, God was still in control. That's about as fine a day anybody can ask for." Ann walked over and kissed him. "Mmmmm, I knew there was a reason I bought spearmint toothpaste."

Her good mood spread to Patrick. Soon, he was fully awake and setting the table. Ann served the pancakes and slightly mangled eggs while Patrick made the coffee. They were early for once, so they determined to enjoy the morning.

After breakfast, Patrick retrieved the paper. They split the paper, chatted, and lingered over second cups of coffee.

The doorbell rang.

"Who could that be?" Patrick asked.

"I'll get it," Ann offered.

Patrick got up as well. "With all the weird things happening, I wouldn't put it past some maniac to rush up waving a pistol and screaming bloody murder."

Chuckling at his wild imagination, Ann walked to the door and peeked through the hole, finding Angela Kiverson standing there clutching a purse. The young woman's grim expression and death-grip on the purse told Ann something was definitely wrong.

Puzzled, Ann opened the door.

Without comment, Angela dug a pistol sporting a long silencer from the depths of her purse and pointed it at Ann.

Ann's heart raced as her right hand shot out to the left of the gun, grasped the muzzle, and shoved right. Had the girl been holding the gun firmly Ann might have snapped her wrist, but instead, her left hand soon had the gun pointed back at Angela. The simple disarming tactic was standard self-defense. This version—the Ann Duncan panicked special—was about sixty times faster and a hundred times more potent than the training exercises.

Well, at least, someone plays things straightforwardly.

Seeing the pistol, Patrick charged past Ann and seized the young woman's wrist. Thinking better of the move, Patrick said, "Hold her. I'll get some handcuffs."

Nodding, Ann handed the gun to Patrick and turned to their prisoner.

The girl recovered enough wits to start

screaming for help.

"That's right, keep screaming. It'll bring the police here faster," Ann muttered, quite sure Angela wasn't hearing a word.

"You've got no right to hold me!"

"Rights? You want to talk rights? All right, let's talk rights," Ann said, letting adrenaline and anger harden her tone. She hoped Patrick would hurry even as she forced the girl to a good handcuffing position. "Pulling a gun on us gives us lots of rights!"

Patrick returned with a pair of cuffs, and Ann applied them to the girl's wrists. Then, together, they lifted her up, guided into the kitchen, and sat her in a chair.

"Hello, Miss Kiverson," said Patrick, once they had taken seats at the table. He tucked his phone away.

"This wasn't exactly the meeting I had in mind when I hoped to meet you," Ann said dryly. She folded her arms. "Would you like to explain things now, or wait until the police arrive?"

The girl sat sullenly.

Ann sighed and topped off her coffee cup. She put a hand to her forehead and absently blew into the liquid.

A loud, insistent banging heralded the arrival of Agent Morrison and Agent Piker.

It's going to be a very long day.

"Come in!" Ann called.

Preferably before you break down my new door.

Patrick got up as the two agents entered the kitchen. "Ah, welcome to our humble abode," he said, bowing theatrically. "Meet the guest of honor: Angela Kiverson."

Agent Morrison's face registered surprise, shock, and awe when he saw their prisoner. Ann hid a smile behind her coffee mug. Despite a deep scowl, Angela was still a beautiful young woman, a fact obviously not lost on Morrison.

Ann made more coffee while Patrick filled Morrison and Piker in on the recent excitement. Piker soaked up every word, but Morrison's attention stayed fixed on Angela Kiverson.

Five minutes later, the police arrived.

Ann answered the door.

"Are you Mrs. Duncan?" inquired a crisp voice.

"Yes, please come in," Ann replied, stepping back to give the officers room to enter. "The girl is waiting in the kitchen. Her name is Angela Kiverson."

"I'm Officer Bessler, and this is my partner Officer Doren. We received a call about an attempted assault with a deadly weapon," said the taller of the two men.

Ann led the way to the kitchen. "That's the weapon," she said, pointing to the table.

"Help!" Angela wailed, bursting into tears. "These people tried to kill me!"

Ann looked perplexed, but Patrick smiled and shook his head. "That's very good, Miss Kiverson. You should consider an acting career when you get out of prison."

The officers and agents took turns trading ID badges and introductions.

"Would you mind coming down to the station to answer some questions. It'll save us time if you fill out a full report right away," said Officer Doren.

"Huh?" grunted Morrison, his attention elsewhere.

"We weren't involved," said Agent Piker. He repositioned his thick glasses.

"Oh," said Officer Doren. His gaze darted around the odd assortment of FBI agents.

"Of course, we'll come. Let me just get

369

my things for work," Ann said, referring to herself and Patrick. She had been so busy watching Angela that she had neglected to finish her preparations for the day. She quickly got her handgun from the safe and strapped it on. Her hand hovered over her car keys. Finally, she grabbed them. "I think we should take separate cars today," Ann said to Patrick.

Patrick turned to the other agents. "Could you tell Morgan we'll be late this morning? I could call him, but I'd prefer it if you delivered the message in person."

Morrison nodded, but Ann doubted he had heard the request. Piker drew himself up to full height, which was still a good two inches shorter than Ann, fixed a determined look on his face, and nodded. He turned on his heel and waved for his partner to follow.

What a fine pair, Ann thought as she climbed into her car and followed the police to their headquarters.

Ann, Patrick, and Angela were questioned separately, each explaining the exciting morning as they saw it. As expected, Ann and Patrick's story matched perfectly, and the girl's tale differed. Quick background checks helped clear Ann and Patrick of wrongdoing.

Afterward, they watched the tail end of Officer Doren's interrogation of Angela.

That girl's as cold as ice when she gathers herself.

"May we speak with her?" Ann asked.

Officer Bessler nodded. "Leave your weapons here and go on in."

They surrendered their guns for the second time that day.

"Oh, and the girl called a lawyer," Bessler warned.

Ann winced, squared her shoulders, and mentally prepared to face down a suited shark.

They were ushered in and found a dark-haired man in a slick suit hovering over Angela's left shoulder.

The man straightened. "What *are* they doing here?" he demanded. His Southern twang slowed the question, making it sound like the police had done something especially despicable. "They'll upset my client."

Clearly enjoying himself, Officer Doren said, "Mr. Ceriven, I'd like you to meet Special Agents Julie Ann and Patrick Duncan." Though his face was professional, Ann detected a gloating tone.

He certainly has no love for this lawyer.

Doren stood and gestured for Ann to take the chair facing Angela and her lawyer. The police officers retreated to the side to enjoy the show.

Patrick gave Angela and the shark a piercing once over. Ann sat down, smiled politely, and proffered her hand for a shake. Grudgingly, Mr. Ceriven held out his hand as well.

"The agents have some questions they'd like to ask your client," Officer Doren said.

"Yes, we would like—" Ann began.

Ceriven cleared his throat. "You will address your questions to me, if you please."

"I don't please," Ann snapped.

The man's jaw dropped. Obviously, he wasn't used to being denied.

Ann speared Angela with a glare. "I had a gun pulled on me this morning, and I want to know why."

"You have no proof," argued the lawyer. "Did anybody witness this alleged attack?"

Your client. Her gun. Our house. No proof? Alleged attack? This should be interesting.

"My client says you two attacked her,"

blustered the lawyer.

"That's right. I forgot that *we* attacked *her* in *our* home," Patrick quipped, echoing Ann's thoughts.

"Precisely. Then you called the police with your wild tale," he blundered on, regardless of whether or not he was making any sense.

"You think we called the police so we could have the pleasure of conversing with you?" Ann asked, one eyebrow quirked upward. Her hand moved to massage away the lawyer-induced headache.

You flatter yourself, Mr. Ceriven. Personally, I'd rather converse with a brick wall.

"Why did you attack us?" Patrick asked Angela patiently.

"I told you not to address my client!"

This is getting us nowhere. Okay, Ceriven, the gloves come off ….

Chapter 16:
Swift Revenge

Police Headquarters
Kensington, Maryland

"Angela—" Patrick began again.

"You will address her as Miss Kiverson, or I'll have your badge number and go straight to your superior!" blustered the lawyer.

Doesn't this guy ever stop talking?

"We're not in the army, Mr. Ceriven," Ann reminded. "Besides, the sooner we get answers, the sooner we leave."

"Angela, we know it was an act of desperation," Patrick said softly. "We just want to know why."

What are you getting at, Patrick?

"What's going on?" Ann prompted, addressing the question to Angela. Her mind worked furiously to arrange the pieces of the puzzle. Her question met with stony silence.

"Kevin's been playing dangerous games," Patrick commented.

"He's been so careful. Why this sudden

attack?" Ann asked. Inspiration struck, triggering another question. "Where's your little brother?"

Angela flinched and fear flashed across her face, telling Ann she had struck a nerve.

Patrick pounced on the opportunity. "What happened to Ben?"

To Ann's surprise, Angela started crying.

"Now see here! You've upset my client. Leave this instant. I won't allow—"

Shut up! Ann thought furiously.

"Shut up!" cried Angela, stunning the room into silence.

"Angela, darling, I'm here to help. Remember, you don't have to answer—"

"I said shut up, Ceriven!"

You go, girl!

"Look, just leave," Angela ordered. "I want to talk to them. *Alone.*"

The disappointed officers and deflated lawyer meekly filed out.

"I'm obligated to tell you this conversation is still being recorded," Patrick pointed out.

Wiping her eyes, Angela drew several calming breaths and looked around the room as if searching for where to begin. "Kevin has been wild lately." She blew out a long breath. "He wants revenge against you two for—for our family, especially our mother," she added, staring hard at Ann.

"Go on," Ann urged.

"Yesterday, I found out how far he'd go to get to you," Angela whispered.

"How far?" asked Patrick.

"He's crazy!" Angela's eyes welled up with tears.

Ann laid a calming hand on the girl's arm. "Hey, easy. Take a moment to collect your thoughts. Tell us exactly what happened."

"Ben tried to warn you, but he was betrayed. Rat called Kevin instead. And Kevin even paid him!" Angela's voice shook with anger. "When I found them, Kevin was beating Ben."

"Where is Ben now?" asked Patrick.

"I can't tell you! Kevin will kill Ben if you try to save him."

From what Ann knew of Kevin Kiverson, he had probably already justified the fratricide.

"That's why I attacked you," Angela stated flatly. "If you had died this morning, Ben would behave and Kevin would leave him alone. Then maybe life would be normal

376

again."

That's wishful thinking.

"What is Kevin planning?" Ann wondered.

Angela shook her head. "I don't know. Did you contact Ben?"

"No, but we certainly would have met with him," Ann replied.

Angela paled and her dark eyes glistened with more tears. "Kevin had a letter from Ben, addressed to you. It didn't say much, but Kevin freaked about it anyway."

"When did this happen?" asked Patrick.

"Yesterday! Please, save Ben!" Angela begged.

"We'll do our best," Ann assured.

"Please, do whatever Kevin asks. It's the only way!"

"Do you have any remorse about attacking us this morning?" Patrick asked.

"I would do anything to save Ben from Kevin."

Angela's love for Ben was touching, but her actions confirmed Ann's conclusion that the whole family needed a few thousand hours of counseling. Ann gripped the girl's right hand and considered her response. She glanced at Patrick and received a nod. "You have our word, Angela. We'll do everything we can to save Benjamin."

"Thank you," came the whispered reply.

They left Angela and went to work.

"I'm glad Joseph wasn't home for this morning's fiasco," Ann said, setting her purse down on her desk.

"What's on the agenda for today?" Patrick asked from his doorway post.

"Oh, the usual," Ann replied. "There's a raid scheduled on the Yeritchi house later. We can go if we want. Also, as you can see, there are a few hundred papers stacked on my desk that I haven't even looked at yet."

"Think you'll be bored?"

"Nope."

"Good luck," Patrick said, waving farewell.

"Who needs luck when we have God?"

Chapter 17:
Interesting Offer

Second Kiverson Residence
Chevy Chase, Maryland

"This is *your* fault!" Kevin bellowed. His fist connected with Ben's already sore cheekbone.

Ben had stopped protesting an hour ago. The terrible feeling gripping his gut had nothing to do with his brother's beating and everything to do with Angela's absence.

She tried to save me.

"You know what? I'm going to kill your FBI friends," Kevin said coldly.

Ben shook his head listlessly.

"And you know what else? They're going to come here because of you."

That hurt. Ben was sick of everything being his fault. He had spent a long, irrational time believing he could have stopped his mother's suicide.

She was disappointed in me. If I'd been a better son, she never would have taken her own life! That and other desperate thoughts had whirled around his head. No sooner had he conquered such thoughts, Angela's trouble started.

Can't I do anything right?

***

Duncan Residence to Parker Residence
Kensington, Maryland

The rest of Thursday passed quietly. Ann and Patrick participated in the raid, which went off without a hitch. Jacob Yeritchi and two underlings were apprehended without a single shot fired.

After a peaceful dinner, the Duncans visited the Parkers. Rachel and Ann escaped to a quiet room with Caitlyn Rose, where they could talk in peace while the baby slept.

Jon and Patrick wrestled the boys, built couch-cushion forts, engaged in Nerf wars, and otherwise wore themselves out. Once the boys were tucked in, the men went down to the basement where they sparred for a while before Jon taught Patrick some computer tricks. Jon knew he could make a good hacker out of Patrick but settled on legal maneuvers for now.

Finally, the Duncan's returned to their empty home. The keen sense of loss renewed their resolve to see the Kiverson case closed with all possible speed.

Friday dawned cold and wet. Ann and Patrick ate a hasty breakfast of toast with cream cheese, scrambled eggs, and black coffee, since they had forgotten to pick up more milk. Ann did her quiet time, and Patrick spent twenty minutes praying. They sauntered into the office slightly wet from the spitting clouds but in good spirits.

***

J. Edgar Hoover Building, FBI Headquarters
Washington, D.C.

That morning, Ann gained some ground in her paperwork war, and Patrick finished a few reports. They attended a brief meeting together, but otherwise saw little of each other. At lunch, they discussed some of the important cases while dining in Patrick's office. Then, Ann returned to her office and sat behind her desk to begin the afternoon work. Her phone rang, and Ann's hand froze above the pen holder.

It's him.

She had been wondering when Kevin would get around to finishing his game. On the fourth ring, she picked the phone up, and said, "Hello, Kevin."

"Hello, Julie Ann, you've been busy. Congratulations on being alive. You and your husband make quite a team. I'd hate to split you up, but I must." Kevin's voice wasn't even filtered.

"Get to the point."

"Well, since you cheated me out of Round Three, I added Round Six. But that round's only for your husband. Would you like to hear it?"

"Do I have a choice?"

He chuckled. "Round Six is full of tricks. I'd offer you a treat, the chance for a meet and greet, but I have better things in store. In fact, I have a chore. Find the body of your wife, and it might spare your life."

Chills ran up and down Ann's spine.

God, help me keep my nerve.

"You are a very sick man."

Kevin laughed the deep-throated, maniacal laugh of a villain. "You see how trusting I am? And here you are insulting me again!"

"Why are you telling me Round Six?"

"I thought you'd like to know," Kevin

said. "Besides, I'm going to make you swear to keep this information to yourself."

"What could possibly convince me to agree to that?" Ann wondered, not liking the confidence in his tone.

"My sister told you that Benjamin is with me, did she not?"

"She did."

"Splendid. Allow me to repeat Round Five: You enter Round Five, only if you're still alive. If I have my way, that won't be the way you stay. You'll come to me; that I can guarantee. But since I'm a good sport, I'll make your death nice and short."

"Allow me to repeat: Why are you telling me this?"

"Come now, Agent Duncan, you're an intelligent woman. Quit stalling. You won't be able to trace the call anyway. I've got the latest anti-nosy-government technology. I had hoped to pick you off by now, but out of my sense of honor, I let you live at the end of Round One."

"That's generous of you."

"I see your good humor has returned. Between you and me, Ben wasn't supposed to be the hostage, but I like this twist of fate. I had intended to take one of your friend's kids."

Ann knew he meant the Parkers. Anger made every muscle tense. "Leave them out of it, creep."

Kevin laughed again. "Weren't you listening?" he asked in a tone full of scorn. "Here's the deal. You come alone—on foot—to each street sign I text you. Eventually, I'll send some people to fetch you. When you get here, I'll let you see my brother. I'll even tell him what a hero you are. Hugs, kisses, tears, et cetera, and then, you can die with a good conscience."

"I still don't get the part that forces me to come to you," Ann said, trying to fight the feeling she would soon do something stupid.

"Agent, I'm tired of our conversation. Here's Ben."

"Don't come for me! Don't—"

Ann gripped the phone harder, and her heart lurched at the panic in Ben's voice.

"My brother's distraught about being the bait, though I can't see what he's got against seeking justice for our mother."

"I didn't kill your—"

"It doesn't matter what you think," he cut

in icily. "I've kept my word—unless of course you don't come and prove me a liar, but that's beside the point. My point is you're an honorable woman, Agent Duncan. I believe you promised my sister you would save dear Benjamin. Well, here's your chance."

"Do I have your word that Benjamin will not be harmed in any way by you, your associates, or your family?"

This could be a ruse.

Ann doubted it. Kevin Kiverson followed his own weird logic.

"I'm not anxious to kill my brother, only willing to do so if you force my hand."

"Is that a yes?"

Sighing deeply, he said, "Fine, fine, have it your way. I solemnly swear not to hurt Ben in any way, shape, or form as long as you keep your end of this deal."

"That means he goes free with enough money to get to someplace safe, right?"

"Fine again."

Dread blossomed within Ann. She paused and drew in a bracing breath. "When do I start?" She closed her eyes and prayed silently. Her mind whirled through options, but she couldn't get past one fact.

I gave my word.

"You accept? Wonderful! I was beginning to fear I'd have to kill you the hard way. You'll receive the first text momentarily. Send no messages and leave no notes. If anyone else shows up, you'll watch my brother and all three of the Parker kids die before I kill you."

"Such sweet promises," Ann said bitterly as she hung up. Her bluster was a complete sham. Inside, she was shaken to the core.

Dear God, protect me. Please keep Patrick, Benjamin, and the Parkers safe as well. You have numbered my days ... if my time is to end today, so be it.

Chapter 18:
The Trail

FBI Headquarters to D.C. Streets
Washington, D.C.

What do I do?

Ann's mind raced, desperate for the slightest hint of a plan. She gazed around her cluttered office as if trying to absorb inspiration from the walls. She needed some way for Patrick and the others to follow eventually but not too soon. She didn't want to further endanger Benjamin. Ann scrawled a note and left the digital recorder on her desk primed to the proper spot. That, at least, would tell Patrick what was going on.

How do I get them to follow me if not by sight?

"The tracer," she whispered.

Things clicked together.

This is crazy!

Ann rummaged through her desk until she came up with a thin rubber glove. Quickly, so as not to lose her nerve, she dismantled her cell phone and removed the tiny tracer.

"Yuck."

I never thought I'd need this.

After reassembling her phone, Ann cut off the glove's longest finger. Hoping the thing would be all right, she tucked the tracer into the newly liberated rubber finger. She briefly wondered if she would feel anything when Jon or Patrick activated the tracer. Pushing the thought aside, Ann tied a knot as far down as she could and trimmed off the excess glove.

"If criminals can do this, so can you," Ann said, dubiously eyeing her creation.

This had better be worth it!

Without further ado, she pinched her nose and carefully swallowed the contraption.

While she changed shoes, Ann contemplated taking her gun. She figured whoever came for her would take it or simply dump it somewhere, leaving another clue for Patrick.

Of course, there is the chance some kid will come along and shoot himself with it.

Ah, quit borrowing trouble.

You've got quite enough of it already. Never leave the office without your gun.

A few minutes later, Ann got her first text

message, so she exited her office and proceeded to the assigned street as slowly as she dared. It was a fine balancing act. Kevin would wait until he knew she wasn't being trailed. The more time she took, the more time her husband had to catch on and launch a rescue. Expecting him to follow her convoluted trail might be a stretch, but it was better than nothing. As soon as she touched the first street sign, the next one appeared on her phone.

Someone's watching me.

Ann had expected as much, but the notion still bothered her. She got through two more signs. When she touched the fourth, she realized she was getting into a shady area of DC. A bevy of street toughs eyed her with interest, calculating if she was worth their time and effort.

Come on, Kevin, pick me up before somebody else kills me.

As if summoned, a black sedan drove up at breakneck speed.

Ah, my ride—

Ann cut the thought off and jumped back to avoid being flattened by the car but made no other move to escape. To her surprise, the car sped past her toward the bus stop a block down. Her phone beeped, alerting her to a new street sign. She knew without checking that it would be the one on the corner by that bus stop.

A woman sat in the plastic shelter mere feet from the sign. Ann gasped and took off down the block.

I can't believe I'm chasing them! What is wrong with me?

She nearly halted when two large men in matching dark suits and sunglasses exited the car, but she conquered the fear and staggered on.

I must look like a drunk.

The two men were arguing with the woman.

That's right guys, just watch the show, Ann thought indignantly at the gang members.

"Halt!" she shouted.

What the heck am I doing? I need to lay off the movies.

"Mind own business, lady," ordered one of the thick-necked, blond men. He didn't even bother looking at her.

Good advice. I really should run.

The short woman futilely slapped at the

other beefy man.

He looked bored and miserable. His broad hands were raised defensively. "Stop! We no wish to hurt—"

"Then let go of me, you brute!" the woman wailed. She continued slapping him.

Ann figured it probably wasn't bothering the man, but she didn't want to wait for him to lose patience with the woman's feeble blows.

One well-placed swat will knock her senseless.

Drawing a few calming breaths, Ann cleared her throat and said, "You have the wrong woman."

Her statement seized the attention of all three. They froze and stared at her like she had worn a bathing suit to a wake.

Ann fumbled in her pockets for her badge. "Didn't your boss give you a picture of me?" she asked, making a valiant effort to hold her voice steady. Finding the badge, she flipped it open so the men could see it.

"He say to take agent woman with brown hair on this street," said the man, now pinning the woman's arms to her sides.

The woman twisted toward Ann. Her eyes were wide with fright, her once-neat brown hair stuck up at odd angles, and her face flushed from the struggle.

"Let her go," Ann demanded.

The man's partner leaned forward to study the badge.

"She's right."

The other man released the woman.

"You're all crazy!" the woman hissed as she ran off. "I'm calling the cops!"

Ann winced and shook her head.

That's not exactly something you want to announce in this neighborhood.

Sometimes, Ann amazed herself, and other times, such as now, she just plain bewildered herself.

Someone ought to teach that woman to be more careful.

Hmmm, that's good advice.

I should take notes.

Wordlessly, Ann pocketed the badge and stood very still, unsure how the rest of this would pan out.

Finally having their real target, the men wasted no time. One stepped behind Ann and quickly removed her suit jacket. She stiffened. Next, he slipped a blindfold over her eyes.

It's a bit late for that precaution.

Someone removed her watch and bound her wrists behind her with duct tape.

Oh goody. Well, I'm having loads of fun—ouch! Easy on the hands, I may need to break something with them later, like Kevin's face.

Next, Ann felt herself lifted up like a doll.

Yikes.

"Uh, is this really necessary?"

Without answering, they removed her shoes, gun, and hairclips but purposefully left her ID badge. Then, they carried her to the car and unceremoniously shoved her into the back seat.

The whole kidnapping, including the conversation, took place in three minutes or less.

There's efficiency for you ... What did I get myself into now?

***

J. Edgar Hoover Building, FBI Headquarters
Washington, D.C.

"Agent Duncan?" called Special Agent George Baker. He took one look at the strange assortment of objects occupying Ann's desk and bolted from the room. Thirty seconds later, he reentered with Patrick on his heels.

"She was here a few minutes ago, I swear. I went to get some coffee and walked right by. She was on the phone."

Patrick glared at Baker. "Did she sound upset?"

Where are Piker and Morrison?

He wanted to blame them, but Patrick knew they were precisely where they should be. Ann had given everybody the slip. Growling, he took a swing at a filing cabinet.

"I don't think so ... a bit tense I guess ..." Baker was left to wallow in his questions as Patrick hastily tossed him out of the office.

Patrick called Jon as soon as Baker left. "Jon, I need you up here right now. Ann's gone, but I think she left us some clues. I'd feel better if you were here." He hung up before Jon could protest and frantically paced Ann's tiny office until his friend arrived.

"Hey, Patrick," Jon said, sailing into the room. He whistled as his eyes swept over the objects on Ann's desk. "What was she doing?"

Patrick picked up the glove with the missing a finger. Without a word, he hit play on the recorder. The short conversation made Patrick's blood boil.

Why, Ann? Why?

"I don't like it," said Patrick, pacing again.

"Look," Jon said holding up a piece of scrap paper that had been face down.

It read: PLEASE FOLLOW.

Patrick stopped pacing and hit the dented file cabinet again. "She knew I'd stop her from going. This is crazy! She's crazy!"

"What are you raving about?"

Patrick picked up the fingerless glove. "You remember those tracers you put in our phones? Not the call tracers, the other ones."

"Yes." Jon's eyes widened. "Oh …"

"Yes, oh! She swallowed it." Patrick threw the glove back onto the desk.

Jon flew out the door and returned with two trace finders, all business now. "There's another tracer in her office shoes, but I doubt they'll let her keep the shoes so I guess she was smart to swallow the second tracer."

"She should've been smart enough to not go!" Patrick grumbled, clenching his fists.

"Come on," Jon said urgently. "We can follow her." He didn't need to spur Patrick on.

Ripping off his blue tie, Patrick grabbed a few extra gun clips from Ann's desk, and strode out the door with purpose. Cell phone already plastered to his ear, Patrick barked orders at Piker and Morrison.

Jon ran to catch up.

***

Prearranged Pickup Place
Washington, D.C.

After a short ride, the men removed Ann from the car. One clutched her elbow tightly.

Yeah, right, like I'm going to try and run now.

The sun had finally come out of hiding, and Ann felt the early summer heat beating down on her head.

And here I thought Mondays were supposed to be the universal bad day.

She stood silently for about thirty seconds before asking questions she really didn't expect answers to. "So how much are you making for this job? What got you into kidnapping? When's Kevin coming? Do you even know who hired you?"

The man not holding her, sighed and answered in a thick accent Ann still couldn't quite place, "Man offer much money for you."

Gee, that's nice to know.

The first man added, "This was urgent business for Mr. Kiverson. He promised four thousand cash American money."

"Money nice but not best part," said the second man.

Ann turned her head toward him, even though she still couldn't see him.

"Mr. Kiverson promised many future jobs if this one is well," explained the man holding her arm.

"Sort of like a job interview?" Ann wondered.

Ignoring the question, the second man said, "Soon, we bring families to America, land of free."

I don't believe it.

Ann chuckled.

"What funny?" the man challenged.

"You're breaking the laws of the country you wish to live in. Don't you find that the tiniest bit counter to your ideals?"

"What these words mean?" asked the second man. He sounded further away now as if he had taken a few steps away.

Ann countered with a question. "Why did you leave your country?"

"Is dangerous," said the man holding her.

"That's what I mean. You want to bring your families to a safer place, and yet you're making this place less safe."

"Having a nice chat with my help, Agent Duncan?" Kevin's cold voice interjected from behind her.

She flinched.

Why didn't I hear a car?

"Yes, as a matter of fact, I am."

"I should shoot you here and be done with it," Kevin mumbled. "It would make my life much easier."

"Yes, but it would also break your word. Something, I believe your 'help' would take an interest in," she countered.

"Where's your dashing husband?" he mocked.

"Where's your brother?" Ann shot back. The bright sun was brutal. Sweat trickled down her back.

Keep him talking.

"Safe and anxious to meet you."

"And I'm anxious for him to leave you," she muttered.

Kevin concluded his business with the two men, thanked them for their service, and promised to call on them in the future.

He's a regular business tycoon.

"I shall now escort you to my happy home," Kevin announced. She could hear the feral grin in his tone.

Hurry up, Patrick. Now, would be a peachy time to step in!

***

Kidnapping Site
Washington, D.C.

The shoe tracer led Jon and Patrick to the kidnapping site. Patrick looked over the scene. Some delinquents sat on nearby steps. He was surprised to find Ann's suit jacket, gun, hairclips, and shoes sitting in a neat pile.

That's odd.

"What happened here?" Jon called out to the gang.

"Some dudes argued with a woman," one kid offered.

"Yeah. Then, some other chick ran up like a maniac and they started arguing," added another kid.

Maniac equals Ann, I think.

"What'd she say?" Patrick inquired so fast that the words became one. Luckily, these less than shiny representatives of the next generation were well versed in the art of nonsensical language.

"Don't know," answered the same boy lazily.

"They let the first chick go and took the second one," another teen spoke up helpfully.

And you just watched!

"How long ago?" Patrick demanded, scooping up Ann's personal effects.

"Fifteen minutes," said the leader with a slow shrug.

"Thank you," Jon said hurriedly.

Why didn't the kids touch the gun?

They got back in Jon's car, and Patrick studied the display screen showing the second tracer. "They've stopped."

"We should be careful. We don't want Kevin to know we're following."

"This may be our best chance to get Ann back!" Patrick argued.

"I know, but the recording said she'd be taken to Benjamin Kiverson. If that's true and we wait, we could rescue him as well," Jon pointed out.

"What will keep Kevin from breaking his word?" Patrick demanded, glaring at his friend.

"God," Jon returned solemnly.

Patrick felt so helpless that he couldn't think straight. He shut his eyes and prayed while Jon followed Ann's signal.

Lord, help us find her!

Chapter 19:
Jon Shines

Kidnapping Site
Washington, D.C.

Jonathan Parker cared deeply for Ann as his wife's best friend and a sister in the Lord, but he wasn't her husband. Thus, he had the advantage of being able to think in this desperate situation. Had it been Rachel in danger their positions would have been switched. Once upon a time, Ann and Patrick had rushed to rescue Rachel. Now, it was his turn. Patrick could follow the tracking device alone, but Jon would never abandon his friend at such a time.

Lord, protect Ann. Joseph needs his mother.

"The signal's moving toward us," said Patrick. "Jon, get us out of here!"

Jon hid the car in an alley. When the car carrying the signal passed, they saw it was a sleek, gray sports car. Jon waited tensely for the signal to gather a good lead before following.

About a half hour later, the signal stopped moving.

"I've got it," Jon announced triumphantly, smiling for the first time in the last few hours. "I'm going to send the location to the SWAT teams. It's going to take them some time to deploy though so I think we're on our own."

Patrick then used some of the skills Jon had taught him.

"We'll get her," Jon reassured, praying he was telling the truth.

***

Second Kiverson Residence
Chevy Chase, Maryland

Kevin removed Ann's blindfold as soon as they stepped into a spacious, well-furnished house. Everything from the framed paintings to the ornate doorknobs spoke of money.

Crime does pay, thought Ann, working hard not to look impressed. *Oh, don't be materialistic.*

She shook her shoulders and tried to flex some feeling back into her hands, which Kevin had left bound.

"Do you like my home?" Kevin's dark eyes sparkled with the power he wielded.

"Is it your home or does it belong to your father?"

"I guess it's mine since my father's in prison," he said irritably.

Such a strange family.

Kevin's tone said he cared for his father, and he seemed quite willing to kill her to avenge his mother. Yet he was also holding his own brother hostage.

"Come on in. You can talk to Ben before I kill you."

Now there's hospitality for you.

Mutely, Ann followed Kevin through the surprisingly cheerful house. Ann had pictured a dismal wreck that would belie the family's true nature. The tasteful decorations scattered about suggested a woman's touch.

"Ben, I have a visitor for you. Wake up!"

Ann walked in as Kevin hauled his brother upright on the couch. She gasped. The left side of Ben's face was one big bruise.

Kevin's handy work.

Other than his face, Ben looked fine. He wore a miserable expression, but Ann saw no permanent damage. His hands, which had been duct taped together in front of his body, looked as stiff as hers felt. His ankles had also been immobilized with tape.

"You shouldn't have come," Ben mumbled. "Not for me."

Ann walked closer. She wanted to wrap the poor kid in a hug and brush the errant locks of hair away from his black eyes. Her sore arms complained about remaining bound. "Are you all right, Ben?"

"You shouldn't have come for me," Ben repeated. Despite his efforts, a few tears slipped down his face.

"Quit whining!" Kevin ordered. "And stop crying like a little girl."

"Ben, you know Kevin would have gotten me here anyway," Ann assured the youth. She half-shrugged, making her arms tingle. "I'd have come for anybody."

"Yeah, she's got a hero's complex," Kevin pointed out bitterly. "Some hero."

"I tried to save your mother, Kevin," Ann said wearily. It took some effort, but she met his accusing gaze head on. She was tired of wrestling with this issue. She had spent many hours feeling miserable for not being quick enough. Well, she could leave the blaming to Kevin now.

"He won't listen," Ben murmured. "I tried

to tell him it wasn't your fault."

"All right you've had your conversation. Say goodbye."

Picking up on the malevolent tone, Ann turned to face Kevin and shuffled left to stand between the brothers.

"Let him go first," said Ann.

"I said I'd let him go, but I didn't specify when," Kevin answered with strained patience.

"What good is it to hold him?"

"I should kill both of you, starting with him just to—"

The house phone cut him off.

"I'd better get that." Kevin hesitated. "Brice is supposed to call," he muttered to himself. "You two wait here!"

He ran from the room.

Kevin's absence was a relief, but Ann still had problems. She could probably dash out of the house, but that would leave Ben in a bad spot. She considered dragging the boy with her, but Kevin had a gun and wouldn't hesitate to use it.

They must've bought the handgun value pack.

Alone she would have been hard-pressed to escape and with Ben it would be nearly impossible.

Suddenly Patrick materialized before her. Ann sucked in a sharp breath. Patrick's features were as cold and concentrated as she had ever seen them. Swallowing a joyful welcome, she nodded in the direction Kevin had gone. The proximity to freedom made Ann throw all her effort into breaking free of the duct tape.

"Let me help," Ben whispered. His cold fingers tugged at the tape binding Ann's wrists.

***

"Mr. Kiverson, my name is Jonathan Parker. I have a business proposition for you."

"Who are you and how did you get this number?" Kevin demanded. He hit the speaker button and griped his gun tightly.

"It doesn't matter who I am," Jon returned. "All that matters is your immediate surrender."

Kevin scoffed and glared at the phone. "To whom?"

"Me," said Patrick. He drew back the hammer of the gun for the ominous click.

Kevin's head jerked up.

"To the nice man holding a gun on you.

He's already very angry with you for threatening his wife, so I suggest you make no sudden moves," Jon advised.

Kevin's hand tightened around his gun even more, draining the blood from his fingers.

"Go ahead. Give me a good reason to shoot you," Patrick dared, holding his gun steady.

"You won't have to push him far," Jon warned.

Patrick walked around the kitchen table, making certain to stay out of Kevin's reach. He ordered Kevin to place the gun on the table and gently slide it away. He then ordered Kevin to kneel and cross his legs behind him.

He was about to apply handcuffs when Ann said, "Allow me." She plucked the handcuffs from Patrick and expertly used them on Kevin. Then, she switched places with Patrick so he could search for other weapons.

Late as usual, Piker and Morrison crashed through the front door with the Chevy Chase Village police on their heels.

Officer Crippen took charge of Kevin without a word while Officer Russell listened as Ann introduced everybody.

"Kevin Kiverson is the source of the trouble," Ann finished. "Benjamin Kiverson is in the other room," she added, pointing. "Go easy on him. He's a victim, and he's had a rough week."

Officer Russell nodded. "Will you be coming down to the station to file a report?" he asked, looking first at Ann and then at Patrick.

"Yes," Agent Piker answered matter-of-factly.

Agent Morrison said nothing, but his jaw locked as he glared at Kevin Kiverson like the man was a new species of slime mold. Morrison took it upon himself to escort Kevin none too gently to the squad car. Officer Crippen rambled through the Miranda rights, perfectly content to let the young agent handle the prisoner. Agent Piker went to collect Benjamin.

"We'll be right there," Ann promised Officer Russell.

Taking the hint, the officer nodded and slipped out to assist Agent Piker.

Ann's gaze settled on her husband. A lump rose in her throat. It was Patrick's move. He stood with his hands hanging limply at his sides. His eyes radiated fright and anger, pain and relief, hurt and joy.

Several moments passed.

Patrick shut his eyes tightly, balled his hands into fists, and took a deep breath. He met Ann's gaze and stepped forward. "I missed you," he whispered, pulling her into a warm hug. His voice was thick with emotion. "You had me wo—"

"You had him worried sick!" declared the phone.

"Hi, Jon," Ann said.

Patrick maneuvered over to the phone, still refusing to let go of her. "Goodbye, Jon," he said, disconnecting the phone. He breathed a sigh of relief and looked at her.

Ann was delighted to see Patrick's good humor return. Up to this point, she had tenaciously held to the fear that their relationship might be strained by the Kiverson case. Her fears melted at the pure, sweet love burning behind his eyes.

"Alone at last," Patrick murmured. He kissed her like he hadn't seen her in a decade.

Chapter 20:
Heavenly Father

Police Station
Chevy Chase, Maryland

On the way to the police station, Ann, Patrick, and Jon sent up prayers of thanksgiving for the case's successful conclusion.

Assistant Director Lance Morgan was there waiting for them, flanked by Piker and Morrison. "You two are giving me gray hair," he said with a mixture of amusement and irritation in his dark eyes.

They spent an hour telling and retelling the tale from every possible angle.

"May we speak to Ben?" Ann asked, when it appeared that the case had been talked to death.

"I see no reason why not," Officer Russell responded. "We were about to release him, but your guys said to hold him until they had a crack at him too."

Ann nodded and followed Officer Russell to the interrogation room where Ben sat sullenly. Her heart hurt to look at his hopeless expression.

"I—I'm sorry," Ben stammered.

"You're not responsible for your brother's actions," Ann said.

"We were told you even tried to warn us," Patrick added.

"I did, but I failed ... like I did with everything else."

"Thank you for trying anyway. It means a lot. It must have taken a lot of courage to go against your brother," Ann said.

What else can we say?

Ben shrugged. "What's going to happen to me?"

"How old are you?" Patrick asked. He knew from reading Ben's file, but he wanted to get the boy talking.

"Sixteen."

"Well, to start, the prosecutors will probably try to pressure you into testifying against your family." Ann didn't like the position that put the young man in.

He deserves better than this.

"Do you want me to?" Ben asked. His gaze flicked from Ann to Patrick and back again several times.

"Do what you think is best," Patrick replied.

"That may not sound like much, but we'll help as much we can," Ann added, glancing at her husband.

There I go again, giving my word to a Kiverson.

She could see Patrick's hesitation, but he nodded slowly, then more confidently.

"You're not alone, Ben," Patrick encouraged.

"What do you mean?" asked Ben. "My father and siblings are in prison. My aunts and uncles don't care. My mother's dead."

"Don't you have any family to turn to?" asked Ann.

A pensive look crossed Ben's face. "I guess there's always Aunt Hannah."

"Who's she?" prompted Patrick.

"Aunt Hannah lives in Michigan. She didn't agree with Grandfather on anything. She ran away in her teens and never returned."

"Could you stay with her for a while?" inquired Ann.

"Probably," Ben said with a shrug. "Last I heard she and her husband were having money problems. I remember my brother laughing about Uncle Jim being fired." A troubled look crossed his face.

"What's wrong?" Ann asked, trying not to look alarmed.

Ben shook his head, and his expression turned angry. "I think Kevin got Uncle Jim fired. My father sent Kevin to bring Uncle Jim and Aunt Hannah back into the fold, but they turned him down flat. It wounded Kevin's pride."

"You think Kevin got your uncle fired for revenge?" Patrick asked.

"Yes, sir. Father always said Kevin was a hothead," Ben said.

"You hold your father in high regard," Ann noted.

"I do." Ben sighed deeply. "My father understands me better than anybody. He wants me to be like the rest of them, but he says I'm free to make my own choices. I guess he won't be around anymore to protect me."

"Your earthly father may be in prison, but you won't be alone," said Ann.

"God is an ever-present heavenly Father and He loves you," Patrick assured. He pulled out a business card, reached for Ben's hand,

and pressed the card into it.

Ben looked uncertain, but he didn't pull away.

"Have you ever called upon the Lord?" Ann asked.

"No, my father said religion was another way to separate people from their money."

Ann grinned at the description.

Even Ben cracked a smile. "I think he was jealous of rich TV preachers. We were never a churchgoing family."

"So, you've never heard about Jesus Christ?" Ann asked, surprised.

I thought everyone was taught that.

"There is evil in the world, Ben," said Patrick. "You know that. God is perfect, but humans are not. We became imperfect when sin entered the world. There had to be a sacrifice to pay for all that sin, so God sent his only Son to live perfectly, die as a sacrifice, and rise again. We're still sinners today—every single one of us—but recognizing this fact is half our battle. Once we acknowledge sin, we can turn away from it and accept Christ's sacrifice."

"He died in our place, Ben," Ann murmured.

"The gift is there, you have only to accept it," said Patrick. "I know that doesn't make sense right now, but think about it. Call us if you have any questions. They don't have to be about religion."

Ann felt like cheering, but she settled for a reassuring smile.

At least, we got him thinking. Father, draw near to Ben. Be his heavenly Father.

***

Davidson Residence
Fairview, Pennsylvania

Ann and Patrick spent Saturday on a road trip to her parents' house to pick up Joseph. After greeting her parents, Ann picked up her son and let the scent of freshly powdered baby soothe her.

Ah, the sweetest scent ever, Ann thought, hugging Joseph tightly.

"Baby hog," Patrick accused.

Taking the hint, Ann reluctantly handed over the baby and watched Patrick close his eyes and hold him.

Her mother took the opportunity to tackle her with a tight hug.

"I was so worried!"

I know, mom. I'm sorry about that.

415

"Everything's fine. We caught the bad guy," Ann reassured.

But the danger never really goes away.

She argued with her pessimistic side. *Forget the worry and enjoy the peaceful moments.*

Epilogue:

Sunday's paper answered Mrs. Briant's burning questions about Agent Duncan's odd behavior. Though some criticized the Duncans for playing Kevin Kiverson's game, Mrs. Briant knew they had saved her sons.

Sadly, four days after his arrest, Kevin hung himself in his prison cell.

Benjamin Kiverson turned traitor to his family and saved many lives in the process. With the Duncans' help, he contacted his Aunt Hannah and Uncle Jim who happily took him in. After much soul-searching and countless conversations with the Parkers and the Duncans, Ben accepted God and threw himself into learning more. He became a doctor and spent years serving alongside his Christian family in foreign lands.

Angela Kiverson spent several years in prison for her role in the Kiverson crime ring, but the Duncans refused to press assault charges against her. She got a GED and a counseling degree and worked closely with children who have rough upbringings.

On the Monday after that hectic Friday, Ann and Patrick wrote up reports on the Kiverson Case. Meddlesome lawyers might keep the case officially open for years, but the Duncans still felt a deep sense of satisfaction as they mentally slapped CASE CLOSED over their reports.

After signing and delivering the reports, Ann and Patrick had a lovely lunch of hotdogs and walked through the park hand-in-hand.

THE END

Thank You for Reading

I hope you've enjoyed this Heartfelt Cases story. If so, please leave a review. I would love to hear your thoughts.

My email is **devyaschildren@gmail.com**.

Visit my new website (juliecgilbert.com) for audio excerpts, music playlists, and more.

Social media links:
Facebook:
www.facebook.com/JulieCGilbert2013
Twitter: **twitter.com/authorgilbert**
Bookbub Partner link:
www.bookbub.com/authors/julie-c-gilbert

www.ingramcontent.com/pod-product-compliance
Lightning Source LLC
Chambersburg PA
CBHW070350260626
47161CB00001B/94